Moon Under Water

Also by Loreena M. Lee

Satin Shoes
Libros Libertad

Within These Bonds
Libros Libertad

Kitchen Tales
Cordillera North Publications

Dragons I Know
Illustrated Children's book –with Eleanor Ryan
Ryan Publications

Moon Under Water

Loreena M. Lee

Copyright © Loreena M. Lee 2014. All rights reserved.

No part of this book may be reproduced, stored in a retrieval system, or transmitted by any means without the written permission of the Author.

This is a work of fiction. All of the characters, places, organizations and events portrayed in this novel are either products of the author's imagination or used fictitiously.

Published by:
Cordillera North Publications
www.cordilleranorth.com

Library and Archives Canada Cataloguing in Publication

Lee, Loreena M., 1940-
    Moon Under Water / Loreena M. Lee

ISBN 978-0-9784472-9-8

Cover illustration by Loreena M. Lee
Design and layout by B.Rodda Visuals

"Sweet is the voice of a sister in the season of sorrow."
Benjamin Desraeli

"Extraordinary things are always hiding in places people never think to look."
Jodi Picoult, My Sister's Keeper

1

He was gone. Dropped face down into the cabbage soup during lunch on Monday. It took a bit of scrubbing to get the stains out of the tablecloth. Tomorrow, Friday, the old man would be put to rest. No more little squeezes with his dry, bony fingers, but then again, perhaps no more job, either. Eva didn't know what the future held in store, but if she couldn't work here for some reason, there would be other places.

She was beginning to think that employers considered it their right to take liberties. Her last one at least was considerate enough to make her a proposition before he invited her to his bed. That was a whole other story, one she didn't want to linger on too long. This one, too elderly to do much but dream about his virile youth, had made a few feeble attempts. It was almost laughable. She was at least two inches taller than he, younger and stronger. Yet, as the provider of her monthly stipend, he felt entitled to extra privileges which were his to take without repercussion. To be fair, it only amounted to a few pinches and pats, just enough to annoy. But still.

Eva ran the feather duster along the gilt frame of the hallway mirror and paused. Removing her headscarf, she shook out her short bob and considered her reflection. The tan she'd acquired from days off spent at the beach complemented her sun-streaked, summer-lightened auburn hair. Agatha had been right: it was a treat to spend time by the sea, and had surprised Eva with a picnic supper on her nineteenth birthday. They had sat on blankets in the sand and watched her nephews build roadways for their toy cars. They shared birthday cake on picnic tables looking over the sapphire ocean that merged into an azure sky. It was a paradise compared to the dry summers of their meagre homestead where the moisture oozed out of your pores until you felt like a sack of bones rattling in the wind.

Dark brown eyes flecked with green stared back at her from the ornate mirror. You have nothing to complain about, they said; you're here now, and you'll never go back. With one last swipe at the mirror, she balanced the handle of the duster on her shoulder like a baton, and entered the dining room which had been re-arranged to accommodate the guests coming for tea tomorrow. She should check the silver tea service to make sure it didn't need a touch up. Everything should be perfect for the funeral reception.

The silver teapot shone her distorted reflection back at her. Picking it up, she breathed on a spot next to the spout and buffed it with her sleeve. She gave it another stern scrutiny and set it back on the tray. Checking the blinds for dust, she straightened the damask curtains. Through the window she could see that the rain had eased somewhat, and silver-lined holes in the heavy clouds displayed patches of blue.

Across the street, a man in a brown raincoat, hat pulled down, shoulders hunched and hands in his pockets, stood looking toward the house. He had stood there, off and on, rain or shine, for the past week, just for an hour or so at different times of day. There were many unemployed men wandering about the city, living from hand to mouth. Jobs were hard to come by, and panhandlers were everywhere. Perhaps he was gathering his courage to come to the door to ask for a handout, or to offer his services in exchange for a meal. Somehow she didn't think so. Short in stature, his portly girth suggested he wasn't wanting for sustenance. On the other hand, if he was new to the game, had lost his job as so many had, he might be too humiliated to ask for a handout.

She considered again how lucky she'd been to get this job. When she boarded the train from the broad plains of Alberta to the coastal city of Vancouver, she hadn't thought about what she would have to do to make her living. She simply assumed she could find employment as a domestic, or a cook. Even a nanny, in a pinch. Agatha never mentioned the condition of the economy here in any of her letters. She counted her lucky stars that Henry, Agatha's husband, had found this position. He had overheard his boss mention that his friends were looking for a domestic. Jacques and Jeannette DeFraine and their son Claude had been served by the previous housekeeper for over twenty years, until she retired to move to warmer climes. Eva felt fortunate to get the job, and the past five months had gone quickly. She'd worked hard to earn her position, but it was an easy go for the most part. She wasn't a stranger to hard work, and cooking from well-stocked cupboards and cleaning the well-appointed rooms was a joy. Even if she had been unable to find a position when she first arrived, she had family who would take her in, although living off the charity of her sisters didn't even bear thinking about. In any case, she would never have had to face living on the street.

Her attention returned to the man she could see from the window. Should she go out and offer him something to eat? She discarded that thought immediately. Start doing that, she told herself firmly, and there'd be no end to the line-up. There were soup kitchens. They weren't that hard to find.

"Everything ready?" Eva turned to see her employer, Mrs. DeFraine, standing in the doorway. The older woman looked drawn and tired. She patted the finger waves in her grey hair as she looked around.

"Almost," said Eva. "I'm finished in here." She studied the new widow. *As if she had the slightest idea what dust looked like.* In fact, she doubted the diminutive woman had the faintest idea about anything. Certainly not the true nature of her husband, may the old goat rest in peace. But perhaps she did know and chose to ignore it. What could she do about it after all?

Eva was fairly certain that Mrs. DeFraine didn't know anything about household accounts, and would soon be in trouble if left to her own devices. She pushed those thoughts aside for the moment. No sense thinking about it now. She looked at the widow with sympathy. It wasn't a good place to be, but long ago Eva had made a vow never to have to depend on anyone and she was determined to keep that pledge.

Both women turned as a pale, gaunt figure ghosted over to the sideboard and reached for a decanter.

Mrs. DeFraine looked at her son with sad eyes, but pursed her lips in disapproval "Oh, *mon cher*," her soft voice barely above a whisper. "So early?"

"Ah, no *maman*." Claude filled a crystal wine glass more than half full. "It's only a drop." The whine in his voice grated along Eva's nerve ends. Claude's mother gave him a stern look, which he ignored.

"An aperitif is good for the appetite, I've heard," he said. "There has been such a strain these last few days. *Papa* gone so suddenly and all." He smiled charmingly at his mother and sipped from his glass. "Perhaps I can pour a small one for you? You haven't been eating at all well of late. This may help."

"You know I have had a small sherry before dinner, only. I see no reason to change my habits just because your father is not here. He would prefer that things go on as always in his absence, of that I am sure. You might do well to consider that."

"But you see," Claude gestured with a limp hand, "I am the man of the house now, and as such, I may make my own schedules. I'm sure *Papa* would approve."

You've always had your own schedule, you prissy-assed brat, Eva thought. Mentally rolling her eyes, she tucked the insides of her cheeks between her teeth to forestall any comment it wasn't her place to make. Not her problem, none of her business.

"Excuse me," she said, making for the door, impatient of the subtleties of the wealthy. Especially involving Claude, whose mere presence served to set her teeth on edge.

Eva made her way to the kitchen. Here she was in charge. This was her domain. If she thought her last employer had provided a well-stocked pantry, the DeFraine household stripped her of any such illusions. Here, fresh greens were delivered to the back door twice a week and the local butcher provided the best cuts of meat available. Accounts had been set up and she had been instructed to purchase anything she needed. On the homestead where she grew up, one cupboard with a few items of food in it was considered a bounty. Here, Eva felt as if she'd been given a free pass to the palace.

She gathered the utensils needed for an afternoon of baking. Measuring ingredients into her favourite glass bowl, her eye was once again drawn to the window. The man in the raincoat hadn't moved from his post.

She tucked a floured finger into the edge of the curtain and tugged it back a little to get a better view, careful to stay hidden. The man's head turned slightly, and even though she couldn't see his eyes, she felt as if his gaze penetrated the curtain and was able to see her staring at him. Then he pulled his hat further down and turned away, hands in his pockets, shoulders hunched against the moisture-laden breeze. She watched until he turned the corner and was gone.

She picked up the rolling pin and turned her attention to the matter at hand. An eerie feeling crept upwards along her spine. Logically, there was no reason to feel threatened, or even uncomfortable. *Nonsense*, she chided herself, and gave herself a shake. But the sense of foreboding niggled at the back of her mind as she measured and mixed. This household could be on the verge of change which would affect her place here. That's what was bothering her, of course. The man's perceived predicament served as a reminder: nothing stays the same for long. She had to put forth her best efforts tomorrow. One never knows; if her fancies or delicate sandwiches made an impression on a few people, that fact may be useful for an opportunity for employment if she needed it in the future.

She plunked the lump of dough onto the floured board with a bit more force than required. Rolling pin in hand, she was ready to do battle, no matter the field of conflict. It never hurt a body to be prepared.

* * *

Eva breathed a sigh of relief as she returned to the kitchen with an empty platter. The living room was stifling. Late August's oppressive air lingered outside the open windows, too heavy to move beyond the ledge to refresh the stagnant air inside.

Wiping her brow with a corner of her apron, she reached for the sandwiches stored in the icebox, and arranged them on the platter in concentric circles, sprinkling little sprigs of fresh garden parsley at intervals. Not that anyone would notice, but she was determined to put on the best presentation as possible, just in case someone had the energy to see her efforts.

She took a minute to fan herself before squaring her shoulders and carrying the tray back into the room. In the short time she was away, a few people had taken their leave, making a bit more space for the remaining guests to mingle a little more freely. The late Mr. DeFraine was well known in the community, but she hadn't realized how many friends and acquaintances he had accumulated. Looking around, she wondered how many were really here to pay their respects, or just looking for a free lunch. Like that man beside the food table, for instance. Several sandwiches piled on his plate, a few cookies perched on the rim, he leaned against the wall next to the table, apart from the milling guests, like a chunk of driftwood beached by a heaving sea. He chewed vigorously while he peered around the room from under bushy eyebrows.

Eva observed the man from the corner of her eye as she busied herself tidying the table. Clean shaven, average height, his shirt collar was a bit worn but clean, his suit a respectable black, shiny with wear at knees and elbows. A bead of sweat rolled down his cheek, bulging with a large bite of sandwich, and dropped to the shoulder of his jacket with the movement of his jaw. Perhaps it was just the way he stood slightly apart with a watchful manner, as if he wasn't really supposed to be here. Yes, that must be it. Eva smiled to herself, her suspicions confirmed that there were some who, hearing about the funeral, decided to slip in and take advantage of the situation.

Setting the platter on the table, Eva quickly scanned the room for the widow. Through a gap in the throng, she caught a quick glimpse of her seated near the front window, Claude standing slightly behind her chair, a half-full wine glass in hand. The stranger should have paid his respects on his way in, but she would bet that he had managed to slip in unobserved among the other guests.

None of her concern; seeing to the needs of the mourners was. She gathered discarded cups and plates, stained napkins and various cutlery and turned toward the kitchen. As she twisted slightly, placing a hip against the door to gain entry, she glanced up. The man had been watching her, she was sure of it. The itch at the back of her neck returned; that uncanny feeling that occurs when you know you're under inspection from a hidden source. She shrugged it off, attributing it to the heat and her own active imagination, and concentrated on her duties.

Placing her burdens on the counter beside the sink, she filled the basin with hot water, added soap, and immersed her latest load to soak. There were dishes to do, and heaven knows what amount of tidying after the guests departed.

As she worked, she reviewed the man's appearance in her mind. He did remind her of someone, perhaps the man who had been loitering out on the street, although he wasn't as portly. Mentally, she went down the list of her relatives and friends, visitors to the household and people in the shops she frequented. No one came to mind.

She was hot, she was tired, and the day wasn't nearly over yet. If he was a puzzle she needed to solve, he would have to wait. Very likely he would be no puzzle at all. Her imagination had produced improbabilities before; obviously it was still in good working order. Rubbing the back of her neck with a damp hand, she left the kitchen to gather another armful of used dishes, determined to keep ahead of the game. The man was no longer at the table. A quick scan of the room didn't discover him either. *Well, whoever he is, he's on his way to the front door or already gone. That's that,* she thought. *The mystery of the man is no longer of any consequence, if it ever was.* She chided herself for giving herself a concern, which, truth be told, probably wasn't one at all.

2

The city was much bigger, much more intimidating than Eva had ever imagined. Among the hustle-bustle, each person is just another faceless part of the whole. She had started a new life with a new name here. The man her father had given her to in marriage just after her sixteenth birthday was far away, as was the employer who had betrayed her trust. She was her own person and intended to keep it that way. As the streetcar rattled along the track, Eva gazed out the window at the passing landscape, the clouds balanced over the mountains, the busy streets. *I can belong here,* she told herself.

She relaxed against the seat. She had a day off to spend with her older sister and her family, and she smiled in anticipation of a dinner she didn't have to make. *I won't say a thing,* she told herself firmly. *No matter how much Agatha's cooking could use a little help. I won't even think it.*

While the old man was alive, her employers dined precisely at five o'clock every evening. On the eve of her day off, Eva would lay the table and serve, then was free to go. Jeannette DeFraine was not adept in the kitchen, so Eva left a casserole in the icebox to be heated up for their dinner the next day. The family piled the dishes in the kitchen and on her return, Eva would be greeted with pots and plates covering every available counter and cupboard. A good part of her morning would be spent in the kitchen, up to her elbows in soapsuds, shaking her head at the foibles of those with money enough to have foibles.

Today she had served the widow and her son a light dinner, mostly leftovers from the funeral reception the day before. Jeannette had poked at her food, and Claude was already in his cups. There were enough meals prepared until she returned, but she suspected most of it would remain uneaten. They mourned, each in their own way, but along with their loss, a concern for the future loomed over them like a gleaming guillotine. Previously, their every day had varied little. Now it must seem as if a dark, dread monster lurked just outside their door.

The pity of it is, she mused as she shifted over to allow a portly woman to share her seat, is that some people who know what to do with money don't seem to have any, and some who do have it have no clue how to hold on to it. She recalled that first morning after her interview four months ago. As she walked down the pathway to the gate, she had made herself a promise. One day, she would have a house like that: comfortable furniture, bright windows with both blinds and curtains and a spacious, modern kitchen. She would have a yard with her own apple tree, perhaps a plum or pear as well, all in a row behind a vast vegetable garden. She pictured lilac bushes lining the walkway, heavy with bloom, scenting the air with the promise of spring. A snowball bush in a glory of white blossoms would occupy pride of place in one corner. Endless possibilities. Since that day she felt different. She wasn't changing exactly; it was as if a whole new person began to grow within. She felt stronger and braver. She was young and unafraid of hard work. Anything was possible, and in her very bones she felt she could make her dream come true.

As Eva stepped down from the streetcar, she marvelled again at the ease with which she found it to be a normal way of transportation. No horses to brush down, no harness to put away, no barns to clean. Standing in the rain until it arrived at the stop, or waiting impatiently for others to get their change, were part of the process. Payment, as it were, for the convenience. Basically though, one simply got on, paid a fare, and got off at one's destination.

Even so, she was blessed to have known Rose, the loyal little mare who had pulled her wagon so many miles, who waited patiently in all weather. She recalled the feel of her soft nose, whuffing into her hand for a treat. A twinge of guilt and a lump of loss crept upwards, coiling into a knot in her throat. She was ashamed that she could so easily have forgotten her friend and pictured the round little mare as she last saw her: grazing in a sunny pasture under a cloudless, scorching sky. She chose to believe her friend was happy, well taken care of, and she put aside all feeling of regret. That was another time, another life.

Eva tucked that image with others of her past, and took a deep breath, savouring the sea-tinged air wafting from the ocean. The sun shone from a cloud-sprinkled sky, shrinking the puddles from the recent rain. As the streetcar trundled away behind her, she hurried down the sidewalk to Agatha's house.

She was looking forward to dinner with her family. Meals in the kitchen with the DeFraine's gardener, when he was on the grounds, were laconic at best. A lumpy, withdrawn sort of fellow, he slurped his soup and burped his way out the door, remnants of the meal clinging to his mustache. For later, she supposed with a wry shake of her head. She was grateful she didn't have to watch his open-mouthed, lip-smacking method of chewing his food any longer than it took, but a little light conversation would be nice once in a while.

The gate from the sidewalk stood open, blocked by an overturned toy wagon. Eva righted it and pulled it out of the way so she could close the gate. Turning, she gasped at the man who seemed to have materialized behind her.

"Excuse me," he said. "Can you tell me where I might find the Bellisario residence?"

Heart pounding, Eva could hardly speak. "What?" she squeaked. "No. Sorry—

I don't live around here."

"I didn't mean to startle you." His cheeks lifted; otherwise, she wouldn't have known he was smiling under a luxurious moustache he smoothed with a deliberate gesture. "I'll just keep looking. Thanks anyway." He put his hands in his pockets, and trudged down the street.

Eva walked to the porch on rubbery legs. One thing she missed about the prairies was that you could see anyone coming a good long time before they got there. Here, people bumped into each other all the time, and no one seemed particularly bothered by it. She took a deep breath, telling herself that she'd get used to it, and opened the door.

While she hung up her coat in the hallway, it came to her. The stranger's moustache. Her father had one very much like it the last time she saw him, so she knew how it was supposed to look, but this one didn't seem right. It didn't quite fit right on his face. But that's silly; maybe his mouth was crooked and that's how it grew. She shook her head. *Really,* she scolded herself; *you'll be getting your eyes examined next. Better get your head examined while you're at it; such an imagination.* Resolved to put it out of her mind, she went in to join her family.

"Hey. Look what the cat dragged in," Henry roared. In two strides, Agatha's husband crossed the room and lifted her in a hug with one large, hairy arm while the other brandished a bottle of beer.

"Put me down, idiot," Eva said. "Honestly, you'd think I've been gone for month."

"It feels like that was the last time I had a meal. I'm wasting away to a shadow."

"That explains why I had to let out the waistband on your pants again." His wife crossed her plump arms and leaned back in her chair, affecting an air of long-suffering despair.

A lean figure stood up and stretched, his wiry frame silhouetted against the light. "I always thought cats had more sense," he said. He finished the contents of his glass and set it on the table.

"I'm glad you could be here, Uri," said Eva, ignoring his comment. "It's not often we get the same days off."

He walked over and pecked her cheek. He smelled of whiskey and soap. "You know how it goes. No peace for the wicked."

"Now he's starting to pick up Henry's quips," Agatha groaned. "Bad enough to have one smart-mouth around here, we don't need two."

Uri's wife came from the kitchen, wiping her hands on her apron, wearing a welcoming smile and a dab of flour on her forehead. Heat flushed Dani's pale cheeks, and wisps of hair escaped her light brown braids. Eva noticed the dark circles under her younger sister's eyes, and wondered if she was well, or just working too hard. Or maybe she had something to tell them, and was waiting for the right time. She made a mental note to ask her about it later. It wasn't too far-fetched to hope that she might be expecting. She had married Uri for love, not like Eva and Agatha, who were bargained. Agatha's had worked out, but Eva's hadn't. It looked like Dani's was going to work out too. Dani and Eva had married brothers, but they were nothing alike, and it comforted Eva to know her sister was in good hands.

"Come on everyone," Dani said. "The gravy's ready. Get it while it's hot."

"Wait—something's missing," Eva said, looking around. "Where are those two rascals, anyway?"

"The boys are playing in their room," said Agatha. "And staying out of trouble, I hope. You can go up and tuck them in bed later, if you like."

Eva smiled. "Of course I will."

As they made their way to the dining room, Uri came up beside Eva and put a hand on her shoulder. Speaking softly, he asked, "Heard anything from that brother of mine?"

"Why would I?"

"Well," Uri shrugged. "Aleksy is your husband. Surely he'd care about where you are and what you're doing."

Eva looked at her brother-in-law, her friend, and clenched her teeth, forcing back the flame of anger that flared whenever Aleksy's name came up. "Have you forgotten how it's been between us? I doubt by now he even remembers he's a married man."

Uri gave her shoulder a squeeze. "If you were my wife, I certainly would be very mindful of where you are."

"Well, I'm not. And quite frankly, I don't see the point in my being anyone's wife." She took a deep breath and relaxed the tightness in her belly and the tension in her jaw. She didn't want anything to spoil the day. And she certainly didn't want to cause a rift in any relationship with the people she loved.

Uri held Eva's chair while she sat. Across the table, Dani scowled, and cleared her throat.

"Sorry, love," Uri tried to look contrite as he hurried around the table to hold his wife's chair. "Age before beauty."

Agatha groaned. "Great. Now you have both of them mad at you."

Uri put an arm around Dani, kissing her soundly. She giggled.

"Sit down Uri," said Henry. "On second thought, you can pour the wine while I hack into this roast." He shook his head and grinned. "We fed the boys so we could have a civilized, grown-up dinner. I guess we forgot you were coming." He put a hearty slice of roast on a plate and passed it down. "I hear on the news that there's likely to be war in Europe soon," he said.

"Where did you hear that?" Uri said.

"People talk. I get the news on the radio once in a while. Germany and Poland are involved somehow."

"Well, it likely won't affect us here," said Uri.

Henry piled two generous slices of roast on his own plate. "Probably not. But don't count on it. There are lots of young bucks just dying to get their hands on a gun and get into the fray."

"Dying is right." Agatha stabbed at a wayward carrot. "That's what wars do. Kill people."

"Nothing for us to worry about," said Uri. "Europe's a long ways away."

Eva spooned vegetables onto her plate while she listened. She felt thankful that she lived in a country that seemed removed from the hostilities of Europe. Her heart swelled with love for these people, her family, and her eyes stung. It seemed almost impossible that she should be sitting at this table, enjoying the companionship of loved ones, as if the heartbreak and trials of the past were a story in someone else's book. As the dialogue washed over her, she began to feel detached, as if she were looking at the scene from behind a veil, disembodied and unseen. The room expanded outward, the island of the table floating, dreamlike, in space. Soon she would waken in her cold empty bed and her cold, empty marriage. She shivered.

"Care to pass the gravy?" said Agatha. "The serving-maid took the afternoon off."

"Sorry." Back in the real world once again, Eva reached for the gravy and spooned some over her potatoes before passing it on. She poked at a lump in the sauce and reminded herself sharply not to say a word. She glanced at Dani. The flour on her forehead was explained; no one but her little sister could make gravy that almost needed to be chewed.

"What are you smirking about?" asked Uri.

Eva raised her head and looked around the table. "Nothing much," she said. "I'm just happy to be living here in a civilized country and not overseas where they're always bickering about something."

"You're right. We should show more gratitude for our blessings." He put down his fork and raised his glass. "I propose a toast. Here's to us. May the future bring us more of the good things in life." From across the table, he looked straight at Eva. "…and may we remember to appreciate what we have."

"Changing the subject, how was the funeral yesterday?" Agatha said.

"I didn't actually attend." said Eva. "There was too much to do preparing for the luncheon. I had a lot of people to feed. Kept me hopping, I can tell you—good thing I always allow for more. As it is, there were even some leftovers."

"I wonder what the DeFraines will do now. From what I've heard, the missus is all froth and feathers, and that son of theirs is useless."

"I haven't heard anything yet." Eva put down her fork. The roast turned tasteless in her mouth. "Time will tell. I just hope I'm not out of a job."

"If that happens, you could come stay with us until you find something else," said Uri. "We have lots of room in the new place. Right, Dani?"

"Of course." Eva noticed a shadow pass over Dani's eyes. Reaching for her wineglass, her sister broke into her familiar, sunny smile. "Any time. You're always welcome."

3

The rain continued all week. A steady, doleful drizzle that made a person despair of ever seeing the sun again.

'Too much rain can make your bones mouldy', her mother used to say when the droughts lasted too long. Eva wondered what she'd have to say about this seemingly never-ending deluge. Remembering her mother brought back the aching lump in her chest. She pushed it away, determined to look to the future and not let the past haunt her until she became as sad and mournful as the scowling sky. She tightened her jaw, watching the drops slither down the glass. Like tears.

"You want any more coffee?" called Agatha from the kitchen.

Eva pulled herself away from her wistful thoughts. "One cup is my limit," she said. "I'll come and help you clear up the breakfast dishes."

Agatha sat at the table, stirring her coffee, looking pensive. Eva put her cup in the sink and joined her. "Penny for your thoughts?"

Her older sister sighed. "Overpriced by half." Her tone had a wry note, and Eva couldn't decide if that indicated a hidden concern.

"I was just thinking about Dani and Uri." Agatha put down the spoon and sat back. "Wondering how they're doing. They work so hard."

"I can't shake the feeling that there's something not quite right with those two," Eva said. She had tried to be tactful, Dani had no answers to give her. Perhaps Dani wasn't ready. Or maybe there was nothing to tell.

Agatha shrugged. "They seemed all right to me. Maybe they're still adjusting. After all, they haven't been married that long."

"True. But…I don't know. I don't like that Dani looks so…well…drawn. I don't know how else to put it."

"I thought she looked a little peaky too, when I saw her yesterday. I didn't think anything of it. Sometimes we just have a bad day. Or maybe it's her time of the month."

After dinner the day before, Uri had continued drinking. Dani had sat, looking somewhat distant, while her husband waxed eloquent about his ambitions for a big house and eventual financial success. Now as Agatha sipped her coffee, Eva thought about the two of them, how they had interacted. She knew Agatha was going over the scene in her mind as well.

The tick of the wall clock had a hollow echo in the silence. Henry had gone to work early, and the boys were upstairs, building bridges with their Meccano sets. As Agatha gazed out the kitchen window at the rain, Eva studied her sister. Small and dark, she had become round and rosy since the birth of her children. She had not always been so easy to understand while they were growing up. But since their mother's death, they had become close: understandings exchanged, aid freely given. Dani, on the other hand, strong as she appeared on the outside, seemed likely to have the same fragile demeanour that had defined their mother, who had died in childbirth when Eva was only fourteen.

"I'd forgotten about it until just now," Eva traced a coffee stain on the table with her finger. "But in the last letter I got from you, you said that Dani may have a surprise. Any idea what it was?"

"Oh, that. She thought she was pregnant. Turned out it was a false alarm. A lot of excitement for nothing."

"Do you suppose Dani is like Momma? When she gets pregnant she'd be inclined to have difficulties? I'd hate to think she might not survive having her own child—after everything she's been through—everything we've been through."

"Anything's possible, I suppose." Agatha spread jam on the last piece of toast, brows drawn together in thought. "Maybe we should pay her a visit. You know, have some woman talk, sister bonding when the men aren't around. I don't think you've been over since they moved. Dani no more finished fixing that place up and Uri put it on the market. This one is just like the last—a run-down old house that Dani will scrub and clean and paint until she can't see straight. You'd probably want to see what he's got her into this time."

"Good idea. I wouldn't mind seeing the new place. When shall we go?"

"No time like the present. I'll see if Mrs. Kurtz next door will watch the boys. We often watch each other's kids." Agatha brushed the crumbs from her fingers and gathered cups and utensils. "And I know a great place to have lunch on the way back."

A break in the grey sky-cover allowed a watery sun to peer out. Wet pavement reflected the trees and buildings. *Like a newly washed floor,* Eva thought. It smelled fresh and clean and…wet. She tucked her arm into Agatha's and they marched in step along the sidewalk. "One thing about living on the coast, we have access to all the water we want." She steered around a puddle. "Remember when we used to pray for rain so that our gardens would sprout or the crops wouldn't wither?"

The air here had a quality and aroma that Eva couldn't put her finger on. Not like freshly washed laundry or scrubbed floors, exactly; this was more like a newly-watered garden, leafy-loamy with an overture of something she couldn't quite identify. She breathed deeply, and decided she could grow to love it here.

As the sisters walked up the street to the streetcar stop, Eva remembered her encounter of the day before. "Is there a Bellisario family living on your street anywhere?"

"Not that I know of," Agatha said. "Mind, I don't know everyone. Just anyone who's anybody. Doesn't ring a bell, though—I would've remembered that name, for sure. Why did you ask?"

Eva explained the encounter yesterday as she was coming into their yard.

"He was probably on the wrong street. Some people don't know how to read maps or remember directions."

That was probably it, thought Eva. She fought the puzzle into the back of her mind and fumbled in her purse for the right fare.

"Have you heard from Billy?" Agatha asked, as they found their seats.

Eva smiled. The tall, bespectacled young man had accompanied her on the train from Alberta, acting is if he was her bodyguard and guide, and had become a good friend. "I got a letter from him just the other day," she replied. "He's still doing well in his job in the camp but they're at the mercy of the weather. They get a lot of snow where they are and sometimes the horses can't haul the cut trees to the sawmill. They might have to close down until spring thaw."

"Will he be coming down for a visit then, do you think?"

"He didn't say. Just that he'll keep in touch. And the usual stuff."

Agatha pursed her lips, but she didn't say anything. Eva could guess what she was thinking—that she and Billy had more than just a friendship. But Eva was determined not to get involved. At least, not for a long time and even then, it would be with great caution.

It seemed to take hardly any time at all before they arrived at their stop. As the streetcar rumbled off, they turned the corner onto a side street. The houses were comfortably close together on narrow lots and most were neatly kept. Between the buildings, Eva glimpsed an expanse of green.

"There's a park behind this row of houses, with a pond," explained Agatha. "More like a small lake. Ducks and swans and geese come and go, and there's a play area for the kids. When we get a break in the weather we'll arrange an outing, maybe a picnic with the boys."

They stopped at a gate in a sagging wire fence and lifted it to push it open. This house had not received the care it deserved. The brown paint was faded, the steps creaked and the floorboards of the porch sagged. The small patch of lawn was overgrown. Agatha rang the doorbell and turned to Eva, anticipation stretching her face into a wide grin. They both knew how Dani liked surprises.

They weren't mistaken. Dani greeted them as if she hadn't just seen them the night before. Grinning through a paint-smeared face, she pulled her sisters into the house.

"We can't stay long," Agatha said. "The neighbour who's watching the boys has an appointment this afternoon, so we'll have to be back in good time."

The pungent smell of oil and turpentine assailed them as they looked around. An ancient, paint-spattered wooden chair held a tin of various-sized brushes. Pieces of cloth cascaded from a cardboard box next to a rickety ladder and rolls of wallpaper littered the floor. Dust motes danced in the wan light of a grimy window.

"I see you're making progress," said Agatha, reaching for a hankie too late to stop a sneeze.

"Gesundheit," Dani said. "Come on in and I'll show you around."

A tour through the rooms displayed Dani's talent for decoration. Her ability to twist ribbons into flower shapes to adorn simple wedding dresses had blossomed into an eye for colour harmonies in wallpaper and paint. The living room was a dusty rose, the floor was polished and the wainscoting glowed like freshly-churned buttermilk. It was a solid building, just neglected: kitchen walls dark with smoke from the wood stove, threadbare rugs on the stairs and in the hallway. Paint peeled from the doorways and wallpaper hung in loose ribbons in the pantry.

As Dani escorted them through the house, Eva looked closely at her sister. What she first thought was dirt smudged on her cheek now looked more like a bruise. Starting to yellow, it obviously wasn't fresh. She wondered why she hadn't noticed it last night. Likely it had been covered with face powder.

"That looks nasty." She touched it lightly with a fingertip.

"Oh, just a little argument with a window blind." Dani flinched but didn't meet her eyes. "I wanted it down, and it disagreed." She looked up and smiled. "I won, though."

Remembering the chaos in the entrance hallway, Eva could well imagine a disaster or two waiting to happen. She changed the subject. "So where does Uri fit into all this renovating and decorating?"

"He gets around in his job. Meets people. He finds out where he can get cheap materials."

"That's how he found these houses," Agatha offered. "His customers tell him about where there's a deal, and he gets in before it has a chance to go on the market."

"He has a lead on some lumber that he can use to fix the front steps," said Dani. "Then, with a coat of paint, we'll be the envy of the neighbourhood."

"Well," Eva nodded with approval. "Sounds like quite an ambitious man you have there, little sis. I remember when Uri came over to help me build that old chicken coop. He brought pieces of lumber he'd scrounged from somewhere. That's what gave him this idea, I'll bet."

Dani's face flushed with pleasure, and she pressed her lips together to hide a smug smile. As her sisters seated themselves around the kitchen table, she poured tea. She opened a gaily painted tin can which filled the room with the spicy aroma of cinnamon and ginger, and passed it around.

Eva declined. She'd tried Dani's gingersnaps before, and wasn't about to take a chance on breaking a tooth. "Someday soon I'm going to have a home I can redecorate. It'll have a big garden and lots of trees. Maybe Uri can find me a deal, too."

"And where are you going to come up with the money for this venture?" Agatha said. "If you ask me, your priority should be to find yourself a husband—preferably one with a bank account—or at least a good job."

"It looks to me like the two of you already snagged the good ones," Eva said. *Well, except for Billy, maybe,* she thought, remembering how well they'd got along on the long train ride over the mountains. *He's a little too young—he won't want to settle down just yet.* Eva had asked herself the question many times: did she really want to share with someone? Her past relationships did little to make her believe that any man would consider her to be more partner than property.

"I had a husband, and look where it got me," Eva continued. "I'll work hard and earn my own money, if you please. Then I get to choose where I spend it."

"Of course." Agatha quirked an eyebrow. "We get to make decisions like that all the time." She dunked her cookie in her tea. "Just how far do you think you'll get without a husband to support you?"

"Women have had the right to vote since nineteen-twenty-something. This is 1939." Eva fought to keep the indignation out of her voice. "I think the country has figured out that women have a few brains and can get along just fine, thank you very much."

Agatha opened her mouth, took a breath as if to launch into a 'big sister' lecture, but paused and popped in the last of her cookie instead. "If you say so."

Her sisters hadn't been here very long, yet they both had their own homes. Could she make it on her own? Did she need a husband to fit into the social norm? Not to say she would turn down an opportunity if it came along. But for now, if she was going to have to cook and clean, she might as well get paid for it. In the meantime, she would live her own life, on her terms. And it cost nothing to dream.

"We'd better get going," Agatha said. "I did promise not to leave the boys with the neighbour too long. Eva wanted to see what you're up to these days, and we thought we'd see if there was anything we needed to discuss without the men around."

"I can't think what that would be," Dani said. "Everything's fine. I have no complaints. Unless there's something you needed…?"

"Maybe I just wanted to have some time with the two of you. You know, like we used to be at home— just us against the world," said Eva.

"Those days are gone, thank goodness," Dani said with a laugh. "But I am glad we're together again. Life is so much better with family."

As Eva hugged Dani good-bye at the door, she pressed her cheek close to the bruise on her cheek. Dani cringed. "Sorry," said Eva. She smoothed her sister's hair and looked into her eyes. "Be more careful will you? I don't want to hear you've fallen off that decrepit old ladder and broken some bones."

"I'll be careful. Promise."

4

Dani closed the door softly and stood at the window. Her eyes filled with tears, blurring the shapes of her sisters as she watched them walk up the street until they turned out of sight around the corner. She yearned to go after them, beg them to let her come with them, let her big sisters care for her as they had when they were children.

The house was thick with silence, except for the whispers she could always hear, echoing through the hallways, curling down from the stairs and drifting into the rooms like wisps of smoke. No matter how hard she tried, wallpaper couldn't cover her sin; scrubbed floors wouldn't wash away her guilt, paint didn't keep the ghost of her youngest sister at bay. If she had just been smarter, looked after her better, taken her to the doctor sooner. She knew she was sick, why had she waited so long before she went for help. If she had been more careful, caring, Tina would still be here. Instead, Tina's ghost wafted through the walls of the house. Even here, instead of staying in her own grave, next to their mother. And that was her fault, too. If she could somehow atone for her lapse, Tina might be able to rest in peace.

If only there was someone she could talk to, but what could she say? She was living in a nightmare of her own making. Uri had been patient at first, listening when she tried to make him understand. He hadn't understood—wouldn't. He laughed, shook his head and said she was simple-minded. He wasn't pleased about having a simple-minded wife.

It didn't matter. Whatever he said or did to her, it didn't matter. It was her fault and what punishment came as a result, she knew she deserved. The pain, as it always did, burrowed into her, twisting her insides into skeins of agony, threatening to paralyze her until she couldn't think.

In the kitchen, Dani picked up the cups and plates and took them to the sink. Taking a damp dishcloth, she wiped the table and the countertop, set the teapot on the sideboard and wiped her hands on the tea towel. At the pantry door, she hesitated just a moment before she entered, removed a cereal box and reached into the back of the shelf. Her hand shook as she found the cool glass of the bottle, half full. She'd need to replace it soon. *Just one,* she thought. *Just enough to dull the pain.*

The café Agatha led them to was a narrow, hole-in-the-wall establishment. A long counter took up half of the space, behind which the rattle of dishes could be heard. A row of tables along the opposite windowed wall overlooked the crumbling street and a view of the harbour.

"You weren't kidding when you said this is a bit out of our way," said Eva, looking around as they took seats at the only empty table.

"True. But worth it for the view and the food." Behind the counter, an oriental man in a greasy apron brought in a tray of freshly-washed glasses.

"Hiya, Chang." Agatha waved, getting his attention.

"Hi yourself, missy Aggie," he called back. "Try our special today—very good—you like?"

"No thanks," she said. "I'll just have the usual. Two orders this time, please."

Chang made a production of looking disappointed. "You must be pretty hungry," he said. He shook his head and finished stacking the glasses behind the counter.

Agatha made a face at him, grinned and took her seat. "It may not look like much," she told her sister, "but here's where you get the best Denver sandwich this side of the Rockies."

"That's not hard," said Eva. She doubted anyone on either side of the formidable mountain range she had crossed to get here would have heard of them. Where she came from, eggs belonged with bacon and toast, for breakfast. But when she thought about the remote homestead and lonely, isolated farmhouses, she couldn't wonder.

The waitress appeared and set two mugs of coffee on the table with a clunk. She took a pencil from somewhere in the nest of frizzy, permed red hair, poised it over her order pad and cocked a hip.

"Two Denver sandwiches, Sheila," said Agatha. "I already told Chang."

"Oh," Sheila popped her gum and walked away. "Gotcha."

"I go through this every time with her. She's like a mechanical doll—can't think past the exact moment she's in. Sometimes I wonder if she's from a different planet."

Eva smiled and took a sip of her coffee. With a grimace, she reached for the cream jug. "Back to this business about our sister," she said. "It feels to me as if there's more than meets the eye in that house. I can't help it. I'm not sure what it is, what's wrong, but it's something. I just know it."

"Well, I can't see anything, for sure."

"I think it would have to whack you over the head before it occurred to you to look beyond the obvious. You're too trusting."

"And you're looking for horned beetles under every rock."

"Do we have horned beetles here?"

"I don't know." Agatha snorted her frustration. "You're missing the point. I just think you should stop looking for trouble where none exists."

Eva leaned back while Sheila delivered their order. The sandwiches each sported a pickle secured with a toothpick, looking like a flagpole on a submarine. The rest of the plate was filled with crisp coleslaw and fried potatoes, steamy and fragrant.

"Smells wonderful," said Agatha.

"Yes it does, and it's a welcome change." Eva reached for a napkin. "After having spent the morning with our sister where something's 'rotten in Denmark.'"

Agatha picked up her sandwich and inhaled the rich aroma. "Good thing we don't live there." Taking a big bite, she closed her eyes and chewed.

"Touché." Eva picked up a crisp potato slice, and popped it into her mouth. "A little greasy," she remarked. "But the food here is a lot better than the first time I ate in a restaurant."

"And when would that be?"

"Some other time—it's a long story. A lot more important is this feeling I have, and what to do about it. If Dani's in some kind of trouble, or she's not happy, or…or…whatever the problem is, I want to help."

"First of all, we don't know that she has a problem, and even if she did, we can't do anything until she asks us, or we find out different. In the meantime, you have your own troubles, and so do I."

"But she's family. I don't want anything to happen to her. We've lost too much already."

"You worry too much. If you're right, and there is something going on, we'll just have to wait until we can help. Just be there for her, if and when she needs us. That's all we can do right now." She reached for the bottle of ketchup. "Let's just enjoy our lunch and the day. If there's something wrong, we'll deal with it when it happens. Right now, concentrate on your sandwich. I guarantee you've never tasted anything like it, but it's not quite as good when it's cold."

Agatha was right. The only thing they could do right now was nothing. Wait and see. Eva picked up her sandwich and looked at it with a practiced eye, analyzing the ingredients. Her first bite confirmed Agatha's opinion of its savoury flavour. She'd have to make it for luncheon when she returned to work.

* * *

Eva put the last dish in the cupboard and sighed as she waited for the kettle to boil. If she hadn't so many dishes and pots to deal with after her day off, she may have found a way to overhear the conversation in the other room.

She had answered the door to a tall, gaunt man dressed all in black, eyes sad in a drooping face which had the good fortune to be propped up by a stiff, old-fashioned collar. Eva had already met the undertaker, so she concluded that either this man had the wrong house, or the business he had here was more bad news.

"Is this the DeFraine residence?" His deep, resonant voice belied his frail appearance. "I'm Herman Shaw, from the solicitor's office. I believe a Mrs. Jeannette DeFraine is expecting me?"

Eva led the way into the drawing room. Her employer sat, book forgotten in her lap, gazing out the window at the September trees luxuriant in their autumn finery. Dust motes played along the soft beam of sunlight that highlighted the silver in her hair and the paper-thin, alabaster hue of her skin. Until now, Eva hadn't noticed that she appeared to have aged considerably over this past week.

"My condolences, madam."

The woman turned slowly, as if her yearning soul reluctantly returned to her body, and regarded the man with a vague, puzzled expression.

He repeated his name. "You were expecting me?" He didn't wait for an answer, but took a seat across from her, next to the window. He opened his briefcase with a snap.

"From the solicitor's office," offered Eva, trying to think of a way she might get to stay and find out what was going on.

"Oh, of course." Mrs. DeFraine's face cleared as she became fully aware of her visitor.

"Some tea?" She turned to Eva. "Make us a pot of tea, please, dear."

Herman Shaw tutted, impatient to get down to business. Mrs. DeFraine's eyebrows went up. He sat back with a conciliatory sigh. "Oh well. If you insist."

Bother, thought Eva, starting for the kitchen. As she filled the kettle and set it on the burner, she grew impatient with concern. This may mean her survival. She felt in her gut that this meeting would end badly, especially for her. As quickly as she could, she assembled cups and saucers on a tray and prepared the teapot.

It seemed to take longer than usual before the water in the kettle came to a boil. She poured the hot water and stacked Mrs. DeFraine's favourite fluted china plate with a few macaroons. Approaching the door to the room, she set her shoulder against it, levering it open just enough to hear the conversation.

"… and of course we'll need the death certificate, and all other relevant papers regarding your accounts that your husband kept here at the house." Herman's deep voice was smooth, persuasive. He projected care and understanding that Eva could feel all the way through the door. She didn't buy a word of it.

"I'll see if I can find them—I'm not sure where they would be, or even if there are any here at all. As you know, I wasn't privy to my husband's business."

"I do understand. But we must get everything in order before we can accurately determine what state his investments are in. As it is, the documents are crucial to the finalization of the estate."

The silence stretched until Eva wondered if they had left the room. Her shoulder was starting to tire. A fly, lethargically looking for one more of anything before its season ended, landed on her hand. She flicked it off with an impatient gesture, catching the overbalanced tray just in time. Herman cleared his throat. "Is there anyone whom you would like me to call? I know this must be difficult for you, so if there's someone who can help, who perhaps had discussed business with him at some time, anyone at all I could get in touch with to get this sorted out?" Pierre was the youngest in a very small family. His older siblings passed on some time ago. "My own brother hasn't spoken to him in a number of years, so I doubt he could be of any help."

"Have you heard from him? Your brother? Surely he was at the funeral."

"Unfortunately he wasn't able to attend."

"What about your son?"

"Oh, Claude has not the interest in business his father had, he's very aesthetic, you see. He is studying for a degree in philosophy."

Eva almost snorted aloud, but contented herself with a silent, disdainful smirk. *Claude can't keep his nose out of a bottle long enough to study anything,* she thought, *much less philosophy.* It had been a source of wonder to her that he hadn't brought home a potential bride already on the way to continuing the family name, until she learned that it wasn't women he fraternized with. It was a good thing his father didn't live to find out that his family name would stop here.

She wished she could continue listening for anything more she could learn, but the tea was getting cold and the tray began to feel heavy. Reluctantly, she opened the door the rest of the way and entered. The room lay in sombre shadow, the light from the window offering barely enough illumination to read by. Herman whisked some papers off the small table between them, and Eva put the tea tray down.

"Shall I pour?" she asked.

"Please." The widow's face was a study in unreadable expression. She sat straight and prim, one hand gracefully placed on the arm of her chair, the other fisted in her lap, knuckles white. Eva admired the way her employer always seemed to be in control, giving the impression of perfect understanding, even though she hadn't a clue what was going on. A talent in itself. An asset to her husband's self esteem and social standing, to be sure. And now that he was gone, her bulwark pulled out from under her as it were, years of training still held her together.

"Sugar and cream?" Mrs. DeFraine asked her guest.

"Both, if you please," he replied.

"Do help yourself."

"After you."

"Would you care for a cookie? Take as many as you like."

"Thank you."

Inwardly, Eva groaned. *This is going to go on as long as I'm standing here. I might as well leave the room and put them out of their misery.*

Back in the kitchen, she finished tidying countertops, folded and hung the tea towels, and took the last oatmeal cookie she had saved for herself over to the window. Looking out at the low autumn sun casting lavender-coloured shadows on the fading garden, she munched as she tried to memorize the details of the scene she feared she would soon see only in her dreams. A soft buzzing ate at her insides; a blurred hum just under her ribs. Absently, she rubbed the spot, recalling the hornet's nest at the back of the yard during the summer. She had heard the monotonous drone, and so had the gardener. He had come back after dark when the insects were all in for the night and the next day the only sounds to be heard were the usual bird-calls accented by the occasional passing bee. Would that this problem could be solved so easily. And the gardener was probably just as concerned as she—possibly more—he had a family to support.

She brushed the cookie crumbs from her hands and sighed. There was no point in worrying about her future here. Whatever fate had in store wasn't worth losing any sleep over. After all, it was possible that things would turn out well, she would be kept on to look after the household and she needn't have wasted her energy.

But she didn't think so.

5

Herman came back twice after that. Each time, Eva contrived to find some domestic chore in close proximity to hear what she could. Now she hovered in the background, ostensibly dusting, straightening blinds or fluffing cushions. There were important financial papers missing, and nothing could be decided until they were found.

At the end of the week Eva opened the door to a new caller, who turned out to be none other than Mrs. DeFraine's elusive brother Louis. A prissy, arrogant little man, eyeglasses perched on the end of his bulbous nose, grey hair surrounding his bald spot like a halo. She was soon to discover that his appearance belied his astute mind and his eagle-eyed surveillance of the surroundings and the situation. As Eva stood in a shadowed corner of the room, twiddling the feather duster over a cabinet that hadn't seen a speck of dust in weeks, the matter was brought to light.

"A Mr. Herman Shaw from the solicitor's office called me," Louis told his sister, whose iron hold on her outward demeanour deteriorated rapidly in the presence of her brother.

"It would seem that the investments your husband made were not doing well," Louis continued. "No, not well at all. And that means that there might not be enough financial support to run this household and provide your 'philosophical' son's tuition. If it turns out, when we find these documents, that this is true, he'll have to withdraw from the college, and you may have to relocate to more modest premises. More modest indeed."

His sister looked at him with the same far-away expression she wore when looking out the window. Her expression suggested she had no idea what he was talking about. Her chin trembled, almost unseen unless one watched carefully, which Eva did in the ornate mirror at just the right angle so she could observe. She couldn't be sure if her employer was fearful of her brother or had a new grip on her determination,

Seeming not to notice, her brother went on, thumbs tucked into the sides of his vest as he paced. "I'm sure it's only a matter of time until this gets sorted out. A very short time, indeed. In the meantime, try not to be overly concerned. Hardly at all, in fact." He waved one limp-wristed hand in the air with a vague gesture of dismissal. "I'll work closely with the solicitor, and you and I can go over the house inch by inch until we find what he wants."

Eva was sure that he would find nothing. As she went about her regular chores, she had poked and prodded, hoping to discover any place where the papers could be discovered. If they existed. Even if she didn't know what they looked like or what was written on them, they were vitally important to a lot of people. Particularly one housekeeper, she thought with a wry shake of her head, who was kept awake nights wondering if she'd still have a job the next time anyone showed up at the door. In her opinion, if there was anything to be found, it would have to be hidden in the walls.

As if he read her mind, Louis said, "Is there a wall safe?" He stood looking down at his sister, hands on his hips. "He must have had a wall safe, don't you think? Yes indeed, an ideal place."

Mrs. DeFraine shook her head, looking puzzled. Eva bit the sides of her cheeks to keep from smiling. Her employer rarely took any interest in the house and its contents, content to leave them to the ministrations of her husband and the hired help. She remained fixated on the welfare and interests of her son; even there she saw only what she wanted to see. But then, why wouldn't the old woman know what was going on in her own house? Eva looked at Mrs. DeFraine with a new perspective she hadn't as yet considered. Perhaps she just didn't want her brother to know how much she knew.

They both turned to look at Eva, as if in doing so, she appeared before them and became the third person in the room.

"Eva, dear," said Mrs. DeFraine, "do you know if there's any such thing?"

Eva turned from dusting the top of a curio cupboard, deciding to play along. She affected a look of surprise as if she didn't realize she wasn't alone. "Pardon?" she said.

"Did you find anything in the house," Louis asked, speaking slowly in case Eva was a little simple-minded. "Like a safe set in a wall, or a place where papers might be kept, in the course of your duties?"

"I haven't come across any papers and the only things on the walls that I know of are the paintings. Mr. DeFraine told me when I was hired that I was never to touch any of the artwork. He was very clear. He didn't want any harm to come to them by accident. They are priceless, he said."

"Hardly priceless, I'd say," mumbled Louis. Then with a brisk nod: "I have an idea," he said. "Come with me, Jeannette; its time we started our search. I think I know where we might locate our quarry."

Obediently, she rose and took his arm, avoiding Eva's eyes. They walked out of the room together. Eva followed at a discrete distance as they entered the master bedroom and closed the door firmly behind them. She stood in the hallway, considering. Should she press her ear to the door and eavesdrop? Probably not a good idea; they might open it suddenly. And Louis would have some questions, no doubt, for which she would rather not have to think up answers.

With a sigh, she returned to the room they had just vacated. There were several paintings on each wall, some with glass, some without. Choosing one at random, she pulled the bottom forward gently and peered behind it. Besides a few clumps of dust clinging to the back, there was nothing to be seen but a patch of unfaded wallpaper. A flame of anger flickered to life inside her. Why did things have to be so complicated?

No point in wasting energy on things that she had no control over. Putting her speculations aside, she entered the kitchen. At least she knew every nook and cranny here; there was no danger of anything being hidden from her in her domain. Every cup in the cupboard, every spoon in the drawer was accounted for. She was beginning to wonder about people and their secrets. She couldn't imagine why her former employer would need to be clandestine, unless he worried that someone would take his wealth away. Yes, that must be it. Well, she was just as happy to not have a whole lot of money to worry about. Having enough to give her a few comforts would be fine with her. And she wouldn't be concerned that anyone would want to take it away from her. That is, and she breathed a wistful sigh, if she ever got to the place where it would actually become a concern.

She had two apple pies ready for the oven when she heard faint voices from the hallway. The front door opened and closed, and she assumed Louis had departed for the day. Throwing her apron over the back of a chair, she went into the drawing room where the widow stood looking out the window.

"Anything I can do?" Eva asked.

Mrs. DeFraine turned, her face a mask, her self-control back in place. "Yes, there is. I wonder if you could attend to the bedroom, please. I'm afraid we made quite a jumble, and I'd appreciate it if you could put it to rights." She sat down in her chair, leaned back and Eva could almost see the tension drain away, leaving her body looking shrunken and frail.

"You look tired," said Eva. "Can I get you a cup of tea?"

Mrs. DeFraine waved a languid hand and shook her head.

"Well, don't you worry," Eva said. "I'll have everything back to normal and dinner on the table before you know it. You just rest."

The bedroom was indeed a shambles. Louis' idea obviously hadn't yielded what they sought on the first try. Drawers were pulled out and not put back properly. The closet had been gutted and clothing was scattered in disorderly piles. Paintings stood on the floor and even the bed had been pulled away from the wall. Eva hoped that they had found what they were looking for, else she could look forward to the task of restoring order in every room as they continued their search. She started with the clothing, taking the opportunity to separate the old man's suits and shirts, folding them into a tidy pile. She'd ask the widow what to do with them—perhaps she favoured a charity or church that accepted donations.

As she went to hang up an armful of dresses in the closet, she paused. A few garments still on hangers were pushed aside and she could see an unusual shape in the back wall. With a finger, she traced the outline, finally feeling an uneven surface. It was a small matter to pull open a panel that hadn't been completely secured. A gap between two-by-fours lined with yellowed newspaper held a broken cobweb and a dustless spot where something had rested. Curiosity satisfied, she returned to the task at hand with a strange flutter in her middle, as if relief and fear were vying for position under her rib cage. The papers seemed to have been found at last—she hoped that now things would be resolved and she could go on, either finding her position secure, or looking for another.

* * *

A week went by without incident. The sun shone with the kind of clarity that only occurs in autumn, as if the earth wanted to leave a reminder of the glories of summer to sustain her tenants while they shivered in the doldrums of winter. She heard snatches of news about the conflicts in Europe; Canada had declared war on Germany and was sending troops overseas. It seemed far away, nothing she needed to concern herself with, and she listened to the broadcasts as if they were a serialized drama.

After breakfast on a glorious Saturday morning, Eva cleared the dishes, Mrs. DeFraine and her son sat in the sunroom with their coffee, and like the proverbial bad penny, the lawyer, Herman Shaw, turned up at their front door. He stood on the doorstep, looking as he always did, sad and apologetic. The fresh, crisp air wafted into the room, replacing the lingering odour of toast and bacon. Eva breathed deeply, preparing herself for what was most likely the day that events would come to a conclusion. Good news or bad, she wondered. She studied him closely as he entered, but as usual, his demeanour wasn't about to give her any indications at all.

Eva showed him into the sunroom and wished she could have hung from the ceiling so she could listen to their conversation. As it was, she needn't have worried. Within minutes, Claude, the son so woefully unsuited to become the man of the house, burst out of the room. He stomped up the stairs, the boom of his bedroom door being slammed rattling the teacups on the drainboard. His childlike bursts of temper were common, and usually allowed him to get his own way. It sounded like this might have actually been the first time he'd been well and properly thwarted, and if he wasn't happy, no one else would be, either. That told her all she needed to know.

* * *

Eva placed the last of her meagre wardrobe in her suitcase, and looked around the room she had enjoyed these many months. A warm, comfortable place, simple but elegant, where she had felt safe and at home.

Mrs. DeFraine had been kind and apologetic. "I do hope you'll be able to find another position," she said. "I will leave this letter of reference with you, and I hope you'll be able to settle in somewhere soon. I would be glad to help any way I can."

"Thank you— and don't worry about me," Eva assured her. "I'll stay with my sister while I look around. I'm just sorry things didn't work out. I've enjoyed working here."

Eva had made plans. It wouldn't be an ideal situation, but Eva had confidence she could find a position quite quickly. Much as she loved her sisters, got on with them reasonably well, she was horrified at the thought of living on their charity until she could support herself again.

"We'll certainly miss your pies." Her former employer paused, gazing out the window at the garden.

She'll miss more than my pies, Eva was sure. The older woman would miss the status she enjoyed when her husband was alive, this house, and the steady, secure mediocrity of her life.

Louis had taken the household in hand, and was even now making arrangements, but for what end, she wasn't privy, except that she knew they could no longer afford to live here. Eva wondered if she'd ever learn what would become of Claude in the future. He'd locked himself in his room for days, sent for his meals and tried to empty the liquor cabinet in one long, dark afternoon. He'd spent the next day in bed with the blinds drawn and the door locked, and the following day he packed a small bag and departed. He left the front door and gate open, as if to have a way prepared for his return, just in case things changed and went his way. So far, there had been no further sign of him, but rumour had it that he had enlisted in the army. Eva couldn't imagine the spoiled, wilful young man marching to anyone else's drums; but then, stranger things occurred all the time. What the final outcome would be she may never discover, but for now, all she could do was tuck the last of her wages into her handbag, and try to be optimistic. All the goodbyes had been said; it was time to move on.

She would miss working here. A few short years ago, the bare, unadorned little house that she had entered with her new husband had been a slight improvement on the desolate home she had shared with her family. After she left her bleak marriage, the farmhouse she had worked in was better, but nothing compared to this. She had definitely come up in the world. It was easy and such a pleasure to care for a home where wealth allowed the finer things. She had learned a lot, foremost being that this is how she wanted to live: where there were tools and materials to work with and the results of her labours were appreciated.

With a strange feeling that she had done this before, she closed the lid of her suitcase, secured the lock and looked around for the last time. At the bottom of the staircase she paused a moment, listening. The ticking of the hall clock counted the minutes softly, alone in its relentless record of the progress of time. Once she closed the door behind her, that sound, the comforts of the rugs and furniture, the bright kitchen filled with the aroma of sirloins, cinnamon and rich, herb-laden soups would be gone forever.

When she reached the gate, she glanced back for a last look at the garden, committing the shrubs and trees to memory so that someday she would be able to fashion her own place in a similar manner.

As she turned and began to walk to the streetcar stop, she saw a familiar figure standing under a tree across the street. The man who had haunted that corner over the past weeks stood in the shade, looking off in the distance at some scene known only to himself. He was such a familiar figure she was tempted to wave goodbye to him, too. The idea brought a smile. In her thoughts, she wished him well, and hoped that he too would find a better life soon. She shrugged off the encroaching depression and squared her shoulders. The only place to look now was to the future.

6

Agatha put the last breakfast cup in the drain and dried her hands on her apron. Eva should be coming downstairs any minute. Should she tell her? She'd been wrestling with herself over the problem for a week, and wasn't any closer to a decision. But what if….

It all started on her way out of the Doctor's office, (it was only an upset stomach, not another pregnancy), when Agatha felt the need to share the good news. What better to do than drop in and surprise Dani, certain her sister would welcome a break from her decorating labours, not to mention a bit of female company. But when Dani opened the door, Agatha saw that her sister didn't seem to be herself—almost as if she had been drinking: a glazed expression, a bit unsteady. But it was too early in the day, and Agatha had seen that Dani only ever had a drink or two on any given occasion. Dani's eyes were red-rimmed and swollen, and her hands clenched and unclenched as if she fought some inner demons.

"Are you alright?" Agatha asked, very much aware of her role as older sister, mentor and giver of free advice to her two younger siblings. A position she was beginning to enjoy more and more as time went on.

Dani bit her lip, tried a smile and failed. She stood in the doorway, one hand on the latch as if she'd forgotten how she came to be there.

"I have some good news. Also, I thought I'd see what else you've done to the house since I was here last time. You don't mind, do you? If you do, just say, and I'll be on my way," Agatha peered closely at her sister; noting her dark and distant expression, her hair dishevelled around her pale face. "Looks like this isn't the best time—we can always visit another day, if you'd rather."

Dani stood, mute, and Agatha sensed her pain. If she had any doubts that there was something amiss with her little sister, the quivering chin dispelled them. This would be a good chance to put her experience and more worldly opinions to good use, getting to the bottom of the issue and putting it to rights.

"Here, now," said Agatha, pushing past Dani and hanging her hat and coat on the hallway valet. "Have you got the teapot on? I'll make us some if you haven't." Taking Dani's arm, she led her into the kitchen. The remains of lunch lay on the table and chairs stood as if their occupants had only just risen. A fly buzzed with busy intent from crust to crumb, ostensibly trying to determine the best place to land and dine.

"Sit. I told you that you were working too hard, and just look at you. You're a wreck." Agatha bustled to the stove, grabbed the kettle and gave it a shake. "And the paint fumes are probably getting to you as well." She filled the kettle and put it back on the stove. Small alarm bells started to ring in her head as she worked and her stomach tightened. She had a feeling that whatever was going on had nothing to do with paint fumes, and she wasn't going to like what she was about to hear. She pulled a chair around to face Dani and took both her hands in hers.

Agatha kept her voice soft, as if she were speaking to a skittish kitten. "You know, don't you? That I'm always here if you want to talk about something? Whatever it is, I promise that we'll work it out together."

A single tear crept down Dani's cheek from beneath her lowered lids. A deep, unsteady breath made her slight body shudder.

"Okay, listen. I'm not being nosy, really. I just want to help." Agatha rose and went to take the kettle off the stove. She prepared the tea and brought the pot to the table. "I know there's something wrong. Just look at you. Where's that bright smile, that joy you always have? I want to know what happened to take that away. I want to fix it."

Silence covered them like a heavy cloak, broken only by the intermittent dripping of the tap. Tendrils of worry clawing at her gut, Agatha poured two cups of tea. She put one in front of Dani. "Let me help you fix it, Dani. Please."

Between shuddering breaths, Dani began to speak, softly, and Agatha strained to understand her mumbled words. "Uri came home for lunch today; he does sometimes. He had been in a bad mood all week, short and snappish, finding fault, blaming me for all sorts of things I did wrong." She looked up at Agatha. "I tried so hard, really, but I couldn't seem to do anything right." She looked down at her hands, twisting the corner of her apron with trembling fingers. "I tried to please him, but everything I did just made things worse. He's probably right, though—I guess I'm just incompetent, I can't seem to—to do the right thing." She sighed. "At night, I dream of Tina, our sister dead because I couldn't help her. She was so young. I bundled her up and took her to Eva. By the time we got to the doctor's, it was too late. I waited too long." Agatha could see the pain in her eyes, and her heart ached for her.

"She haunts me in the shadows of every room, proof that I can't be counted on when it matters most. No matter how hard I work, no fancy wallpaper or pretty paint will make up for her death. My fault. So Uri is right, I'm hopeless."

"That's not true," said Agatha, gripping her sister's hands tightly as if to pass on some of her own strength.

As if she hadn't heard, Dani continued. "Uri hardly spoke to me during lunch today. When he was done, he just sat there, staring at his plate. Then, suddenly, he put down his fork and looked at me. He had the strangest expression. He kept looking, and I thought he was going to say something, but suddenly, he got up, and grabbed me by the arms. He yanked me to my feet...." Dani stifled a sob, took a breath. After a minute, her voice steadied. "I asked him what was wrong. He looked at me as if I had—I don't know—done something really awful. His face was all twisted up, he looked so angry. I got scared."

Dani looked up at Agatha, the pain in her eyes going right to her heart. "Here," Agatha said, putting the cup of tea into Dani's hands. "Take a sip. Take your time." Agatha's heart was beating so hard she was almost unable to hear Dani, her voice a whisper in the silent kitchen.

"He threw me to the floor. He—he forced himself on me. He was so rough." She looked away. "He didn't have to do that. I would have given him anything, gladly. He knows that. I was so shocked, so scared." She gulped down a sob. "He hurt me."

"When he finished, he got up and stood there, looking down at me. Then he told me to get up. I started to—I was shaking so bad. He put a hand on my shoulder to stop me. Then he said, 'Perfect. That's just where you belong. On your knees. And you should thank me.' And then he smiled. He didn't even look like the man I married. My Uri. He looked like someone else. Someone I didn't know. I didn't know what he wanted or why he was doing this."

"Oh Dani," said Agatha. "I'm so sorry."

Dani blew her nose into her hanky and took a deep breath. "He wanted me to thank him. He kept repeating it—kept telling me, 'say it'. I tried, but I couldn't say anything. I tried to figure out what I could have done wrong, why he would treat me that way, but I couldn't think, couldn't speak. I just knelt there, feeling as if the whole world had stopped." She gasped a shuddering breath. "Finally, he shoved me and my head hit the table leg. Then he grabbed his coat and left."

Dani's shoulders slumped even further and she hung her head, a last tear dripping from the end of her nose. "I don't understand. Why would he do that? I keep wracking my brain to see what I might have done wrong, but I don't get it. I don't know what to do."

Listening to her sister's halting explanation, Agatha realized with horror that she had no idea how to fix this.

Now Agatha leaned against the counter, as troubled as she was a week ago when Dani had told her what Uri had done. She rubbed her forehead, trying to help her thoughts sort themselves out. Eva would be moving in with Dani and Uri in a few days, the small suite in the basement finally ready for occupancy. *Forewarned is forearmed*, she said to herself. *But I could be putting my nose where it doesn't belong.* It felt as if there were two people in her head having an argument.

Eva would be coming down the stairs any minute; she had to make a decision. Supposing he had actually done what she said he had. Agatha found it hard to believe, and so would Eva. Uri wouldn't do anything like that, surely. Not the Uri she knew. So where does that leave Dani? Was she telling the truth, or is she imagining these things, driving herself insane with guilt so that the imaginary becomes real?

Agatha had tried to persuade Dani to come home with her; they could talk to Eva, and between them they could figure out what best to do. But Dani had refused. Don't bring Eva into it, she pleaded, until Agatha finally promised. It was my own fault, she said; I'll work harder to make things better. She loved him didn't she, and he loved her. He didn't mean it. He would apologize, she was sure of it, just wait and see. And then things would be all right again.

Horsefeathers, Agatha fumed, which she did each time she brought it to mind. *If someone treated me like that, I'd be out that door so fast. The whole thing is ridiculous.*

What was she going to tell Eva? She and Uri might well be friends, but she should know what was happening. He wasn't anyone's friend if what Dani said was true. Even if Dani had made her promise not to involve Eva, she should at least be told that their little sister is distressed and unhappy.

But maybe if Eva was told, her anger would make her do something drastic, and wouldn't it be better to have all the facts beforehand? When she went to live in their house, she would surely discover the truth, and then they could go ahead with whatever needed to be done. On the other hand, if Eva found out that Agatha knew what happened and didn't tell her… Agatha sighed, and rubbed her temples. *Please,* she prayed to Whoever Was Listening. *I need some kind of sign to guide me to what I need to do next. This is giving me a headache.*

Shaking her head, Agatha took a deep breath. She had to make up her mind.

At the top of the stairs, Eva gripped the bannister as the nightmare replayed itself behind her eyes, settling at the back of her throat with a sweet, metallic taste. Dani painting the walls of a room, the same spot over and over, replenishing the supply with her own blood which she vomited into the paint tray each time it was empty. The blood glistened, oozing in glutinous rivulets to disappear into the rug. Eva had dragged herself out of the dream. Awake in the shadowy room, she watched as the raindrops, like the blood in the dream, slithered down the glass until a watery light pronounced the morning.

Feeling exhausted and haunted, she guided her steps down the stairs with a white-knuckled hand, wisps of the nightmare swirling in her head like wood smoke on water. She willed her mind to turn to the task at hand. She would have to work hard today to convince her new employer that she could do the job. Taking a deep breath, she walked into the kitchen.

"Penny for your thoughts, big sister," she said, reaching for the coffee pot. It wasn't like Agatha to stare out a window, chin in hand, looking vaguely pensive, when there were counters to clean and dishes to wash. "I'll just have a quick cuppa and be on my way."

Agatha turned from the window, reluctantly it seemed to Eva, and bustled to the stove, reaching for wood from the box to stoke up the flame. "With or without bacon this morning?" she asked.

"Just some toast," Eva said. She peered closely at her sister, but decided it was her tired eyes playing tricks on her, making her imagine that Agatha was not quite herself this morning. *I'm the one out of sorts,* Eva thought.

Probably looking for sympathy. She remembered one of her mother's favourite sayings: 'misery loves company.'

She decided to shrug off the haunted feeling. She reached for the jug of juice. "I don't want to be late for my job. Chang is giving me a chance at the short order station today. I wouldn't wish trouble on anyone, but the cook being off work with whatever's ailing him gives me a chance to show what I can do. Maybe he won't want the old guy back. After all, he's practically on death's doorstep as it is—he's got to be close to 80 years old. I'd best get in there while I can."

Agatha reached for the knife and carved two slices from a loaf of bread. "This will just take a minute," she said. "You can't work on an empty stomach."

Eva barked a laugh. "No chance around that place. I can gain 5 pounds just licking my fingers."

Bread slices in the toaster, Agatha turned to her sister, wrinkling her nose. "Ewww....I don't want to know what you do when the customers can't see you." She smiled. "But I'm glad things worked out. All those lunches we shared at Chang's restaurant have paid off. I'll bet he was glad that you were looking for work just when Sheila quit."

"I'll be trying to do two jobs for a while until he finds a new waitress. Although I heard that Sheila might be trying to get her old job back."

"She's pulled this before," said Agatha. "Chang has always taken her back."

"Well, she's a good waitress, I'll give her that," Eva said. "Not too bright, but somehow I can't imagine the place without her, and I guess most of the regulars feel that way too."

"They'll get over it if she doesn't come back; in no time there'll be lineups for your pies and tarts."

"Let's hope so." Eva took one of the toast slices and walked to the hallway. She held the toast in her teeth while she put on her coat.

Agatha followed her sister. "Eva, I need to talk to you."

"Can it wait? I'm going to be late if I don't catch the streetcar." Eva tied a scarf around her head and pecked her sister's cheek. "We'll talk tonight. I promise."

On the porch, she thought about an umbrella, but decided against it. Her scarf would do to keep her head dry on the short walk to the streetcar stop and then the restaurant. Her mood continued to lighten as she walked to the corner, munching on her toast, planning on what she would do when she got to the restaurant. The rain had stopped, but the streets were still wet. Eva had quickly learned the adage the local residents often quoted about living on the coast in the winter: 'If it isn't raining, wait a minute and it will be'. Rain or not, this was going to turn out to be a wonderful day; she could feel it.

A lone man stood waiting at the trolley stop, reminding Eva of the one that had appeared daily at the DeFraine residence. She wondered if he could be one and the same. As she took her place in line, he turned to her and smiled.

"Lovely day," he said, tipping his hat.

Eva opened her mouth to reply when she felt a hand on her shoulder. "Hello Evelyn," said a voice she thought she would never hear again. Startled, she dropped her toast and stood frozen in stunned surprise.

7

At first glance, Horace Bradford hadn't changed, but there were dark circles under his eyes and he looked as if he had lost weight. She stared at the tall man, her former employer, wondering why he was here instead of his homestead in empty plains of Alberta. Just for a moment, she remembered the dark winter nights they had read together in his kitchen, the long fingers that should have held a violin instead of a plow, and how he had betrayed her. She bit her lip, willing herself back to reality. Fury rushed into her lungs, cutting off her air so she could barely speak. Heart thudding in her chest, she wrenched out of his grip and turned, stepping back and bumping into the man with the hat. She hardly noticed. "How did you find me?" she managed to croak.

Bradford smiled, a bit smugly, she thought. She stared at him, hoping to find something in his eyes that she knew he wasn't capable of. *He thinks I'm no better than one of his brood mares. Well, I have escaped from his pasture. He doesn't own me. Whatever deal he's got this time, I'm not interested.*

"My friend here is a very good private detective," Bradford said, indicating the other man.

"Philaberto Stellegadis at your service," he said, stepping forward, bowing and tipping his hat with a theatrical flourish. "You can call me Phil."

Eva peered closely at the man, then suddenly recognized him. "You've been spying on me," Eva said. Fury sang through her until she trembled. "All this time I've felt sorry for you, thinking you were out of work and on the streets."

"Awfully nice of you to be concerned," he said. With a smile, he folded his hands over his ample stomach and rocked back on his heels. "And I must say, you do serve a right tasty luncheon."

Eva narrowed her eyes and poked an angry finger in the middle of his chest beneath his garish, blue and red bow tie. "You were at the funeral reception. You were spying on me."

"Calm down, Evelyn," said Bradford. "He was just doing his job."

Eva rounded on him. "Don't call me that. My name is Eva. Eva Smith. And I'll thank you to go back where you came from and leave me alone." She turned as the streetcar pulled up to the stop, but Bradford caught her arm and Phil stepped in front of her, smiling amicably, blocking her escape.

"No matter what you call yourself now, you're still Mrs. Evelyn Smeniuk."

"Exactly," she spat. "You were supposed to arrange the divorce. So you didn't hold up your end, did you? There's no further business between us."

His hand tightened on her arm. "But there is," he said. "We had an agreement and you left before it could be finalized. Apparently, you didn't fully understand the terms." His eyes glittered like damp pebbles, and Eva could hear the streetcar pull away. Apprehension pushed bile into her throat, making her chest sting. The streetcar rattled around the corner leaving an ominous silence in its wake.

"Now look what you've done—I've missed my ride," she said, more calmly than she felt. "I'll be late for work."

"Oh, that. Don't worry. You seem to have forgotten you already have employment."

Eva glanced around. There were few people on the street this early, and the three of them were alone on this side. Across the road, a lone woman hurried along the sidewalk, head down, opening her umbrella against sprinkles of rain. Eva took a deep breath and lowered her voice. "I won't have it long if I don't show up this morning."

"I meant that you are still working for me," he said in an even tone. "I didn't dismiss you, and I don't like my housekeepers running off without even a by-your-leave."

"And I don't like being kept a prisoner, while promises are made and not kept. If you need a formal notice, here it is: I quit. Now get out of my way." She stepped away, only to be blocked once again by Phil who moved in front of her in one smooth motion. And this time, he wasn't smiling.

She turned, looking to Bradford as he spoke. "Yes, promises were not kept. But let's not argue in the middle of a public sidewalk about who didn't keep them. Instead, we'll go where we can have a cup of coffee, out of the rain, and discuss this like reasonable adults."

Eva tried to move around Bradford, but he took her arm.

"Let me go," she said. "The deal is off. There's nothing more to say."

"Not true. We need to talk." He looked at her intently. "Look— I haven't had breakfast, my feet are wet and I'm chilled through. I was beginning to think you wouldn't be coming, that this was the wrong day, but I see my man here is good at his job." His voice softened. "My hotel has quite a decent menu in their dining room. You really must join us. I insist."

"Please. I must go. People are expecting me." She tried to pull away, but his hand tightened. She could feel Phil's presence at her back, blocking her from running even if she managed to wriggle out of Bradford's grip. "I don't want to go anywhere with you."

"Aw, now that's too bad. I've missed your company." He stepped closer; she could feel his breath brush against her hair. "We had some lovely evenings together, didn't we? After all this time, I'm sure we could find many things to talk about. We could 'catch up', so to speak."

He began to walk, pulling her by the arm. She stumbled along beside him, feeling helpless tears evaporating in hot indignation. She could hear Phil chuckling as he followed behind.

"For heaven's sake," she said. "What do you want?"

"Be patient." His voice softened but not the hold on her arm. "Let's just talk this out. We'll have a nice civilized breakfast, and just chat. Okay?"

They walked away from the streetcar stop, away from the safety of her sister's house. Around the corner they approached a battered blue sedan, fenders rusting, bumper hanging at an odd angle. Phil opened the door and Bradford finally let her arm go after he helped her into the back seat, getting in beside her. Phil wrestled with the handle on the driver's side. Finally, he yanked it open and got in.

As the motor coughed to a start, Eva slid across the seat until she was against the door, as far from him as she could get. There was no door handle. "Where are we going?"

"I told you," he said. "Back to the hotel. I'm starting to grow a fungus standing around in this bloody rain."

"You're forcing me against my will," she spat. "This is assault. Or kidnapping, or something. You've no right to do this."

He looked at her and sighed, as if she was an errant child too stupid to understand. Reaching over to pat her hand, he said, "Try and be patient, my dear. You'll understand soon." Smiling, he sat back. "If you'll remember, I do much better with explanations when my stomach is full." He sighed again. "I do miss your flapjacks."

Eva folded her arms across her chest and glared at him. There might be nothing she could do at the moment, but whatever he wanted of her, she intended to make sure he didn't get it.

The hotel lobby and dining room were gloomier inside than the day was outside, even with the heavy drapes drawn back from the tall windows and the wall lights gleaming bravely at intervals. The glow of the central chandelier, with its myriad of tiny lights and reflecting crystals, barely penetrated the hushed, cheerless atmosphere. The dour desk clerk nodded greetings; his expression suggested he might burst into tears at any moment. The waitress showed them to their table as if she directed a funeral procession.

Bradford manoeuvered Eva into a corner by the wall, and he and Phil took seats on either side. She placed her hands in her lap, and gazed out the window. She remembered her employer, Mrs. DeFraine, who stayed composed, if a little vague, during any event be it crisis or not. It used to annoy Eva that the old woman seemed to remain calm no matter the circumstance. Now she understood how effective it could be.

When the waitress came with the waffles Bradford had ordered for them all, she glanced briefly at her dish and looked away again.

"Eat up," Bradford said. "You've got to keep up your strength. Fainting from hunger will only complicate matters." He poured syrup and placed the container in front of his companion. Phil had been busy slathering globs of butter on the waffles and now he grabbed the pitcher and poured the rest of the syrup over them.

Eva watched, fascinated, then turned her head slowly, regarding Bradford with hooded eyes. "I'm not hungry," she said. Her stomach disagreed with a loud growl, the sound seeming to travel to the surrounding tables. With a sigh, Eva picked up her fork. She looked at the empty syrup dispenser, and reached for a pat of butter instead. She might as well have a bite or two; if only to keep her mind sharp. She knew from experience that Bradford wouldn't say anything until he had finished eating, when he would be ready to tell her why he would travel all the way from the next province to find her. Was it to persuade her to go back, or was there something else?

She stabbed her fork into the waffle and picked up the knife, glaring at her captor as she cut off a piece. He saw the gesture, smiled slightly and forked up a large mouthful, chewing with gusto.

She took a breath and tried to think calmly. She wouldn't give him the satisfaction of seeing her frightened. She wasn't scared, really, she told herself. Just angry. Mostly.

At length Bradford put down his fork and signalled the waitress to refill his coffee cup. "That hit the spot," he said. "Now I suppose you want to know what brought me to this fine place."

Finding it easy to remain expressionless, she raised her head and looked at him. Her anger kept her as rigid and cold as she needed to be.

"You remember what our bargain was?"

She didn't answer.

"Well, just to refresh your memory, we agreed that you would give me a son, and I would see to your divorce from your husband. While neither of us fulfilled our part, you must remember that I said I would take care of my end once it was established that you had taken care of yours."

The waffle sat like a stone in her stomach. Anger sent out tendrils of heat, but she pushed it down and locked it away. With a firm grip on her emotions, she put down her fork. "There was no place in our bargain that said I was to be your prisoner. You kept my sisters' letters from me. You forbade me leaving the farm." Frustration threatened to loose her anger. She ignored it. "What did you think would happen? That I would just stay there and be your meek little slave?"

"I was afraid you wouldn't hold up your end, and you would leave. And I was right."

"Well, what did you expect? Our bargain didn't include exclusive ownership. As far as I'm concerned, the deal is off."

"I don't agree." His demeanor became stiff and his jaw set in a stubborn line.

"Too bad. Maybe you made the whole thing up just to get me into your bed." She sat back in her chair, putting on the most disdainful expression she could muster. "Also, there was nothing in writing. No legal papers between us. So you don't have any legal claim on me."

He relaxed slightly. "True. But we made the bargain in good faith."

"Which you didn't show much of." She tried another tactic. "Look, maybe I can't conceive. In all those months, there wasn't anything to show for...." She shrugged. "And anyway, there was no guarantee that the child would be a boy. We didn't even discuss what would happen if it wasn't. So if I didn't hold up my side of the bargain, it's likely because I can't. My fault. But I'm still married, aren't I, so I lose again."

"Speaking of which," he put down his coffee cup and folded his napkin, "I wonder if you heard any news about your dear husband."

"Tell me. Did he start divorce proceedings on his own? Because that's the only thing I'd ever care to hear about him."

"I doubt he can manage it now, not that it would even have occurred to him. There was a bit of an accident. Last I heard, he had just come out of a coma. Head injury, apparently."

Taken aback, Eva could only stare. Finally, she asked, "What happened?"

"There was some sort of an explosion in the woods. Apparently, he was hit by a falling tree caused by the blast. I heard about it in town. You remember the way gossip always seems to collect at the trade store, which is where I found out about it. There was another man with him; he was killed. They weren't discovered until the next day. Aleksy barely survived. He's being sent to Ponoka to continue his recovery."

"Isn't that where the sanitarium is? Does he have some sort of brain damage?"

"That would be the place to go to find out, I believe." Again, the slight smile. Eva was beginning to think he liked this a little too much. "I thought you might be interested."

"People who operate illegal stills run that risk," Eve said. "It's not unusual. There's nothing I can do about it. Not then. Not now."

"You surprise me; I thought you'd be a bit more concerned. After all, he is your husband."

Eve looked her former employer over carefully. This was the man who threw her husband out of his house, warned him not to come back, offered her sanctuary from a loveless marriage and a life of loneliness and poverty. She thought he had been gallant and had stood up for her. But he had proven to be more devious than she could have imagined.

"And what do you care—about my husband?" she asked.

8

Bradford smiled and gestured to the waitress to bring the bill. Eva looked at Phil to see if he knew anything. He shrugged and drained his cup.

The waitress arrived and handed the bill to Bradford. As he looked it over, Phil leaned towards Eva. "He told me once that your man Aleksy was a little strange," he said in a stage whisper. "Said he didn't condone perverts, that's why he booted him off his property. Don't know what he meant by that, exactly. Never met your man, myself." He shrugged again and sat back. "Beats me."

That wasn't any help. How would her husband or his condition matter to this man? Wait a minute—pervert? Sure, Aleksy was somewhat strange, but she always thought he was just a little quirky—as far as she knew. Besides the fact that he was an indifferent husband, stayed away from the farm for days. That didn't make him a pervert. Sort of vague, maybe. A loner? Although he always seemed to have another fellow with him, come to think of it, so he did have friends. She remembered a dark young man who was with Aleksy a lot, more so after she left him. Her mind skittered away from any further thought; just someone he worked with, she decided. Everyone needs a friend.

Or maybe he once wronged Bradford, who was looking for a way to get even. If Bradford did have something against Aleksy, it was no concern of hers. Or did Aleksy have something he wanted, and she was to be the pawn? *As if Aleksy cared enough about me for something like that,* she thought. So that's not a reason. But does Bradford know that?

When the waitress brought his change, Bradford took Eva's arm, pulling her up from her chair. She wriggled out of his grip and tried to step back. There was nowhere to go. Her mind on how to escape this situation, she hadn't noticed that she'd been hemmed in, effectively blocked from an easy way out.

Annoyed at herself, she vowed to pay attention to the matters at hand. Bradford tucked her arm through his as if they were off for a morning stroll but his grip on her wrist was painful.

She tried to pull away from his grasp. "If you don't let me go, I'll scream for help," she said, teeth clenched against the pain and her fury.

"Go ahead," he said, chuckling. "Cause a scene, if that's what you want." He increased the pressure on her wrist. "I can assure you, you'll regret it. Best you come along quietly, and hear what I have to say in private."

Obviously, he had it all worked out. It might be best to do as he asked and play along. For now. Her indignation was beginning to fray around the edges. After all, he had stood up for her when Aleksy came to take her home. Aleksy wasn't very enthusiastic, she remembered, but he was exercising his right. She was, after all, his legal wife. He'd even brought a lawyer with him. Bradford had protected her and given her a job. At the time, entering into their agreement seemed the right thing to do. Maybe she should have stayed and tried to make him understand that she couldn't live in total isolation. So maybe it would be fair to give him a bit of her time just to listen. Perhaps she owed him that.

He steered her toward the stairs. On the second floor, they turned left. The carpeted hallway sucked up the sounds of their footsteps and the dark walls and ceiling absorbed the dim light cast by the wall sconces. As they walked, Eva's mind skittered about, looking for a way to escape this predicament. This was beginning to feel like a waking nightmare. She shoved the gnawing rodents of doubt into a corner of her mind and concentrated on giving him a fair hearing. She had a new life, a job, and she didn't intend to give it up, just because of some agreement, real or imagined.

They stopped at one of the doors and Bradford unlocked it, his hand on her back propelling her in ahead of him. He muttered something to Phil, then closed the door, leaving the two of them alone. A small lamp cowered in the corner, throwing a faint circle of light, enough to make out the shapes of a bed, dresser and stuffed chair.

Bradford threw his coat and hat on the bed. Jingling the key in his pocket against some spare change, he walked to the window and pulled back the heavy, brocade drapes, displaying an array of scowling clouds behind a lone steeple.

"Not much of a view today, I'm afraid," he said. "You can't see the mountains at all. The city's quite a sight when the sun's out."

Eva rubbed her arm. She would find bruises there tomorrow. "How long have you been here?"

"As soon as Phil was sure you were the one I was looking for, I came straightaway. It's a pleasant ride by train, don't you think?" Still staring out the window, he rocked back on his heels, hands in his pockets. "I'm looking forward to the trip home."

"And when will that be?"

"I have tickets for the 4 o'clock."

"Tickets?"

He turned and sat down in the armchair, steepling his fingers. "You will be coming with me, of course."

Eva folded her arms across her chest and thrust her chin forward. "I'm not planning on it."

Bradford stood and beckoned her to take his place in the chair. "Please. Have a seat. Hear me out. I know you'll agree I'm right."

Eva remained standing. "Look here. I've made a new life. My family is here. I have absolutely no desire to leave—especially to go back to that godforsaken place in the middle of nowhere."

"You don't miss the prairies?" His expression was all innocence, his voice smooth, almost playful. "Oh, come now. The long, quiet winters, the hot summers? You traded it all for this constant rain, this—this—isolation in a place teeming with strangers?"

Eva didn't answer. Instead, she gave him a long look, then sat on the edge of the chair, back straight, arm draped over the armrest with as much grace and decorum as she could muster. Her former employer, Mrs. DeFraine, would be proud of her display of aloofness and control. With one hand, she smoothed the lines of her housedress and pulled her coat closed, knowing it was no defence against the chill she was beginning to feel in her bones. She raised her chin and glared at him with the most defiant look she could muster. He had no concept, she fumed, of the isolation and loneliness she had endured, first in her family home, then in her husband's house, and at last when Bradford tried to keep her from leaving his homestead. One thing for sure, if she went back the seclusion would be her death. Here at least, she had family. People. Possibilities.

"Unfortunate," Bradford continued. "I thought you would see reason." He rounded on her. "There's still the question of our agreement."

"There's nothing to discuss," Eva said, exasperated. "It's over. If neither of us kept up our end of it, is there anything further to say?" She let out an frustrated snort of breath, throwing her hands in the air. "We've been over this already. Several times. I don't see it going anywhere." She pinned him with a look. "Unless there's something here I don't understand...?"

"Like what?" He raised his eyebrows, all innocence.

"Is this something to do with Aleksy? Are you trying to get even with him for something he did? What's going on between you two?"

"As little as possible. I don't associate with him in any way. People like him should be put away." His eyebrows drew down in a dark scowl. "Permanently. He's exactly where he should be."

Eva peered closely at him. In all the long months she had been his housekeeper, he had never been so forthcoming. Perhaps he didn't have the need for much conversation then. Now that it appeared he wanted something very badly, the words came easily.

"This has nothing to do with Aleksy," he continued, waving a dismissive hand. "I only told you about him to let you know what's been going on since you left. This is about us."

"There is no 'us.'"

"Just listen." Eva could hear a barely contained anger in his voice. He began to pace, another action totally out of character to the man she had known. "It's very important to me that I have a son. Someone who can take over the land. I've never married, as you know, and you're the first woman I've met who has any appeal in the slightest." He stopped, looked at her with narrow, piercing eyes. He took her chin in his hand, his face close to hers. "You're strong, capable, and smart."

She twisted out of his grip. "I'm not one of your brood mares."

As if he hadn't heard, he resumed pacing. "It's the perfect solution: I want a son, you want freedom. Simply, we help each other."

"You don't understand—I'm already free," she stood, trembling with rage. The devil take Mrs. DeFraine and her cool resistance. "And it's obvious I can't give you what you want. So I don't see any need to continue this conversation. So if you don't mind..." She went to the door, taking her damp headscarf from her pocket and tying it on. He made no move to stop her.

She jiggled the door handle—when had he locked it? "Unlock this door and let me out," she yelled, turning to him with fury in her eyes, yanking on the handle again.

Bradford sighed and shook his head as if she were a willful child. "Here, don't be ridiculous," He came to her side and put his arm around her shoulder, his fingers biting into flesh through her coat as he guided her back to the chair. "Just sit down. Think calmly about it. It's the best thing for the both of us."

Standing with her legs braced firmly against the chair and her arms crossed, Eva resisted his attempts to make her sit. She was shaking with anger and frustration. Finally, she took a deep breath and calmed herself enough to speak. "This is insane. You're keeping me here against my will. I want nothing more to do with you. Let me go."

Bradford reached for his hat and overcoat. "The train doesn't leave until four. Plenty of time for you to think things over. Perhaps if you have some peace and quiet, you'll be able to understand the situation more clearly."

He unlocked the door and opened it. "I'll be back soon," he said. Eva made a move toward him, but he tipped his hat and quickly slipped out. Mouth open in astonishment, Eva heard the key in the lock, his muffled footsteps receding, then silence. She yanked the knob to satisfy herself that it was indeed locked. Furious, she aimed a kick at the door. Pain sprang up her leg from toe to knee.

Limping back to the chair, she collapsed, heart pounding, and bit back a sob. Her stomach clenched against the fear crawling over her nerves like bluebottle flies on a corpse.

Her mind began to race and she felt panic rise, but she took a breath and closed her eyes, focusing on finding something she could do. Turning to the window, she looked down at the street below. She tried to lift it open, but it wouldn't budge. Pressing her head against the glass, she could see a corner of the fire escape several feet away.

On the street below, pedestrians bustled back and forth, going about their day, unaware that there was anything amiss above them. Look up, look up, Eva sent out a mental plea. If by some chance someone should glance up, others would stop to see why and she could try and get their attention. Agatha told her about that once, and she hadn't believed her; didn't think that folk were so easily led. Then one day on her way to her sister's house, she saw a man standing on the corner, hands in his pockets, looking up. Without thought, she looked up too, in time to see a crew of men bolting the last letter of a sign into place. When she turned to go, three more curious passers-by had stopped to watch the procedure. She had shaken her head with a laugh at the time, but now she wished that there was someone out there putting up some kind of sign, hanging from a window ledge, jumping off a roof, anything that would make people stop and look up. She could wave, gesture or pound the window, then perhaps help would come and get her out of this mess. As it was, being on the second floor, she could beat on the window until her hands bled, and no one would hear anything.

Defeated, she leaned her head against the glass and fought back tears. Stop it, she told herself, stop feeling sorry for yourself. You should have screamed and run while you had the chance. She reached for her hanky and blew her nose. Her throat hurt from trying to keep anger and self-pity from letting her lose control. Crying wouldn't solve anything, and being riled up would get her nowhere. *Keep your head on straight and bide your time. Something will come up; keep believing and it will.*

Her stomach growled. She hadn't eaten breakfast and had only nibbled a little of the food Bradford ordered for her. It must be nearing lunch time. Her bladder reminded her that she had neglected it, too. *Oh damn,* she thought. *Should have insisted on using the toilet.* Maybe there would have been some way to get away then. She eyed the sink, hanging against the wall near the corner, and remembered one of Agatha's stories about travelling with the boys, and how they were afraid to go down the hall at night. She had lifted them up so they could relieve themselves at the sink. Agatha had rinsed it out well, and trusted that the chambermaids at the hotel were efficient in their duties after they checked out the next day.

The silent room closed in on her. Eva's head felt swollen, as if it would explode like dandelion seeds in a summer wind. She sat down in the chair, leaned back and rested her feet on the edge of the bed, crossing her ankles. She would just have to wait, and if she was lucky, it wouldn't be too long. Otherwise, she wouldn't be responsible. She wasn't used to being idle; she should be up doing something. Her thoughts were clearer when her hands were busy. About this time she should be walking her feet off at the restaurant, alternating between waiting tables and the kitchen. What would Chang think had happened to her? Would he have called Agatha to find out where she was? If so, maybe Agatha would be worried enough to call the police. Would she even have a job, when she got out of this mess?

And get out she would; she was determined. She felt the anger rising and she tamped it down. Take a breath, she told herself, no sense wasting energy. Keep your wits about you. The more she thought about it, the more resolute she became. She crossed her arms and set her chin. She wasn't going back, wasn't going anywhere with that man. Period.

9

This was her fault. She'd been too trusting. She shouldn't have allowed things to get this far. Anger grew, threatening to boil over as another thought occurred to her. Why would she trust anyone who had hired someone to spy on her, watching her every move for weeks? What had she been thinking?

She kicked the side of the chair, wincing when the pain spread along her foot. Taking a deep breath, she told herself to calm down. Yes, she should have known better; until now, the men in her life hadn't been very honourable. Her father sold her in marriage, her husband all but deserted her, and her employer tried to control her every move. Not a good foundation for trust. She must be really naïve to think that any of them would have her best interests in mind. *Okay, breathe,* she told herself. *You can't think straight if you're angry. What's done is done. Now you'll have to try and figure out how to get out of this mess.*

Eva put her head back on the chair, took several deep breaths and tried to relax. Trickles of fear were beginning in the pit of her stomach and her head whirled with possibilities. She stared at the ceiling as if the answers were written there. Anger and frustration coiled, threatening to spring, but she refused to let them take over. In all the time she worked for Bradford, she couldn't recall him being very talkative; now he seemed changed, as if—as if something had happened. He had sounded a little desperate.

That was nonsense. What could he possibly be desperate about? Having an heir? Any woman might be a likely candidate—why her? The questions rolled around in her mind until they came up against Aleksy. He must be connected to this somehow. Maybe he was dead, and Bradford lied to her. After all, with him out of the way, there would be no means to bargain on his end. She would be free and clear and wouldn't have to lose nine months of her life (and untold time after that, if she produced a healthy child) in payment for something that was no longer required.

Yes, she decided, Aleksy must have something to do with it. But why would Bradford go to the expense of tracking her down, coming all this way to find her? She mulled these thoughts over while ghostly shadows cast by the wan light shortened and then began to lengthen on the walls. She hardly noticed the passing of time; it was later in the day than she thought. Subtle noise from the street below barely pierced the hush of the room. Then even that faded away. She closed her eyes and breathed deeply, feeling her body relax, letting her mind search for answers.

She jerked awake, neck cramped from her position in the chair, body damp with sweat. How long had she dozed? A key rattled in a lock. She rubbed her forehead, feeling a headache start to grow. The door opened and Bradford entered, leaving the door unlocked this time. She straightened and flinched away from him as he approached.

"Were you asleep?" he said. "Sorry to wake you. We should go."

Ducking under his arm, she rose and stood with her back against the wall, calculating the distance to the door. "I've told you. I'm not going anywhere with you. You've no right to…"

"Yes, I know." He held up a hand. His voice was subdued. "And you were right. I, uh, had time to think things over while I was out." He took off his hat, holding it by the brim in his two hands. The room filled with a strained silence. Finally, he said, "I'm sorry."

"What?"

"Come on. Let me take you home. Phil is waiting outside with the car. He said he won't mind driving you back to the streetcar stop. Or wherever you want to go." His lips twisting in an ironic smile, he added, "…for a fee, of course." He held up one hand. "…which I've taken care of already."

"Well." Her planned retorts, recriminations, pleas and demands broke into pieces and skittered off in all directions. She searched his face for some trace of a lie, a ruse to make her do what he wanted. She found none, but a small voice in her head cautioned her to be wary. She puffed out a breath. "All right." She straightened her coat, anxious for this to end then remembered that her bladder had other ideas. "First, I'd like a minute to freshen up."

"Of course." He gave her an enlightened look. "How stupid of me." Walking to the door, he said, "It's just at the end of the hall."

He accompanied her down the darkened hallway, gently holding her elbow. "I didn't mean to be such an old bull about things," he said. "I was angry over the way you left and wanted an explanation. I wanted to know why. I wanted you to come back and honour our agreement, and I figured you'd see reason right off." They stopped at a door at the end of the hall. "It was the wrong way to go about it, I realize that now. I came up a day late and a dollar short, I guess." As she opened the door, he said, "Sometimes I can be such an idiot. If I knew how to do things better, maybe you wouldn't have left in the first place."

She had no answer to that. Did he really see reason, or was this just another ploy? Should she trust him? Best to be on her guard, she decided. Gratefully, she entered the small, high-ceilinged room and closed the door.

When she came out, he was leaning against the wall, hands in his pockets. He immediately straightened, "Ready?" he said as he offered his arm. Eva pretended not to notice and preceded him down the stairs.

The rain had stopped, leaving the sidewalks shiny with reflections of the shop windows. Phil stood with one foot up on the running board of his car, cleaning his fingernails with a large, sharp-looking pocket knife. As they approached, he looked up and his face changed from a serious, brooding scowl to a bright, welcoming smile. He flipped the knife closed and put it in his pocket, turning to open the back door all in one smooth movement. He motioned for her to enter.

"You go on," Eva said, taking a step back. "I'll make my own way home."

"Evelyn…"

She opened her mouth, but before she could correct him, he said, "Sorry. Eva, Phil is going to take me to the station before he takes you on home. It's too late for you to go in to the restaurant, but I'm sure he'll take you there if that's what you want. In the meantime, I have a train to catch." He reached for her hand, patted it. "You understand. They have their schedules…"

Eva snatched back her hand while a bitter taste flooded her throat. She looked from one to the other, feeling trapped. Two against one. "I'll be fine—really. I can find my own way."

"Please," Bradford's eyes were pleading. "I'd like to make sure you get home safely. It's the least I can do."

She was so tired. Would this never end? She was beginning to feel desperate and cranky. "Most of the day has been wasted. I'd just like to go home."

"And I'm sorry about that," he said. "Truly, I am."

"It's getting late," Phil told them, pulling out his pocket watch. He hurried around to the driver's side. Startled, Eva felt Bradford shove her into the back seat, his hand firm on her arm. He settled in beside her. As the car pulled away from the curb, Eva shifted towards the window, stifling her anger, wanting this ordeal over with and her own life back as quickly as possible.

One wiper squeaked against the windshield, making her nerves prickle as they drove through intermittent showers of rain. Out of the corner of her eye, Eva peered at the man she had worked for, shared a bed with and trusted. His long-fingered hands rested loosely in his lap and he stared straight ahead, wide-brimmed hat shading his eyes, mouth pressed in a grim line. Sudden fatigue made her bones melt against the seat. Why couldn't she have just fallen in love with him? It would have made things so much easier. Was there something wrong with her? Maybe she just couldn't trust any man enough to feel anything deeper than a vague fondness. She thought about her sister Agatha and her husband. They were nothing alike. Her sister, petite and rosy; tall Henry, always ready with a joke. They were so easy with each other, stepping together to their own special music in the dance of daily life. She would like to do that one day, but until now, no one had a song that touched her heart. She sighed, gazing at the water droplets streaking diagonally along her window until the car came to a sudden halt.

"We're here," Phil announced from the front seat.

The sprawling station loomed through the misty rain. Eva remembered her arrival a few short months ago. She hadn't been prepared for the bustling scenario that greeted her when she and her friend Billy got off the train, much less the cavernous terminal with its marble floors and soaring ceilings. Never having been further from the sparse homestead she grew up on, or the wooden sidewalks of the village, the buildings of the city took her breath away. It was as busy as ever now with uniformed soldiers, families, and working men with places to go or come from.

Bradford opened the door, then turned back and held out his hand. "You'll come in, won't you? It would mean so much if I could have your company until it's time to go."

"I thought we agreed…" Phil began. Bradford scowled at Phil and raised a hand. "I'm sure it's all right." He turned back to Eva. "Say you'll come. Please."

The pleading tone of his voice made Eva pause. She felt confused. What was he doing? He had never begged for anything in all the time she was in his employ. Warning bells rang in her head.

"Please," he said again. She studied his face. He looked hopeful, waiting for her to take his hand.

"And then I'm going home," she said. Anything to get this over with. They were in a public place; Phil could see them from the car. Maybe they could part on friendly terms. After all, he did come all this way. And just for her…

What was she thinking? He'd lied to her, kidnapped her; she just wanted this to be over. She slid out of the car on her own. "Let's say goodbye here. No hard feelings?" She held out her hand.

Bradford took her arm, placing her wrist in a painful grip. Taken by surprise, Eva was pulled up the wide steps and across the plaza. She struggled to keep her balance and tug her hand free, but his grip tightened, numbing her arm with pain. "Wait." She said. "This wasn't the deal." At the entrance she tried to stop, but Bradford kept walking, dragging her along.

"You didn't think I'd let you go that easily, did you?" he stopped, leaning so close she could see a drop of perspiration in the shadow of his hat. "Really, Eva, I'm very disappointed. I thought you'd be smarter than that."

I thought I was too. Eva fumed, not sure if she was angrier at him or herself. "You're right. I was stupid to trust you." She tried again to pull her arm out of his grasp. "Let me go. This is one of the reasons I left. Now you know."

Bradford smiled, his eyes cold and threatening. "Your sister has two little boys," he said. "If you don't come with me now, Phil has instructions to see if perhaps that may be one too many for her."

"What?" Eva was stunned. "What do you mean?"

"Come with me now—quietly—and everything will be as it was. I promise. If not…"

Eva heard the words he spoke, but the meaning didn't penetrate. She felt unable to move, paralyzed with fear.

"I don't understand."

"You don't have to. Just do as I say, and everything will turn out as it should." Still smiling, he drew her a few steps more into the station.

"Stop. Wait a minute." She pulled against him, making him stop with her. "Are you saying that if I don't come with you, Phil will harm my nephews? Would he do something like that?"

"I didn't say that, exactly, did I? He has his instructions. He knows what to do. And you wouldn't want anything to happen to those two little boys, I'm sure." She twisted around in time to see Phil's car pull into traffic. "I'm not really sure what he's capable of, but I do know he's very good at what he does." His breath brushed her ear as he leaned towards her. "Walk away from me, and all it will take is a phone call."

"You wouldn't."

"Try me."

Eva watched the car disappear, then turned to Bradford, fear filling her with a hot fury. She could feel her face flush with anger, and her lungs burned as she struggled to breathe.

"Come along," Bradford began walking as if they were on a Sunday outing. "We have a train to catch."

All her frustration, fear and anger exploded outward. "You sneaky, fork-tongued liar!" She wrenched free and began to beat him with her fists, calling him every name she ever remembered her father using, and a few she'd picked up since. He managed to grab one hand, reached for the other as she flailed at him, her blows landing wherever she could reach. "Let go!" Frantically twisting in his grip, she kicked out with her foot, hearing the thud of her leather shoe against bone as she connected with his shin. Agonizing pain shot through her foot and leg, already sore from lashing out in the hotel room. With a yelp, he loosened his hold. The split-second was all she needed. She twisted away and started toward the entrance.

And hit what felt like a stone wall. "Whup! Watch where yer goin', lady," a gruff voice said. A cloud of cigarette smoke stung her eyes, and she inhaled a lungful of stale sweat. "What's the problem, here?" A tall, heavily-bearded man squinted at her through a haze of cigarette smoke.

"Get out of my way," she said. As she tried to step aside, she felt Bradford's hand on her shoulder. Whirling, she kicked out again, but met only air. She staggered back, then regained her balance.

Bradford's voice was as soothing and calm as if he were talking to a skittish mare. "You must excuse my wife," he said, putting an arm around her. "She's a little nervous around trains."

"I'm not your wife," Eva yelled at him, twisting away. "And you're a…a…" Rage prevented suitable words from reaching her mouth. "Get away from me. I wouldn't go anywhere with you if you were the last man on earth."

"Now, now. Just calm down…" Bradford began.

The bearded man took a step back, hands in the air. "I don't mean to fetch up in the middle of no family spat," he said. He shifted the cigarette to the other side of his mouth. In a distant part of her mind, Eva wondered how he managed to do that without disturbing the long curve of ash that hung from the end.

She was jerked back to reality as Bradford reached for her. In a panic, she looked around for something, anything, to use as a weapon. Her heavy old purse would come in handy now, and she vowed never go to outdoors without an umbrella again. All she had were her two hands and feet, and enough anger to give her strength.

As Bradford approached she stepped toward him and pushed with all her might. Caught off guard, he staggered backward.

Two men behind him blocked his fall. Another man stopped next to them, ready to help. "You okay?" said the taller one. Bradford regained his footing and pushed him away, glowering. The tall man stepped back and straightened his glasses. Eva's eyes widened in amazement.

"Billy?" she said.

10

"Eva? Hey. Whoa." Billy raised his hands, palms out. "What's going on?"

"Eva," Bradford bellowed. "We're going to miss the train."

With two quick steps Eva put Billy between her and her tormentor. "I'm not going anywhere with you," she said.

Bradford reached for her, clutching at her sleeve. "Eva…"

Billy put a restraining hand on Bradford's arm. "You there, fella—you deaf or something? The lady said she wasn't going with you."

Bradford shook his arm free, looked from one to the other. "There seems to be some misunderstanding—"

"Yes, there is," Eva's voice was tight with tension. She folded her arms and glared. "You don't understand, so I'll tell you one last time: I'm not going anywhere with you." Her heart was still racing and she couldn't seem to get enough air into her lungs. "Go away. Please. Just…go away."

They scowled at each other. People who had stopped to gawk started to move off, travellers streaming by their little group like water around rocks in a river. Eva felt numb, as if her body was disconnected from her head.

For a brief moment, Bradford's eyes flashed sharp with pain, then he scowled, rage once again darkening his features. "Remember what I said." Taking a couple of steps back, he turned on his heel and limped into the jostling crowd, a serious bruise no doubt forming from the toe of Eva's shoe. Eva stood frozen as he vanished from sight, his words tightening her stomach with fear.

"What was that all about? Who was he?" Billy turned to face her. The other men stood by, the slighter one with his hands in his pockets, the other looking her over through eyes slitted against a steady stream of smoke.

Eva waved her hand in a dismissive gesture, surprised to see that it shook slightly. She took a deep breath. She had to get to her sister. If she tried to explain now, Billy might want to call a constable or even try to go after Bradford. There was no time for any of that.

"What did he mean by, 'remember what I said?' Was that some kind of threat?"

Irritated, she shook her head. "I've got to get back to my sister's," she said. "I've got to warn her."

"About what?"

"I can't explain right now. I have to go." She rose on tiptoes, craning her neck to locate the way out. Thoughts scrambled around in her head. *I've got to get to Agatha. We have to figure out what to do.* Without looking back, she followed a stream of people toward the exit.

"Wait," Billy said, running up and stopping her with a hand on her arm. "Maybe we can help. Do you need a ride? Maybe Jacob here could drop you off." He turned to his friend who trailed behind him, licking the seal on a freshly rolled cigarette as he walked. "Eva, this here's Jacob. He's letting me stay over at his place for a while, 'til I find work for the winter."

"Pleased ta meetcha," Jacob said, lighting up and exhaling a cloud of blue smoke. Billy was taller than Jacob by a head, and while both men were unshaven, Jacob had the breadth of years on Billy's youthful slenderness. He stuck out his hand. Dirt was imbedded in the wrinkles of his skin and deeply entrenched under his fingernails. Eva gave him a weak nod, and mustered a smile, keeping her hands in her pockets. "I'd appreciate a ride. Yes. Thank you. But we need to go right now." She started again for the door. She didn't have time to indulge in niceties; the desire to hurry dominated her thoughts.

"What do you say; shall we give the lady a ride?" The men quickly caught up and matched her pace.

"Whereabouts are ya headed?" Jacob asked. Over her shoulder, Eva gave him the name of her sister's street.

"That ain't too far," he said. "N' it ain't much out of our way. I can take ya where you're going right easy."

"That would be great," said Billy. "Wouldn't it, Eva?"

"As long as we hurry."

"By the way, this is Tom," said Billy, indicating his other companion. Tom took off his hat and nodded, revealing a shiny bald head with a fringe of straggly grey hair, reminding Eva of damp work-socks strung on a clothesline. A bump of chewing tobacco created the only smooth area in his weather-lined face.

"Hiya," he grinned at her, exposing long yellow teeth.

As they approached the entrance, Billy asked, "Who was that fellow?"

"My former employer. I'll tell you all about it later." Before he could say more, she asked, "What are you doing here?"

"We just came down from camp. It's freeze-up now and there's three feet of snow. Our train was a bit late. Good thing Jacob waited for us."

They waited on the broad steps while Jacob went to get his vehicle. The rain had stopped, but the clouds hung bunched together, surly and threatening.

Eva couldn't imagine what other bizarre event could happen in one day. Billy had been on the same train, keeping her company on the twelve-hour trip from Alberta. Now, with him turning up at the place where they had last said goodbye, she felt as if they were continuing where they left off so many months ago.

A battered pickup truck rattled up to the curb, pulling her thoughts back to the present. Billy threw his duffle in the back among crates, boxes, various-sized pieces of lumber and an assortment of rusty machinery.

"Let's go then," he said. "You coming, Tom?"

"Pay no mind about me," Tom said and spat a stream of tobacco juice into a potted shrub already besieged with cigarette butts and dead leaves. "I'm for the other direction, but I can get me where I gotta go by streetcar if needs be." The older man tipped his hat to Eva. The men shook hands all around, with much back-slapping, and "see ya soon's". Eva's stomach tightened with impatience, but she pressed her lips together to keep from screaming at them to hurry. Billy helped Eva into the cab and with a cough and a hiccup from the engine of the ancient pick-up, they were on their way.

She supposed it was some archaic act of chivalry that put women in the middle: protection, wild animals or simply stopping them from falling out. She would prefer taking the risk of landing on the hard pavement to sitting between Billy and the malodorous Jacob who had waggled his eyebrows at her as she got in. Billy could have sat in the middle—then she wouldn't have to share space with the gear shaft that rose from the floor of the truck. The door did rattle loosely as if it would open any minute, spilling anyone sitting next to it out onto the road. Billy held onto the handle, just in case.

The engine of the old truck groaned with effort, beginning to climb a slight rise. Eva cringed as Jacob reached over to the floor shift to find a lower gear. She gritted her teeth as his hand 'accidentally' brushed her thigh on the way back to the steering wheel. She tried to distract herself by looking out at the busy streets.

She thought back to the day of her arrival; how in awe she was of the hustle and bustle of the city. The vast, flat prairie she left behind had horses, wagons and, very rarely, the occasional vehicle. Here, there were no horses and wagons and empty spaces. Never in her wildest dreams had she envisioned the noise and traffic that constantly occupied the streets. It was busy and crowded, full of purpose and energy. Even the clouds looked different. Heavy with moisture scented with the salt-tang of the sea, they surged against the mountains and pressed against the land, held back only by the tall buildings. She thought she'd never get used to it, but of a wonder, now she felt as if she'd always lived in the rain forest, the wide prairie starting to fade from her memory like an early-morning dream.

The truck lurched over another bump and she wondered if they'd get to their destination in one piece. She couldn't shake the feeling that Bradford might be bluffing again. Should she believe him? Was all this panic to get home and warn her family just another ploy? The whine of the engine grated along her spine. The effort of keeping her legs away from the gear shaft and the driver made her tense and uncomfortable and the springs in the truck seat threatened to break through the thin leather. Walking would have been easier. Her stomach growled, reminding her of the long day with little food. She put her arm through Billy's and hung on.

Billy looked over at her, concern in his eyes. "You look properly wrung out," he said. "What exactly did happen anyway? Was he rough on you?"

"He was my employer when I left Alberta to come here," she said. "He had some kind of skewed idea that I was his property, and he came all this way, to—to claim me."

Eva began to relax for the first time in hours. "I was on my way to a new job this morning. *Was it only this morning? It felt like a week at least.* When I got to the streetcar stop, that man was waiting for me." She rubbed two fingers on the bridge of her nose. The last thing she needed was a full-blown headache. "I can't imagine what my new employer must think of my not showing up on the first day. I'm not even sure I still have a job."

"Don't worry," Billy said. "It'll all turn out, you'll see. Soon's he understands what happened, I'm sure he'll give you another chance."

Eva managed a weak smile and braced herself from falling against Jacob as the truck turned a sharp corner and started down the street where Agatha lived. The already gray day was losing what little light it had, and the headlight beams danced along the uneven pavement.

"It was good of you to do this, Jacob," said Eva. "I hope you're not going too far out of your way."

"Naw. Makes no never mind—one route is as good as the next, and we're here now anyways. It's a bit of a drive no matter how you look at it. Me, I got a couple acres down by the river, just outa town, between here'n New Westminster. It ain't so far from here in the grand scheme of things." Jacob shifted his cigarette and this time the long column of ash fell on his shirt. He brushed it off with a casual hand, not taking his eyes from the road. "It's a bit damp in the spring, and the outhouse tends to float when the river is high, but I do a little fishin' when the turnips don't grow." He chuckled as he shifted gears. Eva and Billy exchanged a look, and Billy smiled and shrugged.

With a wrench of the wheel, Jacob swerved the truck over to the curb. "Here y'are," he said, with one more swipe at her thigh as he put the truck into neutral. Billy pulled down the door handle and pushed. Nothing happened. He tried again, a little harder, with the same result.

"Give it a good yank, son." Jacob flicked his cigarette butt out the window. "Sometimes it sticks."

With a dark look, Billy took Jacob's advice and this time the door opened. It seemed there had been no danger of anyone falling out after all.

As Billy helped Eva down, a car pulled up to the curb in front of them. Henry got out and broke into a big smile as he approached.

"Hiya, sweetheart," he said to Eva, giving her a quick hug. "That old Chinaman let you off early?" Before she could reply, he looked around at her companions. "And who have we got here?"

Eva made introductions all around.

Henry nodded to Jacob. When it was Billy's turn, Henry grabbed his hand, shaking it with enthusiasm. "Billy," he said. "Aren't you the one I met at the train station when Eva arrived here? I heard you went up north—logging or something."

"Camps are closed for the winter," Billy said, massaging his hand. "We got three feet of snow dumped on us already. I'd just got off the train when we bumped into Eva and gave her a ride."

Henry looked from Billy to Eva. "What were you doing at the train station?" he asked her. "I thought you were starting a new job today. You decide to fly the coop instead?"

"It's a long story." She started toward the house. "I'm glad you're home—I have something very important to tell you and Agatha right away." She reached for the gate latch.

"This sounds important," she heard Henry say. He swung his arm in an encompassing movement. "C'mon in then, and take a load off."

"Thanks, but I should get along," Billy said. "I'd love to hear the story, too, but I'm staying with Jacob here until I find work. Maybe I can come by for a visit some other time."

Eva paused at the gate to see what was going to happen next. She was anxious for Henry to come inside, but she knew that once he settled in to a conversation, there was no moving him until he was done.

"Looking for work?" Henry's smile grew even broader. "They're hiring down at the foundry. Can't get enough workers since this war business started. If you're interested, I can give you all the details."

Eva groaned inwardly, apprehension making her stomach burn. She wanted to hurry into the house but she needed her sister and brother-in-law together when she told them. Knuckles white as she held onto the gate, she waited.

Billy looked over at Jacob, who was rolling another cigarette, then turned back to Henry. "Thanks. I'm bunking up with Jacob, but I could come back once I get settled in."

"No need, boy," Henry said. "We can put you up, and you can get right to it. I've got some connections, and if that place doesn't work out, I know of a couple more. If you'd like to give it a try, I'll drop you off on my way tomorrow."

"That's a mighty generous offer, Henry," said Billy. "What do you think?" He looked up at Jacob. "Mind if I give it a try?"

"Tell ya what," Jacob put up a hand to end the discussion. "You just go on ahead. That sounds a lot easier than what we were gonna do. We can meet up somehow when you're done."

"You sure?"

Jacob shrugged and flicked a hand in dismissal. He struck a wooden match, grinning as he looked from one to the other. As he lit the cigarette, the glow of the flame gave his face an ominous mask. Eva suppressed a shudder.

Billy hauled his duffle bag out of the back of the truck. "Thanks for all you've done, Jacob—be seeing you soon." With a wave, he shut the door and stepped back.

Jacob pulled away, honking his horn as the old truck complained its way down the street, trailing a cloud of blue smoke. As grateful as Eva was for the ride, there was no way she would ever intentionally seek out the old man's company. He appeared to have a sleazy side to his generosity and she didn't want to find out which side of him was who he really was. She sighed. Was there no man out there she could trust? That was a question for another time; there were more pressing concerns. With luck, she'd never see him again, and she puffed out a relieved breath as the truck disappeared around the corner.

With Henry and Billy at her back, she pushed open the gate to her sister's house.

11

Drawn by the smell of frying pork chops, Eva headed for the kitchen, tossing her coat on a chair. Agatha stood at the stove, pot lid in one hand, poking a fork into a pot of boiling potatoes with the other. Eva's mouth watered, reminding her that she'd had little to eat all day.

"Where are the boys?" she asked.

As if in answer, her two nephews raced through the kitchen on their way to the hallway. Eva backed up against the door jamb just in time to get out of their way. They clattered up the staircase, chasing each other into their room. The door slammed against their giggles and all was quiet.

"Guess that answered your question," Agatha said, replacing the pot lid. She shook her head. "Lordy, I hate these rainy days. I'll sure be glad when the sun comes out and they can roar around outside. What did you want them for?"

"I didn't." Eva sagged against the wall, relief draining her muscles of the strength to hold her up. "I just needed to know that they were safe."

"Safe? Those two?" Agatha snorted. "They're gonna break a few bones, if not their silly heads, one of these days." She paused, shaking her head. "Boys." Still holding the potato fork, she peered at Eva. "Why? What's wrong? Chang give you a bad time your first day and you're looking for some peace and quiet?"

"I didn't make it to the restaurant," said Eva.

"What?"

"When's dinner, darlin'?" Henry stalked into the kitchen and gave his wife a peck on the cheek, easily avoiding the fork. "Set another place – I brought an extra mouth in off the street." He looked from Agatha to Eva and back. "What? Someone died?"

"I was just going to find that out, when you barged in," said Agatha. She always made enough for last-minute guests, which she could count on once or twice a week at least. "Go get washed up and we'll eat." She turned to Eva. "What happened? Are you all right?"

Eva shrugged. "Maybe I should save it until the boys are fed."

"Sounds serious," Agatha said, draining potato water into the sink. She turned to her husband, who had paused in the doorway. "Shoo."

Henry stood his ground. "I want to hear this too. Did you get into some kind of mix-up? Or did Chang fire you when you tried to burn the place down?"

"It had nothing to do with Chang or the restaurant. As I said, I never got there. Do you remember Horace Bradford, the man I used to work for before I came out here?"

"Sure, I remember." Agatha waggled her eyebrows and smiled. "It is something you don't want the guys to hear?"

"I think everyone should hear it. I'm not sure about the boys, though. You can decide how best to tell them." She took a deep breath and blew it out. "Bradford was waiting at the streetcar stop this morning. He tried to force me to go back to his farm with him."

Agatha stared at her. "Good grief. That's ridiculous."

"And that's not the worst part," Eva said. "But when I tell the whole story, you'll see." "Let's get this meal out of the way first," Agatha said. She firmly believed that things were better handled on a full stomach. "I can hardly wait."

* * *

It took but a few minutes for everyone to find a seat at the table. Agatha brought in a platter of pork chops and potatoes, and Eva followed with a bowl of peas and carrots. Henry introduced Billy to Agatha and the boys as he passed around the platters. Billy told them all about the logging camp, and Eva watched the boys with affection as they questioned him. "Are there any bears up there?" asked Wally, the oldest. Little Freddy's eyes grew round with awe as he awaited the answer.

"Sure are," Billy told him. "And the trees are so big, six men holding hands couldn't make a circle around even the smallest one." He lowered his voice. "But the bears are even bigger."

"Did you see one?" asked Freddy.

"I sure did. But he was far off, so I wasn't too scared. He passed right on by without catching my scent. Didn't even turn around and wave."

Eva dug into her meal, but after the first few bites, she lost her appetite. The banter faded into the background of her mind as she found herself looking for answers, excuses, and generally trying to define her emotions. Sure, she had been frightened and angry. Mostly angry. And the more she thought about it, the more she smouldered with firmly banked fury. At last the boys asked to be excused.

"Now we can get down to the good stuff," said Agatha, watching her sons disappear into their room, closing the door. "Let's have it, Eva. Looks like you're about to bust."

As Eva spoke, she began to feel as if the whole episode had happened to someone else. Billy's knuckles were white as he clutched his fork in his fist, and she saw a muscle jump in his jaw. Henry's face turned various shades of red, and when she related Bradford's threat to the boys, he'd had enough. "That S.O.B.," he burst out. "I'll…"

"Hold on Henry," said Agatha. "Let's hear it all first."

He struggled to hold in his indignation until Eva was finished. His face a frightening shade of purple, Henry could contain himself no longer. "That bastard," he growled. "I catch him lurking around here, I'll tear him in half and send his parts in different directions." He proceeded to detail other suitable scenarios, some rather gruesome, others creatively contradictory, but sincere nonetheless. Since no one could get a word in, they waited until he ran down.

Agatha had no doubt her husband could produce a formidable front to protect his family. But as much as he'd blustered and threatened, he'd never actually hurt anyone, as far as she knew. It comforted her to know, as she busied herself with clearing the dinner dishes to hide her smiles, that he would do whatever it took to keep them safe.

Finally, Henry slapped his hand on the table and stood up. "That's it," he said. "I'm calling that detective friend of mine. This should be reported. And if he ever tries something like that again, we'll be ready for him." He made his way to the front hall, lifted the receiver from the wall telephone, and shouted a number to the operator.

Agatha filled the sink with water and detergent while Eva and Billy brought in the rest of the dishes.

"Thanks for the dinner," said Billy. "Anything I can help with?"

"You just go on into the living room and put your feet up." Agatha plunged her hands into the soapy water. "We can manage here."

Henry poked his head around the corner of the door. "Carlson said he'll drop by on his way to the constabulary. He's just starting his shift." He jerked his head at Billy. "C'mon, Billy. Let's get outa the way and let these women do what they do best."

Agatha and Eva exchanged a look and Agatha rolled her eyes. They worked on in silence. Finally Agatha said, "The boys will be fine. Remember what Henry told you – he'll make sure nothing happens to them." She smiled to herself, remembering her husband's reaction when Eva told them about Bradford's threat that Phil would harm one of his two sons. "Henry looks after what's his. His family is his dearest and his foremost concern." Agatha's voice softened. "And that includes you."

Eva managed a slight smile as she reached for a cup to dry. "I just wish the detective would hurry and get here." The cup slipped out of her hand and crashed to the floor. "Sorry. I'll get the broom…"

"You won't." Agatha took her sister by the shoulders and steered her to a chair beside the table. "You just sit. You've had a rough day and you're all done in." She retrieved the broom and dustpan out of the pantry closet, pointing the dustpan at her sister. "You need to get some rest, young lady. It's just a cup – I can manage. I'm not in my dotage yet."

"Getting a little bossy in your 'almost dotage', aren't you?"

Agatha swept the shards into the waste bin and took a chair across from Eva. She thought back to all the times they had sat just that way; 'table sharing', they called it. Until now, it was mostly Agatha who shared her hopes and dreams. Bad news was best shared shoulder to shoulder, for comfort. The tables have turned, she thought, chuckling to herself at the pun. She looked over at her sister, who sat, chin in hand, staring off into space. She reached across and put her hand over Eva's as it lay limp against the patterned oilcloth. She was glad she hadn't mentioned Dani's problems this morning; that would have made her day even worse. That would have to wait until they got this sorted out.

"You want to talk about it?"

"Not right now." Eva rubbed her forehead as if to make it focus. "My brain is numb. The world seems as if it's moving in slow motion. And on top of everything else, I don't know if I still have a job."

"I'm sure Chang will give you another chance," said Agatha.

"I'm not. I certainly wouldn't like it if I'd hired someone and they didn't show up. How could I be sure they wouldn't do it again, and if they were responsible enough to even do a good job?"

"If you explained the situation, I know he'd understand. If you like, I'll go with you. I'll vouch for you. I'll convince him you're not just making excuses; that when you didn't show up, it was no fault of your own. It'll be okay, I'm sure of it." Agatha gave her sister's hand a pat and sat back. "You're tired. You'll feel better after a good rest."

"What kind of plots are you two hatching?" Henry stood in the doorway, looking from one to the other. "I had my face fixed for a cuppa," he said. "Guess I'll have to get it myself." He slouched over to the cupboard trying to look as if he'd been sorely mistreated, an expression which made him appear more comical than tragic. Turning back to the doorway where Billy stood gazing at Eva with a concerned expression, he raised a cup and his eyebrows at the same time. Billy dragged his eyes away from Eva long enough to shake his head. Henry shrugged and reached for the teapot.

"My detective friend should be arriving any minute," he told Eva, as he spooned sugar into his tea. "Then it'll be done and we can all get some rest."

Eva rose from her chair and began to pace. "I could do without having to go over it all again," she said. "It's beginning to sound like a weird story that happened to someone else."

"Well, it didn't," Henry growled, the teaspoon making loud clanks against the side of his cup as he stirred. "It may or may not be a real threat but we have to take it seriously." He slurped his tea. "Once we report it, and then if he makes another attempt, Bradford I mean, then we can get rid of him once and for all. The man's a candidate for the Looney Bin, as far as I'm concerned. Maybe if we get lucky, he'll be put away." He put his cup down with a thump. "In the meantime, Agatha and I will make sure that the boys are safe. One or another of us will keep an extra eye on them. If it keeps raining, that won't be much of a problem. They'll be playing around the house. Once the sun comes out, we'll make sure that they're supervised at all times. There's no way that nut-case is going to bring harm to my boys."

Eva shrugged. "It might have been an idle threat, for all I know. Something to make me do what he wanted."

"Don't matter," Henry said with a scowl. "We can't take any chances.

We have to assume he'll do what he said. Anyone who would travel all that way is either a love-sick nincompoop or a demented monster. Who knows what would have happened if you had done what he wanted."

A rap at the door brought Henry to his feet. "That must be him now," he said, emptying his cup in one last gulp. "Let's get this over with."

12

Everyone followed Henry into the living room. He opened the door to a tall man in a worn overcoat who took off his hat as he entered. "Good of you to come, Art." The two men shook hands. "C'mon in and meet the family. This here's Art Carlson, everybody. He used to try and beat me at street hockey when we were young bucks."

Carlson nodded and grinned. "I wouldn't say 'try', exactly," he said in a slow, easy drawl as he handed his hat and coat to Henry. "That was a long time ago, so I can understand if the facts are a little blurry for you."

Henry gave him a sideways glance and opened his mouth as if to protest. Instead, he grinned, pointing to each in turn as he told him their names, then offered him a seat. Carlson took the nearest easy chair and produced a notepad and pen from his pocket. Eva sat at the far end of the sofa where she could watch everyone. She studied her brother-in-law's school chum, trying to imagine them as boys. She knew that Henry had played football in high school, had even been drafted into the fledgling Canadian Football League. She couldn't remember which team. He had told them a few stories about the training camp he'd attended, but had never mentioned hockey. From what Carlson had just said, maybe there was a good reason. It wasn't like Henry to pass up a chance for some kind of witty or sharp-edged comeback.

Carlson and Henry would be around the same age, she guessed, but the lines in Carlson's face and his thinning hair made him seem much older. He appeared to her as if he'd seen a lot more things than a man should. She wondered if that made him good at his job, or too jaded to care.

"So we have threats? Attempted kidnapping?" Carlson said. He looked at each in turn, then straight at Eva. "I take it that it was you that received this supposed threat?"

"There's nothing 'supposed' about it," Eva said. "It was a threat. I didn't think for a minute he was just trying to frighten me into doing what he wanted."

Carlson raised his eyebrows. "And now?"

"He'd said things before, then turned right around and did the opposite. I don't know if I can trust him to tell the truth."

Carlson sat back in the chair, licked the tip of his pencil and held the notebook ready. "How 'bout we start from the beginning," he said. "What was it, exactly, that he wanted?"

Eva's stomach clenched. How many times would she have to repeat the ordeal? She took a deep breath and with her jaw tensed against every word, she began with the meeting at the streetcar stop. Carlson interrupted as she went along, asking questions and making notes. As she repeated the sequence of events, she could almost feel the texture of the waffles on her tongue, the dusty, stale odor of the room at the hotel, the pressure of Bradford's fingers as he pulled her into the station.

"…and that's when we ran into Billy," she finished.

Carlson looked around and found Billy leaning against the wall at the back of the room, arms crossed and brows knitted in a dark frown. "You saw him?" he asked.

Billy nodded. "Yep."

"Hmmm…" Carlson turned back to Eva. "Looks to me like you went along with him. He didn't just grab you and force you into the car, or into the hotel."

Irritation prickled along her nerve ends. "He wasn't about to let me walk away. I tried, but they both hemmed me in. If I had tried to run, they would have grabbed me. He told me if I screamed, he'd just tell everyone that his 'wife' was given to hysterics." Carlson continued to stare at her. What did he want her to say? Didn't he believe her? She struggled to keep her voice calm. "I used to work for the man. I tried to reason with him. I thought I could make him understand, and even thought for a moment he did. But I was wrong." From the expression on Carlson's face, she wondered if he was taking this seriously.

Carlson wrote in his notebook, stared at it a moment, then turned to a new page. "Tell me more about this 'private detective' person. You said his name was Phil?"

"Yes, Philaberto Stellegadis, he said his name was."

The detective smiled and shook his head.

"What," said Henry. "You know him?"

"It's possible, once we figure this out." Carlson said. "A sleazy character like that likely would have crossed paths with us at some time or other. But that's a made-up name people use when they don't want to admit to something they shouldn't have done. Or just don't want to be identified. We used it a time or two, kidding around when we were growing up. I'm surprised you didn't remember."

Henry scratched his head and frowned. "Didn't make the connection. Guess I got all het up worrying about my boys." He looked over at Eva. "And of course, Eva here."

Eva looked into his eyes and read concern, not blame. At least he believed her.

Carlson snapped his notebook closed and put it away. Rising from his chair he looked down at Eva. "We're going to need more than a made-up name, if we're going to track this fellow down. We'd better take a trip down to the station. We've got a young fella who can draw a likeness from what's described to him." He looked over at Billy. "You'd best come along as well. We need to talk a little more about what you saw, and we can do it just as well while the young lady here is occupied."

"Can't it wait until morning?" Agatha said. "My sister is exhausted; she's just had a terrifying experience."

Eva reached out, putting her hand on her sister's arm. "Don't worry about me. It's best just to get this over and done with. I can't do it tomorrow. I have to show up at work or I won't have a job for sure."

Agatha searched Eva's face, noting the skin drawn tight, the slight bruising under the eyes. "Are you sure?"

"Remember that Sunday I came to dinner when I worked for the De-Fraine's? I told you I had met a man by the gate as I came in. He asked for directions. That could have been Phil. Or whatever his name is. I remember thinking that his moustache wasn't quite right. It looked kind of funny and I noted it at the time, but I guess I forgot about it. I didn't think it was important." She gave her sister's arm a pat. "Suppose that really was him? He

83

already knows where you live. I have to be sure I've done everything I can do to help."

As Eva went to get her coat, Carlson said, "This shouldn't take long. We'll get her back home as soon as we can." He motioned to Billy. "You ready?"

Billy nodded, one arm already in the sleeve of his coat. Agatha thought as she watched them get ready to go, that it was a good thing Billy had been asked to help. Otherwise he'd be hanging around, getting underfoot, mooning like a love-sick calf. Eva hadn't known Billy long, but Agatha recognized attraction when she saw it. She smiled to herself as she looked at her sister, and thought, *she doesn't have a clue how he feels.*

She sighed. Henry's instincts to help people were one thing, but she wished he wouldn't keep bringing just anyone in off the streets. But she knew her husband had the bright idea that he could save the world by bringing home every Tom, Dick and Harry he found in order to help them get started. This time, he didn't have a clue exactly what he was starting, or at least helping along. She shook her head. Big man, big heart, but sometimes not so big in the common sense department. But that's why she loved him.

She studied Billy as he held open the door for everyone to precede him, wondering if Eva realized she had brushed her hair behind her ear as she passed him. Her sister could use someone decent in her life that treated her well. That respected her and cared enough to make her happy. In the short time she had known him, Billy seemed kind and patient. Hard work and time would fill out his broad shoulders; his big hands looked capable of the effort needed for a decent life. They would make a good match and if that happened, and if he so much as hurt a hair on her sister's head, treated her like the other men in her life had done, he would regret it. She would personally see to it.

* * *

At the station, Detective Carlson hustled them past the front desk into a small room. A high window looked out on the black sky and a fan moved with lazy circles on the ceiling.

"Sit yourselves down while I get things started. I won't be long," he said, closing the door behind him.

Alone in the silent room, they looked around. There was a small table in the middle of the room and two chairs, one on each side, besides the two chairs against the dull green walls without a poster or sign to relieve the monotony. They chose the chairs against the blank wall and prepared to wait.

Billy could almost touch Eva, but he sat still as stone. His mind made and discarded frantic thoughts, but he couldn't think of anything to say. Anger rose behind his throat every time he thought that she might have been taken back to the prairies and he would never have found her again. He leaned his forearms on his knees and with his fingers laced together, worried at a hangnail on his thumb. He felt Eva slouch in the chair. He remained motionless, his mind a blank, hoping she would say something to put him out of his misery. Glancing out of the corner of his eye, he saw that she had leaned her head against the wall and closed her eyes. He was relieved; she must be tired. There would be time to talk later. He'd make sure of it.

Before long Carlson returned and beckoned Eva to come with him. Billy tipped the chair back on two legs against the wall. *I coulda said something to her*, he thought. But he hadn't, and couldn't think of a thing even now. He clenched his fists. There had to have been something he might have told her that would make things better. Not that she would have listened to him anyway, but he could have tried. She was stubborn and independent, he knew, but somehow he had to make her see that he was there for her if she needed him. He examined that thought, and there it was: more than that of a protector, much more. He'd been herded in, marked for life like a branded calf. There was no escape for him now.

He closed his eyes, remembering the feel of her thigh against his as they crowded into the old truck. Her scent assailed his nostrils and all he could find to put a name to it was soap and crushed rose petals. He had wanted to put an arm around her then, but she had a tight grip on that arm to steady herself as the old truck rattled and swayed along rough streets and around sharp corners.

Carlson came into the room and pulled out a chair. The detective flung his coat on the table, placed his hat on top and sat down across from Billy.

"Well, Billy," he said. "We've a bit to wait while the little lady gives her description of 'Phil' to our sketch artist. Why don't you tell me your story?"

"Not much to tell," said Billy. He straightened in his chair and blinked a couple of times to clear the cobwebs. "Me and a couple of the guys had just got off the train. First thing you know, here we were smack in the middle of a kerfuffle. Turns out it was Eva, of all people. This here fellow was apparently trying to make her come with him, and she wasn't havin' any." He chuckled. "Downright feisty little thing, she is."

Carlson considered the younger man. Billy was a head taller than himself, whereas Eva and he were almost of a height. *She might be feisty*, he thought, *but 'little' she certainly was not.* It was plain to see that Billy admired her. She was a handsome woman, after all. But it wasn't clear how Eva felt about Billy. Likely, she had too many other things occupying her thoughts right now to spare any for him. Be interesting to see how this pans out. In the meantime, he had a job to do. "Give me the names of the men that were with you at the train station."

After Billy told him about Jacob and Tom and what he knew about them from their one summer at the logging camp, Carlson sat back. "Anything else?" he said.

Billy shrugged. "Seems that fellow wasn't 'bout to take 'no' for an answer. He kept trying to grab her." He chuckled. "I recall the first time I ran into her, back before the both of us came out here to the coast. Some crazy duffer had tried to drag her into an alley. Don't know what he had in mind, considering he didn't have much of one to begin with, being the village idiot and all. Somehow he got the idea that she should take a shine to him. She had already whanged him with a rock when I came along. Didn't want no help, though. No siree. She didn't seem too worried. She tells me, 'he's like a hound dog chasing a hay wagon – if he caught it, he doesn't know whether to jump up and roll in it or take a nap. The man is a little simple, anyway. Not too much to be scared of – nothing I couldn't handle.' So I just waited there with her until the local constable came along. She wouldn't hardly let me walk her back to her wagon, even." He shook his head, remembering.

"And this time?"

"This time we all stood around while Eva allowed she wasn't going anywhere with this guy. Wasn't like he was real physical with her, just expected her to do like he told her. He acted like she was some kind of kid and he knew what was best. I made it plain that we were going to stand up for her. Then he says to her, 'remember what I said,' and limps off. Maybe she whacked him one, or maybe he just has a limp. Dunno. I'd opt for the former, myself." He leaned forward, elbows on the table, considering. "Then, we offered to give her a ride on home. That's about it."

"Did you know this fellow?" asked Carlson. He consulted his notes. "Horace Bradford, I think his name is."

"Nope. Never laid eyes on him before. Heard Eva tell that she used to work for him, though. Housekeeper, like she said." Billy wondered why Carlson asked him questions he already knew the answers to. Probably hoping something would slip out that had been overlooked.

'So how did you come to stay with Henry?" asked Carlson. "You a friend of the family?"

"Eva and I somehow ended up on the same train, coming over here from Alberta." Billy scratched his head. "Funny how that happened. It was a long trip, and we spent some time talking about this and that to pass the time. I met Henry when he came to get her at the station."

Billy told him how Henry had offered to find him employment in the foundry. Carlson made a few more notes, then stood. "You think of anything else," he said, "you give us a ring here at the station, or else you can call me at home. Henry's got my number, but here's both numbers just in case." He tore a page out of the notebook and handed it to Billy.

"Come on," Carlson said, taking up his coat and hat and opening the door. "Eva's probably close to being done about now. We'll collect her and see about getting the two of you home."

13

Eva turned over on the small cot, the sounds that murmured through her dreams shredding into distant voices. She was exhausted when Carlson dropped them off the night before and went straight to her room. Now she felt as if she hadn't slept at all. Like bees on a hot summer day, the buzz of conversation circled in her brain until she gave up and fumbled her way out of the covers. Eyes half open, she reached for her alarm clock. The black and white face stared solemnly back at her, hands firmly fixed at ten minutes past two. She turned over, plumped her pillow and noticed the silver light streaming from under the shade. Puzzled, she glanced back at the clock. Still ten past two. The clock had stopped.

The basso mumble of a male voice suggested the men hadn't yet left for work so she still had some time. Even so, within minutes she was up and dressed and making her way downstairs. She could smell fresh coffee and heard the rasp of a knife over toast as she entered the kitchen. In the doorway, she stopped in astonishment. Instead of Agatha's husband or their new boarder, Uri sat at the kitchen table, the last person she expected to see at this time of day. He smiled at her, his lop-sided grin at once familiar and open.

"Ah, you're up," Agatha said. "Please tell me you have time for some breakfast."

"I work at a café," Eva said with a dry smile, still staring at her brother-in-law. "I'm in no danger of starving."

"Surely you can have a coffee." Uri got up and took her hand. His grin disappeared, eyes searching her face as if to spot any changes in the week since she'd seen him last. "I've been worried about you."

Eva drew her hand away. There had been a time when his touch slid sparkles down her spine, but that was long ago, before he had married her sister. She studied him closely; his eyes were red-rimmed and it looked as if he had been a bit careless with his razor. "What are you doing here? Aren't you working today?"

"I heard about what happened and I had to make sure you were okay," Uri said. "Agatha here's been filling me in. I had to see for myself you were all right."

"I'm fine." She couldn't say why prickles of irritation clambered up her spine. Uri was her friend, after all. Maybe she was just tired, and fed up with the whole thing. She didn't even have the energy to wonder how he'd heard about it. She reached for the cup Agatha handed her and sipped, feeling the hot liquid soothe her, making the morning a little brighter. She tried on a smile, gave it up and took another sip.

"I'm running late. Again." Eva turned to Agatha. "I think there's something wrong with the alarm clock."

"You have to remember to set it." Grinning, Agatha put a plate of toast on the table and set a hand on her hip. With her other hand, she indicated a twisting motion. "See: you wind it up, make sure it's ticking, and then….." Eva scowled at her. "…you push the little gadget on the top… Okay, look," Serious now, Agatha set a jar of jam on the table. "It's been a pretty rough go for you lately. Things happen. I'll set the clock to rights for you, don't worry about it a minute longer. You have a little time—at least finish your coffee before you go."

"I'd hoped we could talk," Uri took her arm and guided her to a chair. "I was just telling Agatha here—Dani and I want you to come stay with us. We've fixed up the spare room downstairs and you could move in right away. We were thinking if we got you away from here, away from the boys, maybe it would help. Maybe somehow if you're not here, it would direct the threat away from the boys." She could see a muscle jump in his jaw. "It's you Bradford wants; if he doesn't know where you are, he'd have to change his tactics."

"You're probably right." Eva rubbed her f orehead, willing her brain to work. "Right now I can't think and I don't want to make things worse. I have to get in to work or I may not be employed very long. Since I missed that first day, Chang's been giving me the eye every morning. I don't think he trusts me yet—probably worried I won't show again like that first day and he'll have to hire someone else." She looked from Agatha to Uri, both staring at her. She could see the concern written all over their faces, see how much they cared about her. "Can we talk about this later?"

"Sure," Uri said. "Come on over after work and have a look at the place. There's lots of room, even a spot where you can have a hotplate if you want. You would be able to make your own meals." He paused as Eva cocked an eyebrow at him. "If you want, that is. I know you'll probably get most of them at the restaurant, but still. It'll give you all the privacy you want, and you can get lots of rest." He paused and smiled. "Nobody'll know you're there but us."

Eva sighed. "It's just a café after all, not a restaurant, but when I get my hands on that kitchen, it darn near will be. If I can get some decent, home-made meals on the menu, Chang will have to add more tables." She glanced at the wall clock. "If I ever get there…"

"Chang doesn't know what he's in for if he lets you loose in that kitchen." Agatha nudged the jam a little closer to Eva's plate, and leaned toward her sister. "Promise me you won't tamper with the Denver sandwiches." Eva rolled her eyes, then nodded, indicating she wouldn't change her sister's favourite and one of the best items on the menu.

Agatha sat back. "Anyway, we can discuss your move when you come home." She gave her sister a stern look. "Remember, we need to have a talk anyway."

Eva put up her hands. "Okay, hold your horses, you two." She looked from one to another and sighed. "It might be the best thing to do. Thing is, I'd be worried about you and the boys the whole time. On the other hand the boys might be safer." She sighed, shrugged her shoulders. "I certainly wish I hadn't tangled myself up in this mess. If I had known this was going to happen, I would never have agreed to that stupid arrangement with Bradford." Her finger traced the pattern on the oilcloth table cover. "I was so naïve to think it would be so simple. That he would actually help me, instead of it being just a sneaky way of making me a literal prisoner. He can't seem to understand that he has no hold on me— who knows what he'll try next."

"It isn't your fault," her sister said. "You were young and desperate. And heaven knows you didn't have a whole lot of experience with the outside world, tucked away on that farm out in the middle of nowhere."

"I'm not much older now," Eva gave her sister a sideways grin. "But I've learned a few things. Mostly from mistakes, unfortunately. I've heard they make the best teachers." She picked up a piece of toast and rose from the table. "Now I'd better get going or I'll miss the streetcar." She glanced at Uri. "See you later."

She took one last sip of the coffee and gave Agatha a hug. "I promise we'll talk." In the hallway, holding the toast between her teeth, she put on her coat and fastened a kerchief under her chin. From the corner of her eye, she could see Uri watching her from the doorway as she hefted her purse over her shoulder. With a quick wave, she hurried out the door.

The sky was heavy with clouds, but Eva was so accustomed to it now, she barely glanced up as she hurried along the sidewalk. A chill breeze tried to wriggle its way down her neck, and she automatically put her coat collar up and hunched her shoulders. She concentrated on sorting the clamoring thoughts that jostled for priority inside her head. When she had arrived home from the café last night, Agatha entered her room as she was getting ready for bed. "I know this isn't the best time," her sister admitted. "But I really have to talk to you. It's important. If it hadn't been for all the stuff that's happened to you, I would have sat you down before now. I know you've gone through a lot and you're tired. But I thought I'd just let you know: it's important." Agatha's voice was tight with anxiety, concern making her look drawn and tired. Whatever it was, it was worrying her sister, but Eva didn't have the strength to deal with it at that moment. She'd promised her they would get together as soon as possible. Eva hadn't thought about it this morning, but Agatha's reminder rang in her ears. What else was going on? And what was Uri doing there first thing in the morning? In fact, how did he hear about what had happened so quickly? She thought for a moment. He probably had come to tell her about the room, and Agatha had talked the ear right off the side of his head, every step in great detail. With a sigh, she remembered the words her mother used to say: "It never rains but it pours." If she hadn't been sure what it meant all those years ago, she definitely knew now.

As she rounded the corner, she saw the streetcar slowing down, the doors swinging open. Three people formed a line at the curb. She picked up her pace.

"Eva, wait," said a familiar voice. Eva's heart skipped a beat and her mouth went dry. *This can't be happening*, she thought. She turned around.

The man known as Phil walked toward her and extended his hand. "Wait. I need to talk to you."

Rage and fear stopped her breath. Without thinking, she swung her purse, catching him in the middle of the chest. He staggered back. "Leave me alone," she snarled, and sprinted for the streetcar. The last passenger had climbed in and she leaped onto the step just as the doors began to close. Her heart pounded so loudly she thought the driver could hear it. Taking deep breaths to calm herself, she made her way along the narrow aisle. Falling into a seat, her breathing slowed along with her hammering heart. As the streetcar pulled away, she craned her neck around the man next to her, trying to see out the window. The sidewalk was empty.

She suddenly felt chilled through and closed her coat, gripping her purse hard against her stomach, the pain helping to keep the panic away. Her seatmate was staring at her. She frowned at him and he buried his face in his newspaper. Bold, black headlines announcing the latest stories of war and Allied invasions stared back at her.

Eva reviewed the encounter in her mind. He seemed so reasonable, so polite. He had always been so; his way, no doubt, of putting her at ease before he struck. Anger stirred in her gut, giving her a cramp. She was glad she'd reacted and run. He was not to be trusted, and she wouldn't let him fool her again. The only thing she wanted to hear was that he wasn't going to harm her or her nephews.

That thought made her stop. What if he wanted to tell her he had no interest in them? That Bradford's threats were just that, and he wasn't going to follow up. *Silly*, she thought. He was being paid. Otherwise, what did he think he was doing? Did he think she was so gullible that he could fool her again?

* * *

As the streetcar rumbled out of sight, the man called Phil stepped back into the alcove beside the door of the corner grocery. He leaned against the rough brick, breathing heavily, one hand massaging his chest. After a moment, he straightened his shoulders and reached into his pocket, drawing out a package of cigarettes. He tapped one against the side of the box and lit it, cupping the match's flame against the wind. Inhaling as deeply as his aching ribs would allow, he savored the smoke as it curled from his nostrils. A light drizzle began to fall as he stepped onto the sidewalk, turning his coat collar up as he walked away. Approaching the corner, he felt a heavy hand grasp his shoulder from behind. He tried to turn but a firm grip held him in place, and he could feel a body close to his back, warm breath wafting beside his ear. Something hard poked into his side, just under his aching ribs.

"Don't turn around," said a voice. "We have to talk, you and I."

Phil stood very still. "What do you want?" One hand in the pocket of his overcoat, he could feel his pocket knife next to his cigarette package. He relaxed his shoulders, but his forehead began to gleam with sweat. "You want to talk? Sure. You first."

"Oh, we'll both take a turn. Count on it. Just for now, though, start walking. I know a nice, quiet place to have our conversation, and both of us will learn all kinds of things."

A tiny, grey-haired woman with a cane, bent with age, shuffled toward the curb to wait for the streetcar. She paid no attention to the two men who appeared to be good friends as they walked past her into the grey morning mist and disappeared around the corner.

14

Eva balanced the plates and cups on her left arm while she wiped the counter with her other hand. She heard the door open, but didn't bother to look up. There seemed to be no end to the customers today; they were starting to become faceless.

In the kitchen, she put her order slip in the line and deposited her load of dishes beside the sink. Out of the corner of her eye, she saw Chang watching her out of the corner of his. Her boss was a man of few words, most of them in broken English, but he made himself very clear, and she felt his eyes on her whenever she came in to pick up an order.

She couldn't blame him, really. After all, she didn't make a very good impression on her first day by not showing up. But she was determined to make up for it, and show him she could be a reliable, conscientious employee. Then maybe he'd let her do the things she did best: making the hearty soups, meatloaf and stews that she was sure everyone would soon be clamoring for. In the meantime, she'd do her job well and get to know the regulars.

Backing out of the kitchen, she delivered the latest order to the customer's table, grabbed the coffee pot and placed a menu in front of the new arrival at the counter.

"Coffee to start?" she asked. Her legs were beginning to ache, and she glanced at the clock. No wonder she felt tired; she was well over her shift time, and Sheila was late again. Sheila wasn't an early riser, and was glad to take the afternoon shift, but it would be nice, if just once, she came to work on time. "Coffee will be fine, thanks."

"Billy?" she stared at him as his face came in to focus. He was the last person she expected to see. "What are you doing here?"

Billy smiled as he reached for the sugar. "Having a coffee." He leaned over his cup, sniffed, and reached for the sugar. "Yep, that's it all right."

"You came straight from work?" she asked, looking over his stained hands and smudged face. "…unless you missed your ride or something."

He shrugged. "I told Henry I'd see you home. We discussed it at breakfast, and I made the offer. He had to put in a bit of overtime anyway, so I took the streetcar over."

She put a hand on her hip and frowned. "I don't need 'seeing home.'" I'm perfectly capable of finding my own way."

Billy smiled and shrugged, stirring his coffee. "Like I said, we discussed it this morning."

Eva felt her jaw tightening. "And I suppose 'we' decided what's best for me. Except that no one bothered to include me or ask what I thought. As usual."

The door opened and a man and woman walked in, found a table. Eva grabbed a couple of menus. "I'll be back in a jiff." Giving Billy a meaningful look that plainly said the conversation wasn't over, she started toward the new customers.

Sheila came in from the back just as she was about to give out the menus.

"Gimme those," she said by way of greeting. "Sorry I'm late. Bet your dogs are ready for you to call it quits."

"Thanks." She added to herself, 'it's about time'. Her feet had been complaining for the last hour. Once Sheila had been assured that Eva wasn't after her job, they got along quite well. Eva wanted to keep it that way—no point in upsetting the apple cart.

Eva untied her apron as she made her way to the back to collect her coat. When she came out, Billy had finished his coffee and Sheila was bending over the counter, chin in one hand, a twenty-five-cent piece flourished between two fingers in the other. Eva noticed the amount of cleavage on display and held back a grin. She could see Billy trying hard not to stare and she suspected his glasses were starting to fog up.

Sheila straightened. "I was just about to get this nice gentleman some change." She snapped her gum and fluttered her eyelashes. Billy grinned.

"Keep it," he said, putting on his hat. "Last of the big tippers," Eva remarked as he followed her out the door.

"There's a café a couple of blocks away," Eva said, walking quickly. "I'm going to stop there for a bite."

"Don't you like Chang's cooking?" Billy asked as he hurried to keep up. The rain had stopped, and twilight had settled in, early lights reflecting in the puddles as they walked. "This place isn't too fancy, I hope. I'm still in my work clothes."

"I take that to mean you're coming with me." She glanced over at him, shrugged and sighed. "Lots of working men stop there. I want to check out their menu – see what the competition is. I pass it every day on my way from the streetcar stop. I've been curious, is all."

The café looked about the same size as Chang's from the outside, but the arrangement of tables and counters made it look bigger inside. They found an empty table by the window. As Billy cleaned the rain from his glasses, Eva looked around. She noticed that the table linen was free of stains, a bit thin in spots but somewhat frayed around the edges. The dull metal utensils echoed the colour of the wet pavement outside, but were clean and well placed. All in all, she thought, it gave a good impression. So far.

"You didn't see Uri this morning?" Eva asked.

"Nope. I left kind of early. Why—did he come by?"

"He was there when I came downstairs. He offered to let me rent the suite they just fixed up in their basement."

"So you'll be moving then?"

"I've been going over this all day. One minute I think I should, then the next I'm not so sure." She'd focused on the possibilities of the move, pushing the events of the morning to the back of her mind, concentrating on serving, cleaning and keeping out of Chang's way.

There were only a few patrons at the tables, Eva noted as they were handed their menus. She thought back to the busy tables at Chang's, and she had a feeling that there was no competition here, despite appearances that suggested otherwise. Her suspicions were confirmed as the waitress set their plates in front of them. Eva eyed Billy's greasy food and sighed. He picked up his fork and dug in. *Working men have to fuel up, I suppose,* she thought.

She poked at the pale peas on her plate, took a few bites of the pork cutlet, edges dark brown and curling from overcooking. She tried to avoided the mashed potatoes that drowned in fast-congealing gravy. Billy methodically worked though the contents of his plate with determination, and for the first time she really looked at him. Tall, youthfully slim, his large, strong hands were calloused. His glasses had slipped a little and his broad shoulders hunched as he ate. Sandy hair, discoloured by dust and sweat, brushed the collar of his work shirt, curling a bit there. She caught herself brushing her own hair back with one hand, and reached for her napkin.

Finally, she put her fork down. "You know what I was thinking?" she said.

Billy mopped the last few soggy crumbs from his plate with a piece of bread and looked at her with surprised eyes. "What?" he asked around a mouthful of food.

"How about you go with me right from here to Uri's? I can look at the suite. I've pretty much decided to move in right away, even if I have to hang a blanket up for privacy. I can find something else if it doesn't work out—but this'll be okay for now. Thing is, I still have to get my belongings from Agatha's. There's not much—only one suitcase."

She leaned forward, about to tell Billy about her morning meeting with Phil, but couldn't bring herself to face it again, just yet. Instead, she continued her train of thought. "I think if I go back to Agatha's, and that horrible, creepy man is hanging around and watching, he may follow me, and who knows what trouble he'll start." Her jaw tightened. "I just don't want to give him any more opportunities than I have to."

"Good idea," said Billy, wiping his mouth with a napkin. "I'll go with you and then I'll go back to Agatha's and get your things. I'll tell her what happened. I'm sure she'll be happy to give me your stuff, and I'll bring it to you later." He dropped a bill on the table and rose. "I can get Henry to give me a lift when he gets home."

As they left the restaurant he took her arm. "I think this might be a good idea. Then maybe you and the boys will be safe."

Eva wasn't convinced; she had a feeling that no matter what she did, neither she or the boys would escape until Phil was caught and put away. But she was willing to try anything.

"We can only hope." Eva drew her arm away to pull up her collar against the cool, damp air. Conscious of his warmth as he walked beside her, Eva tightened her jaw, determined not to be distracted. She picked up her pace and walked with purpose in her steps and a lighter heart, determined that the move would help make things better.

* * *

Dani folded the dishcloth and hung it over the edge of the sink to dry. Turning, she surveyed her domain. The kitchen counters were tidy, their surfaces shining in the dull reflection of the ceiling light. Everything in its place. She put her hand on the counter next to the sink. *Even me*, she thought.

The soft ticking of the clock on the wall beside the doorway measured out the seconds, as time wafted onwards through the silent hours of her world. Her gaze turned to the door of the pantry. There was a small respite there, something to help her while away the empty evenings. She stared at it, and thought about a recent possibility. Her next door neighbor, Vivian Clough, had dropped by. She had come on the pretext of borrowing something or other; Dani couldn't remember what.

It was wonderful to have someone to talk to. They had begun to take tea every day or so, and Vi, as she like to be called, told her all about her life with her recently departed husband and her woes in her new role of widow. Dani had listened in fascination, as if she were reading a chapter from a novel. Vi and her husband had travelled down south in the winter and enjoyed a well-rounded social life. Life was grand, declared the chatty, brassy blonde. Until the old bugger, her words, up and croaked on her. He had taken care of her, sure, she grumped. 'Don't worry, he sez to me,' she told Dani with a snarl. 'I'll always be here to take care of you.' She tapped a long, fuschia-coloured fingernail on the table. 'He lied. Now he's not around and I got to take care of everything. I never learned to drive because he said he'd always be there for me. Now I gotta take a taxi cab everywhere. Maybe I'll even have to start taking the streetcar if I can't figure out how to manage the small pension he left me—you wouldn't believe the paperwork.' She sighed with practiced drama. 'I got to learn about a whole bunch of stuff I don't want to know.' She sighed again, blinking back the moisture that formed in her heavily mascaraed eyes.

Vi began to visit every couple of days. Soon she was making herself at home, running a finger along a table, straightening the curtains, refolding the newspaper. Dani thought at first it was because she was upset and nervous, but after listening to another lecture on her colour choices, her inability to organize and her choice of comfortable overalls rather than a flowered housedress, Dani was starting to find her neighbour irritating. She vowed that the next time she came calling, she would find an excuse not to let her in and hear more criticisms. But Vi stopped coming instead. Dani was surprised and a bit annoyed to find she missed her company—but not her annoying habits.

Then a couple of days ago, she'd knocked on Dani's back door. Dani opened it to a widely smiling Vi, her big handbag clutched under one arm, a lit cigarette flourished dramatically from her other hand. "Got time for a cuppa?" she asked. Without waiting for an answer, she strode into the kitchen, leaving a haze of musky violet scent in her wake.

The widow vibrated like a boiling kettle, her cigarette providing the steam, pacing the kitchen and making small talk until the tea was on the table. She sat and reached into her purse with a wink. Pulling out a flask, she poured a dollop into her cup.

"I'm up to celebrating," she said. "You?"

Dani shrugged. It was the middle of the day, but one wouldn't hurt. She nodded. Teacup between her two hands, she sat back and waited for the tirade to start.

"Guess what," said Vi. With a wave of her hand, she shrugged her shoulders, giggled, and sipped. Then she put the cup down and leaned across the table. "Never mind," she said. "You'll never guess anyway." She sat back with a smug smile. "I've met someone. See? I knew you'd never guess. Ha ha—your eyebrows are on top of your head."

Dani had listened and drank the spiked tea while Vi told of the most wonderful man, younger than she by a bit, but who's counting, who had swept her off her feet. He came from quite a wealthy family, but had fallen on hard times. He tried to enlist in the army, but was turned down for health reasons. He hadn't told her what, she said, but she just knew he'd be a hero if he were able to fight for his country. He was going through a bad patch, but he had some ideas, and with a little work and luck in the right places, things would turn around for him. They'd hit it off right away. The two of them talked for hours, making plans to travel, to perhaps move to some exotic place permanently as soon as he was back on his feet. She babbled on and on until the flask was empty and the afternoon had begun to wane.

Dani finally stood, the room spinning a little. "I really should start supper," she said. "Uri will be home soon, and I'll have a hungry man to feed." She giggled. "Wouldn't be happy if there was no food on the table."

With a look of mutual understanding, Vi gathered up her purse and flask. Arms around each other, they walked to the door. They had parted with a hug, happy for each other; although thinking about it now, in the dismal silence of her kitchen, Dani couldn't recall what she herself had to be happy about.

Dani hadn't seen or heard from Vi in the days that followed. Now as she waited in the waning light, she wondered if she should give her neighbour a call to come over, or just pop over to her place for a few minutes. The silence was crawling along her nerves like a nest of newly-hatched spiders. Uri's dinner was in the warming oven. The fire was banked. He usually didn't come home until late, but Dani had a feeling that, with her luck, if she went next door, this would be the day he picked to arrive home early. She didn't like to think about that. She also wasn't sure she was so desperate for company she'd be willing to put up with her neighbour's constant scrutiny. Although since she had met someone, she might be distracted from finding fault. Dani gazed toward the pantry, then at the kitchen door. The clock ticked while she fought to make a decision.

When the doorbell rang, she thanked whatever 'powers that be' for giving her a reprieve. She paused with a hand on the doorknob, preparing her mind to accept another visit with her neighbour. Taking a deep breath, not getting her hopes up, she willed it to be anyone else. With a welcoming smile firmly in place, she opened the door.

15

As they waited for the water to boil, Dani kept up a stream of conversation about her latest decorating projects. Colours, patterns, wallpaper—Eva was beginning to wonder if she ever went out of the house. Dani's wide-eyed surprise and delight when she opened the door made Eva doubt her sister ever had visitors. She'd ask her about it later—or as soon as she could get a word in.

Dani had taken her guests downstairs to see the room, and Eva had been delighted to find it tidy with a small bed, a dresser and an easy chair in one corner. The brightly painted cream-coloured walls set off the warm reds and oranges of the bedspread and chair.

"It's certainly bright and cheerful," said Eva, one hand shading her eyes while she fanned herself with the other. "Warm colours."

"There's only one window down here," Dani said, ignoring her sister's jibe. "I thought I should make it as welcoming as possible." She peered at her sister with a worried frown. "Is it too much? Too gaudy?"

"It's just fine," Eva assured her. "I was only kidding, for Pete's sake."

"Pardon me, ladies." They both turned. Billy stood by the door. They had forgotten he was there. "I should get along if I'm going to make it back before dawn." He looked from one to the other. "What?"

"Why would it take you so long?" asked Dani.

Billy grinned, eyes twinkling. "I was just pullin' your leg. I'll be back in no time." He started toward the stairs. "I can let myself out."

They had come upstairs, saw him to the door and settled in the kitchen. Dani had been talking non-stop. When she finally took a breath, Eva asked, "Does Uri work late very often?"

"Quite a bit." Dani's mood came down several notches. "I can't imagine what a milkman has to do at night, but maybe he has another job, like inside the office, maybe."

"You don't know? Doesn't he talk to you?"

"I asked him once. He says I don't need to know." Dani's knuckles were white as she clasped her hands together on the table. "He says I should just worry about my job and he'll take care of his. That way we'll get to where we're going without getting into a twizzle—whatever that is."

"What is it with our men?" Eva threw up her hands in mock dismay. "Is it just the Smeniuks? Or do all husbands think their wives are too dense and can't be trusted with their 'big dealings'? If you'll remember, I knew nothing about the illegal still Aleksy had set up in the backwoods. For all you know, Uri might be involved in a smuggling ring, or something more ominous. Or maybe he's just moonlighting at another job." Eva looked at her sister and sympathy softened her voice. "Then again, maybe he just doesn't want to worry you."

"Yes, I'm sure that's it." Dani rose, poured hot water into the teapot and took two cups from the cupboard. "He's either working late, or I'm so tired from my day, I'm not sure I'd get the whole story before I nod off."

"It must get lonely at night," said Eva.

Dani tucked her hair behind her ear while she put the cups down. Eva could see the yellowing of an old bruise on the soft flesh of her arm and one below her cheek. "I see you're just as clumsy as ever."

"What?"

Eva pointed to her sister's arm.

"Oh that." Dani's hand trembled as she handed Eva a spoon. "I seem to have a knack for bumping into things. I get so involved, I forget where I am, sometimes." She sat down at the table, her face suddenly bleak and distant. "Thing is—I don't seem to be able to get done. Just when I think I could take a break and do something else, we sell and buy another place and I have to start all over again. I'm not complaining—but there must be a house somewhere that isn't full of ghosts and whispers."

"What do you mean? Do you think these places are haunted?"

Dani shook her head and her voice took on a wistful tone. "Sometimes I think I'm losing my mind. I spend so much time by myself. My mind wanders and…" She sipped her tea. "I could use a holiday. Just one day away somewhere where there are other people and there's no cleaning or scrubbing or redecorating or—or—I don't know. Just some time to myself, I guess."

"I thought you liked making the old look new again," Eva said. "Getting your creative juices flowing and all that."

"I do. Really. It's just…" Dani shrugged, relaxing in her chair. "I'm just being silly. I love to choose the colours, making a room shine after being sad and dingy for so long. It's getting so my best friend is old Mr. Vogt at the hardware store." As she stirred her tea, her eyes darkened and she gazed beyond the room. "I enjoy cleaning windows, letting in the light, seeing the dust motes dance in a newly aired place— it's like fairy magic. You know, sometimes when that happens, I feel like if I get in the middle of the sunbeams and twirl around and around, I'll find myself in a magic land where everything is gleaming bright and flowers scent the air and the days aren't filled with dark shadows and the wretched rain drooling down the windows." She was silent for a moment, looking into a distant scene only she could see. She put her chin in her hand and cocked an eyebrow at her sister, a smile lurking at the corner of her mouth. "I know. There'll come a time when we'll be better off and things will slow down a bit. Then I can take a day for myself."

Eva reached over and placed her hand over her sister's. A wave of affection overwhelmed her. For all the times she had tended to her two younger sisters when their mother couldn't. For all that they had been through together. "Don't worry, love," she said. "Now that I'm here, we'll take that day, just the two of us. As soon as we can. Go somewhere for lunch, do some shopping. Have some us time."

A smile lit Dani's face with the sunny glow Eva remembered.

Dani turned on the lights in the living room, and they brought their newly refilled teacups with them as they settled in to wait. Eva slipped out of her shoes and snuggled into the soft chair, looking around. The lamps cast a quiet, comforting light on the egg-shell toned walls, suffusing them with a golden glow that kept the shadows away. It felt like the kind of room where one could find peace and comfort while the winter wind raged outside. They sat in comfortable silence, sipping their tea, savoring each other's company and feeling safe from the outside world.

Eva imagined herself in a room like this in her own home. Someday she would have that, she was sure. As she envisioned what it would be like, Billy came to mind. She wasn't surprised that her husband wouldn't have been in the picture. She had known from the first that there would never be anything between her and Aleksy. Their arranged marriage had been a false hope from the start. But Billy? She considered: Tall, a little rangy yet, in his youth. Tousled fair hair and blue eyes—a ready smile. A little like the Nordic gods she'd read about, except with glasses. And anyway, he'd told her that his ancestors had come over from Scotland. Would he even fit in a home like this, she wondered, with his penchant for wandering. But maybe if he ever wanted to settle down...

A screen door banged and a gust of wind whirled around their ankles.

"Uri's home at last," Dani said. "We're in here," she called.

"We?" Uri appeared at the doorway. Eva noticed Dani's shoulders tighten. "Oh, hello Eva," he said. "Isn't it a little late for you to be wandering about? Something happen?" He put out his hands as she started to rise from the chair. "Don't get up. I'm surprised you're here, is all." Eva wondered how he could have forgotten his early morning visit, and his offer of a room. Had it been only this morning? It seemed like days ago.

"She's come about the room," said Dani. "She wants to move in right away. Billy's bringing her things over soon."

"Well, good." His grin lit his tired eyes as he shrugged out of his coat. "It's been a long day. I'm for a beer. Anyone else?"

"I'm already sloshing with tea." Eva glanced at Dani who was staring into her cup.

Uri tossed his coat on an empty chair as he left the room. Without speaking, Dani got up, cup in hand, picked up the coat and took it out to the hallway. In moments, Uri was back, a bottle of beer in hand, cigarette dangling from the corner of his mouth.

"I knew you'd see it was a perfect solution, but I didn't expect you to come right over." He slouched into an armchair and drank from the bottle. Wiping his mouth with the back of his hand, Uri nodded. "You did the right thing. You'll be safe here."

"I'm not so sure the boys will be any safer," she said. "I don't know what the solution is, but I did need to find another place anyway, however temporary."

"You can stay as long as you like." He leaned towards her. "I mean that, Evelyn. I want you here. I'll protect you."

"Don't call me that." Eva felt her jaw tighten. "Call me Eva. That's who I am now, and I'd appreciate it if you don't forget it." There was a time when she welcomed his company. He made her laugh, they worked well together and she was grateful for his friendship and support. Lately, she'd begun to feel things weren't so easy between them; she was uncomfortable when she felt him watching her. She hadn't been able to figure out why. She'd worried the problem through the long nights she'd lain in bed unable to sleep and wondered if her own disappointments weren't making her suspicious of everyone.

Uri leaned back, hands up in a defensive gesture. "Sorry. Slip of the tongue." Laughing, he relaxed and took another drink. "It doesn't matter what you call yourself. Anyway, you'll always be special to me. My special person."

"Friend," said Eva.

"If you like. Friend, then. My special friend."

Eva gave up the discussion. They sat, silence opening a chasm between them. Eva could feel Uri's eyes on her, as if he was trying to get inside her brain. She felt irritated, a little breathless. "Where did Dani get to?" she asked no one in particular, trying to break the tension that was beginning to make her jaw hurt. The clattering sounds of dishes and silverware coming from the kitchen answered her question. "Dani, do you need some help?" Having something to do would help to dispel her discomfort.

As if in answer, the doorbell rang. "I'll get it," Dani called as she made her way into the hallway. Eva put down her cup and rose to see if the caller was her sister, or Billy, or whoever was bringing the suitcase with her belongings.

"There you are," Agatha called from the doorway. Eva could see her brother-in-law, Henry, struggling in behind his wife with a suitcase in one hand, balancing a large box with the other. Agatha tossed her hat and coat onto the newel post of the staircase. Her sister looked stern, but then she often did when she was immersed in something. Henry just looked confused, but then when Agatha was on a mission, he usually did.

Eva had been a bit concerned about what her sister's reaction was going to be to her sudden move, but she needn't have worried. Agatha threw her arms around Eva and gave her a fierce hug. "Give us a little notice, why don't you?" she said. Holding Eva at arm's length, Agatha clucked her tongue, then shook her head. A smile lifted the corners of her mouth. "Never mind, we'll just get organized, get you settled and it'll work out just fine."

"Where's Billy?" Eva asked.

"He's keeping an eye on the boys." Agatha poked her head into the living room, nodded to Uri, then turned, facing away from him. "We have to have that talk," she whispered, linking her arm with Eva's. "Now, more than ever."

Henry cleared his throat with a theatrical rumble. "I'm standing here in the doorway, ladies," he said. "Do you mind?"

"Come on in." Dani reached for the suitcase. "Let's take that downstairs and you can see Eva's new place."

"Oh, good." Agatha pecked a kiss on Dani's cheek. "Lead on, McDuff."

Agatha took the box from her husband and followed her sisters downstairs. She put it on the bed and looked around. "Nice," she said. "You should be comfortable here."

"I think it'll be fine." Eva eyed the box. "What's that all about?"

Agatha laughed, and removed the lid. "Henry's aunt died a while back and left us her possessions to deal with. Thank goodness she didn't have a lot, just a few fairly good things worth keeping. This stuff has been sitting up in the attic, gathering dust, and I thought you could make use of it. Most of a set of dishes, what's left of a luncheon set, a few pots and some odds and ends. Uri did say you could cook down here if you wanted, and I didn't think Dani would have a lot of extras."

She turned to her younger sister. "Dani, why don't you go and put the kettle on? I could use a cuppa. The guys are probably in the beer, so just for us, okay?"

"Sure. I'll be right back."

After Dani left, Agatha pushed the box aside, took Eva's arm and sat with her on the bed. "How did Dani look to you?"

Eva shrugged. "Fine. Just a couple of bruises. Clumsy as ever. I guess I shouldn't have worried so much."

"That's not clumsy." Agatha looked into Eva's eyes, her own dark with concern. "When you told me that you felt like there was something going on here that wasn't right. I pooh-poohed you at the time, as I recall. You were right. I should have known better—you're good at sniffing out stuff like that. Frankly, I thought you were being a little melodramatic then. Seems you were right, after all." She stood up, paced a couple of steps and sat down again. "Listen. I came to visit her a while back and caught her at a bad time. She told me that Uri had been doing some strange things. Being abusive. I'm convinced that the only bruises she ever got were from him."

Eva stared at her sister, mouth open. Agatha held up her hand and gave Eva a brief version of the event that had left Dani bruised not only on the outside, but deep down, where her love for her husband cowered in a cage of fear. "Those bruise are man-made. And her own husband is that man."

"Uri? You can't be serious. This whole thing is impossible—it's not even… well, it's just not possible. Are you sure she just isn't twisting a story around for some reason? Maybe she did something she feels guilty about…" Eva felt bile rise in her throat at the thought that her little sister could be so sorely used. Not her of all people. She fought to think clearly. There had to be another answer. But if there wasn't, she would find a way, anything she had to do, to stop this atrocity. Agatha was still speaking, and her words finally penetrated Eva's fogged mind.

"You don't believe she'd lie about a thing like that. Or even make it up?" Agatha asked.

Eva took a deep breath, puffed it out. "No, I guess not. I did suspect something, but I find it hard to believe Uri would do such a thing. He's always been so kind. So caring." She shook her head, searching inwards for some truth. It wouldn't be the first time that she had been disappointed and hurt by someone she trusted. She stood, pacing the few steps permitted in the small room. "Do you think she's delusional? She's always been a little high-strung, but…"

"I know. Moody one minute, perfectly fine the next. As Henry would say, '…up and down like Maggie's bloomers at the picnic.' But you didn't see her that day. You didn't listen to the pain in her words. I did, and believe me when I say you just can't make that kind of thing up." Agatha paused, searching her sister's face, willing her to understand. "People change. That's why I'm so glad you're here to keep an eye on things. See if you can find out what's going on. If she's in trouble, we have to help her."

"Of course. I'll do what I can. Leave it to me." Eva sat back down on the bed, thoughtful, shaking her head. "How could this happen?" she said. Her eyes ranged the room as if searching for answers. She reached out and clasped Agatha's hands. "We'll get to the bottom of this. We have to—for her sake. For both their sakes."

16

Eva brushed her hair away from where the breeze had tossed it into her eyes, and breathed deeply. The air had an undercurrent of cool moisture, laden with the scent of freshly cut grass and trimmed cedar branches. Beyond the dark line of trees, the vast mountain range pressed against the deep blue of the sky, a sight that always took her breath away. She thought of the vast mountain range as guardian against an ancient, foreign foe and felt comforted beneath their mighty reach. The park was almost in her sister's back yard, and she envied them their view.

She pushed off her headscarf and turned her face towards the early summer sun as she walked towards the lake. There were a few other picnickers here and there. She listened to the laughter of children, the faint hum of traffic in the distance, and smiled. Except for the occasional bird call, perhaps one or two animals lowing from the fields or barn, much of her life had been ruled by silence. She had spent so much time in her own company, in what she'd come to think of as the outskirts of nowhere, she was happy to no longer feel like the last person on earth.

Spotting her sister setting out a blanket, she waved and hastened her step. It was the first bright day she could join Agatha and her family at the park as her sister had promised, and she looked forward to relaxing and letting the world continue on without her.

"You're looking sprightly, sister-mine," said Agatha.

"It's the sunshine." Eva watched as her brother-in-law skipped a stone into the lake, laughing at the hoots from his sons when it disappeared after three skips. Billy stood, hefting a small rock, waiting his turn. "Funny, isn't it? When it rains, I become so depressed thinking I'll never see the sky again, but when the sun comes out, all the gloom and doom is long forgotten."

"That's the way it works for most of us. Here." Agatha handed her one of her baskets. "You can put that food out. You're just in time for lunch. The boys will be ready to chew leather; they've been racing around most of the morning." She set out a handful of flatware.

"Good thing your house is so close to the park," said Eva. "I can't imagine how you'd get all this food out here otherwise."

"We have our privileges." Agatha looked at her sister with raised eyebrows. "Where's Dani and Uri? I thought they'd be coming with you."

"They'll be along. They had a few things to do, who knows what all, but they should be here soon. I didn't want to wait for them. I need as much sunshine and fresh air as I can get."

Agatha drew close to her sister. "Very convenient. Do you have anything to tell me?"

"Not really." Eva shook her head. "I haven't seen anything disturbing. They seem to be getting along alright. Uri works long hours, and I see a lot of Dani come evening. But she hasn't said anything. I wonder though…"

"What? Go on—don't keep me in suspense."

"Well, there's this neighbour. Her name's Vi. She comes over from time to time and brings a bit of 'good cheer', if you get my meaning. Once or twice the two of them get a little too jovial. Nothing to be worried about—I don't think. Although I kind of suspect that Dani's been into the sauce a little too much lately. She often mentions that there are ghosts in the house. I haven't noticed any, myself." She allowed herself a wry smile, then sobered as it occurred to her that she hadn't heard anything strange, voices or otherwise, since she left the Prairies. "Except for the usual creaks and groans of a house at night…" She thought for a minute. "Late at night when I can't sleep, I think I can hear soft footsteps above me—in the kitchen." She shrugged. "It's not much, but that's about all I have. It's really quiet, stuffed down in the basement as I am."

Agatha looked disappointed. "Maybe they're on their best behaviour since you moved in."

"Maybe." Eva placed one of the baskets on a corner of the blanket, which threatened to fold over in the breeze. "One interesting thing, though. Remember that family I worked for? The DeFraine's? Well, it's the strangest thing. Vi's a widow, just lost her husband not too long ago, and already she's taken up with this man. Not only is he very much younger than she, but I know him:

Claude DeFraine. The young man who packed up and left when his father died and there was no more money to support his habits."

"Habits?" Agatha continued to spread butter on the buns as she listened.

"I think I told you about him. He was a good-for-nothing, as momma used to say. A lay-about and a drunk. I don't believe he worked a day in his life. He went storming out of the house when he found there were huge debts to be paid off and he'd either have to get a proper education or a job. Heaven knows his mother wasn't able to cope with handling any money if there had been any—and just as well. He would have finagled her around until there wasn't a penny left."

"I remember now." Agatha chuckled. "Small world, isn't it? Looks like he found himself a wealthy widow."

"So it would seem. Not that she's that wealthy, but every little bit helps, I guess. And she is a good-looking woman, in her way. Anyway, that's the only thing of interest."

Agatha put her hand on Eva's arm. "Well, I have some news. We received a visitor the other day, to our surprise. He had quite a story to tell us."

They were interrupted by the arrival of the boys, with Henry and Billy in close pursuit.

"Let's feed this hungry crew first, then I'll fill you in."

"Is it bad news?" asked Eva over the head of the youngest boy who had all but knocked her over in a hug. Henry and Billy approached and stood with their hands in their pockets, grinning in anticipation of the picnic spread before them.

"Depends how you look at it," Agatha grinned. She started handing out plates. "Dig in everyone. There's enough and more to go around."

Eva took her filled plate out of the way and dug in to the potato salad while she wondered if the news consisted of anything that would change her life. As Agatha and Henry bustled about settling the boys, Eva smiled as she remembered her older sister's penchant for the dramatic. Make a person wait long enough and either the news will be such a big relief or so drastic that there's enough time to get prepared. Eva fervently hoped that in this case, it was the former.

"Penny for your thoughts?" Billy stood in front of her, balancing a plate in one hand, a bottle of beer in the other, with his utensils tucked into his shirt pocket. Eva steadied the plate for him while he found a level spot for the bottle so it wouldn't tip. He lowered his lanky frame beside her.

"Agatha has received some news that she thinks I should know about," she said. "She won't tell me until after we eat. Do you know anything about it?"

"Some. I could let you in on it, I suppose, but I don't know who all is involved. Guess it's better if she tells you herself."

Eva nudged him with an elbow. "Spoil sport." She saw his grin and decided it would do no good to push him for information. Trust Agatha to cover all the bases.

They ate in silence, watching the interaction of the family on the blanket. Eva felt the soft touch of Billy's sleeve on her arm as he raised his fork. For no reason that came directly to mind, she became very warm, and she suddenly felt as if she couldn't eat another bite. She lowered her plate and fork and concentrated on trying to breathe.

"Full?" Billy was looking at her, concern in his eyes. She'd forgotten how very blue they were. She nodded, not trusting herself to speak, becoming annoyed with herself at her reaction to his closeness. She'd always felt comfortable around him. Comfortable, like a pair of old shoes or a cozy sweater. This wasn't right. She didn't care for this at all. She took up her napkin and piled her utensils on her plate.

"Here," he said, leaning over and wiping a thumb over her chin. "Missed a spot."

"Thanks." Flustered, she got up and stacked her plate with the others.

Her two active nephews could hardly sit still long enough to finish their meals. If it hadn't been for dessert, which was served when everyone had finished their meal, they would have been back by the pond. A flock of ducks had landed and were floating serenely on the glassy surface, unaware that only thick slices of lemon meringue pie stood between them and an interruption of their tranquillity.

After everyone had eaten, Henry and Billy walked down to the lake and stood smoking while they watched the boys try to create mayhem with the wildlife. The ducks simply moved farther out into the lake and swam serenely on, occasionally dipping for their dinner, as if that was their intention in the first place.

Eva forced herself to not think about anything while she helped pack up the leftovers and tidied the blankets. Agatha wasn't to be rushed, but as she poured them each one last cup of lemonade, she couldn't wait any longer.

"If you don't tell me what the news is," she glowered, "I'll have to get you down and sit on you."

"Oh please, not after such a big meal." Agatha feigned a belch and moved a little aside in mock concern, giving her sister a sidelong look of pretended fear.

"Oh, all right." She settled herself, obviously preparing for a long dissertation. Eva gave her a dark scowl, but Agatha smiled smugly, unconcerned. "Do you remember Uri's older brother, John?"

"He's Aleksy's oldest brother. Yes, I remember him."

"Well, he dropped in to see us the other day. Heaven knows how he located us; we haven't been in touch with any of the Smeniuk family. But there he was, on our doorstep, asking after you."

"Me? What would he want with me? I hardly know him; only met him a couple of times."

Agatha continued as if she hadn't been interrupted. "I asked him in and served him the rest of the breakfast coffee."

"And then what? What did you tell him?"

"Seems he came out looking for you, to tell you what happened to your husband."

"I already know. Bradford gloated when he told me that Aleksy had been injured in an accident and was in Ponoka. That's where they treat people with brain issues do you remember? Mother used to call it the nut house." Eva shook her head and smiled at the memory. "Anyway, he had a concussion or something. Afterwards I thought about it and wondered if Bradford had invented the whole story to get me to come back with him before I found out that maybe I didn't have to. You know, if Aleksy's accident had been fatal, he would no longer have what he considered our 'agreement' to hold over me. I wondered if he wanted me to believe that I'd be saddled with an invalid the rest of my life. I for sure don't know what twisted thoughts inhabit that brain of his. But I would never, ever go back. For any reason."

"Well, that's as may be. Anyway, John said that Aleksy hasn't gained any memory of who he is or how he came to be there. He didn't recognize John, his own brother, when he came to visit. And the doctor told him that with his kind of brain injury, he might never remember anything, if indeed he survives long enough for it to matter."

"So why would he come all this way just to tell me that, I wonder."

"He said that perhaps you'd like to go see him, his being your husband and all. Particularly since he may not have very long." Agatha swirled the last of the lemonade in her cup. "I suspect he may have found out our address from Uri. Surely the two of them have been in touch."

"Yes, but to travel all that way just for that doesn't make sense. Why would he care about me?"

Agatha searched her sister's face. "Sometimes, you can be so thick," she said. "John cared about you. And he cares about his brother. He knew all about him, what he was up to in the deep woods and who he was with, and he felt sorry that you had been thrust into a marriage that neither of you wanted. He knew what kind of life you'd have, and he cared."

"Still…."

"Yes, I know. But I also got the impression that he had something going on with Uri. Maybe he wants to move out here, or maybe they have a business deal of some kind. John said he was going over to see Uri, if we'd be so kind as to give him the address. So I told him where Uri and Dani live and I suspect he'll be over there, probably today or tomorrow. Maybe that's why they didn't make it to the picnic. John is likely there as we speak."

They sipped their tea in silence, watching an impromptu game of catch. The men were certainly not letting the boys out of their sight for a moment. Eva tried not to think of the man who was her husband. She rarely thought of him at all these days; he was part of another time, another life, another world.

"Okay, I'm curious." Eva tossed the dregs of her lemonade that had suddenly become sour and handed the cup to Agatha. "I'll go along back to Uri's and see if John is there. Maybe he has something to say that he couldn't say to you."

"Good idea. If there's anything else he tells you, be sure to let me know. As you say, it seems there's more to this."

"I guess I won't see you until my next day off," said Eva. "So if there's anything new, it'll have to wait."

"You must be able to telephone me from work," Agatha said. "Uri won't get one installed as long as they intend to sell and move again, but there must be a telephone at the café. If not there's a call-box somewhere close, I'm sure." She looked thoughtful for a moment, but then her face brightened. "I almost forgot to tell you—Henry has finally stopped ranting about the telephone. He's been carrying on since we had it installed. Suddenly he's decided it comes in pretty handy after all and I don't have to listen to any more of his complaints about 'new-fangled contraptions', and how next thing you know they'll be sending us to the moon. He may have actually entered the twentieth century, although he was willing to put the horse and buggy behind him in favour of a car without any problem, as you know. Where we lived on the prairie, so far from anything, people didn't have one mostly because there were no lines available, or they were too poor, and Henry kept saying how they survived without one all this time and why did we need one, blah, blah, blah. Here in the city it's practically mandatory. People think you're strange if you don't have one.

"It saves a lot of time, when you think about it," Eva agreed. "It makes sense, and I'm glad he stopped griping about it. But as he says, maybe it'll be the end of civilization as we know it. People will stay in their homes; they won't have to leave their easy chairs to visit their friends and relatives."

"Oh, Eva. You're such a pessimist. There'll still be lots of visiting. How would one get to know one's family, nieces and nephews and the like? And what about family dinners? No, I think it's good in lots of ways. Why, I can just call and ask Henry to pick something up for me that I need from the store on his way home from work." Agatha smiled at the thought.

"See, that's maybe what Henry was afraid you'd do," Eva said. "That can get to be a nuisance. He might lose his job, or his sense of humour, then what would life be like?"

"That'll be the day. And anyway, if he doesn't speak to me for a day or two, it might be a relief. I've heard his tired old jokes so many times I can recite them in my sleep."

Eva noticed that Agatha patted her hair and smiled as she spoke, and couldn't help smiling herself as she recalled the easy relationship they had with each other. She tied her kerchief on and picked up her handbag. "Never mind daydreaming, sis. In the first place, his boss wouldn't like you calling and taking him away from his job. You could get him into trouble."

Trying to look disappointed, Agatha shrugged. "You're probably right. But who knows what kind of earth-shattering difference telephones will make in the long term. We'll just have to wait and see. Right now, I'm enjoying the peace and quiet since he's stopped complaining about it. Anyway, let me know as soon as you can if there's anything else. I'll be on pins and needles waiting to hear from you."

Eva hugged her sister and made her way across the park to the streetcar stop. As she waited for it to arrive, she glanced upward, seeing a ghostly image of the moon in the afternoon sky. As a girl she often saw it, a lonely silver spectre, seeming so close she could almost touch it. She recalled her brother-in-law's comments about sending people to the moon and smiled. That man had such an imagination.

17

Billy threw the ball to the oldest boy, watching the two women on the blanket from the corner of his eye. He saw Eva rise and brush crumbs and grass off her skirt. She turned in his direction and waved.

"You're aunt's leaving, I guess," he said to the boys. "Better wave goodbye."

They all waved, Henry looking over his shoulder at Billy with a knowing expression.

"What?" Billy could feel a flush creeping up his neck from under his collar.

Henry grinned at him and quirked an eyebrow. Billy knew that look. It was the one his mother used to give him when she recognized an excuse before it came out of his mouth. 'Gabriel Liam Alderson,' she would begin, the slanted angle of her eyebrow a clue as to how stern the coming lecture would be.

His little sister had caught on quickly. 'Bril Lee', she would begin, and eventually he became Billy to everyone. Her chubby arms akimbo, she would tilt her head in a manner that made it difficult for him to maintain a sober expression suitable to the scolding she had prepared. Even though they were hundreds of miles away in another province, their voices still rang in his head and hurt his heart with missing them.

As he watched Eva walk across the park, he didn't need anyone to tell him he'd been an idiot. *Billy, you dolt, you did it again—waited too long to speak up during lunch when you had the chance and now she's gone off. You may have to start all over again.*

He'd hoped he would have arranged to see her home and then maybe he could tell her how he felt. Or if that didn't work, make a date to go for a walk so he could take his time to say it right and not blurt out everything at once. Now all the words were still piled up about the middle of his chest, and they'd have to stay there and wait, a pressure under his heart, for another opportunity. "Damn," he said under his breath, a habit he'd formed so his mother and sister wouldn't hear him. Throwing his cigarette to the ground, he crushed it out with his foot. He picked up a stone, threw it out into the lake, sending some of his helpless anger along with it. It plopped with a splash, startling a couple of ducks into flight. Delighted, the boys each picked up stones but the ducks had already retreated to the other side of the lake, saving Henry another lecture on the merits of kindness and restraint.

Billy looked over to see Henry still staring at him with a half-smile on his face. Billy glared back, hoping to forestall any of his friend's ribald or folksy comments. For once, and much to Billy's relief, Henry kept his own counsel.

* * *

The rumble of men's voices greeted Eva as she hung her coat on the hall rack. She paused, listening. She recognized Uri's tone, but the other voice remained unfamiliar.

Uri sat sprawled in the chair, frowning into a glass of rum. A dark-haired man sat across from him and turned as she entered the room. He rose and approached her, smiling. She didn't remember him being so tall. His hair had remained dark, slicked back and tidy, but Eva thought she could spot flecks of gray. *A trick of the light, maybe,* she thought. He wasn't that much older than she was. His eyes seemed tired, and he looked solemn as he returned her gaze. Other than those few things, she decided, her husband's oldest brother looked much the same as when she had last seen him in what felt like another lifetime ago.

"Hello, John."

"Evelyn." In two steps he stood in front of her, holding out a big hand. Irritation prickled along her spine. Why couldn't the past just stay away? She wasn't that person anymore and hated to be reminded of it.

She took his hand and he folded both his hands over hers. They were warm and gentle. She smelled the liquor on his breath, and with surprise, a faint scent of spicy aftershave.

"It's Eva now, please. I changed my name when I left the prairies."

He looked puzzled for moment, then nodded and smiled. "It's good to see you again."

"What brings you all the way out to the west coast?" Taking her hand back, she found a seat on the sofa. The coarse touch of his fingers lingered on her skin. "Did you bring your family along?"

"I've some business here in town." He evaded her question, which Eva understood to mean he hadn't taken a wife yet. "And I need to speak to you about Aleksy—I've been told you've heard about what happened."

"I have. Is there more news?"

John shook his head, chewed on his lip a moment before answering. "I had thought for a moment—only for a moment, mind, of asking you to come back, but I won't bother either of us with that for right now. Instead, I'll get right to the point." He swallowed the rest of his drink, put the glass down, and gazed at something by his feet that only he could see. "I guess you remember our father. He was a hard man, mean as a snake." He sat back, laughed. "But you'd know about that. You had one of them mean ol' bastards for yourself, didn't ya? Any road, he finally got his last calling. My old man, I mean, not yours. Or if your daddy got his, I haven't heard about it. Now about our papa, as I was saying, I don't know a whole lot about the afterlife, 'cept what that skinny old preacher used to lay on us. But I'm hoping, if there is one, Papa gets to his just desserts. And I hope it's damn good and warm for him."

He reached for his glass, saw it was empty. Eva noticed a movement in the shadows, and saw Dani sitting quietly, eyes glinting over the rim of her glass. Eva glanced at Uri. It was obvious he wasn't taken aback by the news that his father had passed on. He was watching her, like always, trying to pretend he wasn't.

"So here's what I'm getting at. Aleksy's in bad shape. Doctor doesn't give him a long time. He doesn't seem to really know anybody, not me, not our housekeeper, Aunt Enna. You remember her. She was quite fond of Aleksy. Of all of us, actually. Like the mother we lost, almost. Thing is, we got a good piece of land, and now it appears to have come down to us. The brothers, I mean." He looked up at her, expectant; she had no idea what he expected her to say and waited for him to continue.

She looked around. Everyone was watching her. Uri drank from his glass without taking his eyes from her. She could see the gleam of Dani's eyes. She took a breath, pushing surprise and confusion aside until she had time to indulge them. "I don't know what to say. Aleksy isn't dead yet. He might live for a long time to come." She smiled at John, pleased that he'd thought enough of her to tell her in person.

"I'll bet you could use a drink about now Eva," Uri said. "Rum and coke?"

Eva shuddered. "No thanks. That stuff will rot your insides." She rose. "I'll just put the kettle on. I won't be a minute."

"Wait." Dani moved from the shadows towards the door. "I'll do it. I should get refills anyway." She turned to look at her husband. "You?"

"I'm good," Uri said.

John handed Dani his glass without looking away from Eva. "Thing is, Uri here has agreed to sell me his portion."

"I got no use for it," Uri said. "I'm not going back; guess I'm a city boy now. Far as I'm concerned, John is welcome to it."

"I need to ask you," John said, his eyes still on her, black in the low light. "Do you know if Aleksy has a will?"

"No reason why I should know that, John," said Eva. "Aleksy and I were never what you'd call close. He never talked to me about his business ventures. I never knew where he went or what he did. I didn't even know when and if I should expect him home for a meal-- or any other reason." To her relief, her voice sounded calm, nothing like the mix of emotions churning around her solar plexus like a load of clothes in a washing machine.

John lowered his head and appeared to study his hands, clasped between his knees, but looked up when Dani came back into the room, two glasses on a tray. She put one on the table next to John, then took the other and walked back into the shadows.

"I have a farm to run," he said. "I may not be able to get away when the time comes, and I'd rather have things set in place when I am able." He looked at Eva, frowning. "If Aleksy doesn't have a will I'm not sure of the legalities. He never had any sons, so I would guess that his portion would go back to the estate. I'm not sure how things work nowadays. I'd have to consult a lawyer."

Inwardly, prickles of irritation started to smoulder. *'He never had any sons' he says*, she thought. *One more thing men take all the credit for when we produce.* She could still see her mother as she lay dying after yet another still-born birth; hear again her father's rage. *And we get all the blame when we don't.*

She took a deep breath and let it out, keeping her temper in check. Smiling sweetly at the two brothers, she said, "We haven't even come to that bridge yet. No sense planning the crossing until we find out what we're dealing with." Eva never expected to receive anything from her husband. The law clearly favoured putting women in the same category as the land. It would have been nice, though, she thought. She certainly deserved to get something out of their bland, sterile relationship. Then she could get her own place here—not be dependent on anyone.

"So you've spoken to Aleksy? Asked him about it?" John's gaze was steady as he sipped his drink. She didn't know what he expected her to say. She could be of no help to him here.

She hadn't noticed when her sister left the room for the second time, and was startled when Dani suddenly appeared beside her to put a cup of tea into her hands. Smiling her thanks, Eva wrapped cold hands around the cup, comforted by the warmth.

"I've tried," John said at last. "But he doesn't understand. He just nods. Then he thanks me for the visit and tells me it's time to leave. He tires easily, I suppose. As I said, he doesn't even know who I am most of the time. I've also talked to some of the fellows that he hung around with, did business with. They didn't know anything. I have an idea there is no will. Quite frankly, I don't think he was ever so long-sighted."

"Yeah," Uri interjected. "Young bucks his age think they're going to live forever. Probably didn't occur to him."

"What about you?" Eva asked, turning to Uri. "What about Dani if something happened to you?"

Uri threw back his head and laughed. "Don't worry—I'll be around for a good long time." He drank from his glass and shrugged. "I'll get around to it eventually. Sooner rather than later, I suppose. Anyways, I don't believe John here would try to put one over on you or me. Only reason he came here is so as to get things straight best way he can. Probably needs to get it done legal because that's the way they do things nowadays. If it were me, I'd be happy with a handshake. I don't think we need to worry about being cheated out of our fair share." He smiled over at his brother. "John's always been the responsible one in the family. 'Ol' Sober-Sides', we used to call him. Always level-headed and serious, that's our John."

Eva didn't think of him that way, recalling all the teasing and snickering they did on the morning after her wedding, but she said nothing. As she gazed at her oldest brother-in-law, she saw the broad shoulders, steady hands and weathered lines of a simple farmer, and couldn't imagine he'd ever do anything or be anyone else than the straightforward man she believed he was.

"I don't picture myself going back there any time soon, so I would have no use for the land. It'll just go to you and you're welcome to it which seems to me will be the case. As far as I'm concerned, there's no point getting my hopes up over something I have no say in."

"Thank you," said John. "I'll go ahead and…" The doorbell interrupted whatever he had intended to say.

Dani jumped up. "I'll get it."

There was just too much Eva didn't know. She didn't want anything to do with the farm; that was certain. Even if there was some remote chance that she would inherit, John was the one who would take care of the land, make his living. She just wished this was over and done, so she could forget about her empty marriage, the poverty and loneliness of the time she spent with a man who neither knew nor cared about who she was. Why would Aleksy provide for someone he hardly knew existed? That made it very unlikely that even if there was a will, which she highly doubted, it wouldn't have anything to do with her.

"Someone here to see you, Eva," Dani said from the doorway.

From behind her sister, Eva could see the tall figure of Detective Carlson. "Evening, everyone," he said. "Sorry to interrupt." He nodded at Uri and John. "I'm Detective Carlson of the Vancouver Police. I've come to ask Eva here, a favor."

"What's this all about, officer?" Uri said, moving to Eva's side.

"Detective," corrected Carlson, looking past him at Eva. "And we just need Eva to come down to the station. We won't inconvenience her any more than we have to—I'll have her back before you know it."

Uri moved closer to Eva and put a hand on her shoulder but she stood up, shrugging him off. "I don't understand," she said to Carlson. "What am I supposed to do?"

"Well, see, here's the thing. We got us a body turned up this afternoon, down at the morgue. Considering what's been going on with you lately, we think you might be able to help us out and provide us with an identification."

18

The main office of the police station didn't bustle with activity as it had on Eva's first visit. The ghostly echoes of busy typewriters and ringing phones drifted like smoke in the eerie silence. Paper-littered desks sat empty but for one man, who appeared to be sorting a pile of files. He didn't look up as they passed. She smelled stale cigarette smoke and old sweat; a musty, sweet-sour odor that she couldn't quite identify settled onto the back of her throat.

"Where is everyone?" she asked. "I thought the work here went on day and night."

"We've just hit a lull." Carlson smiled down at her as he steered her across the room. "Everyone's out and about—duty calls, and all that. Or maybe they're all out on a supper break. Chances are by the time we're done here, most of them will be back and you won't be able to hear yourself think."

The detective guided her through a door and down a flight of stairs with a light hand on her elbow. Along a hallway, a single tired bulb scarcely dispelling the gloom, they stopped at one of the rooms. He entered, indicating she should follow.

"Wait here. I'll be back in a minute," he said. He guided her to a chair and disappeared through another door. She sat on the edge of the seat, took a few calming breaths.

The drive over had filled her head with questions and wound her tightly with threads of tension. Carlson had said little to assure her, had evaded her questions and asked for her patience.

"No sense trying to explain things ahead of time when they may not make sense," he had told her. "It'll just get you all confused and worrisome and I'd rather we keep things simple."

As he drove, she studied his tight-lipped demeanor and decided it would be no use to try to push for answers. She gave up and turned her attention to the street lights of the city as they blinked on in the deepening dusk. But she couldn't keep her mind from trying to sort the few possibilities that presented themselves. Who did she know? Not many people here, certainly, so it must be someone from her past. Perhaps Bradford had returned, and had run afoul of bad luck or some mishap. She admitted to herself that she wouldn't be too sorry if it was him. As they pulled in front of the station, her stomach tightened and her jaw clenched with dread.

She waited now, breathing in short shallow breaths, trying to relax her neck and shoulders. She closed her eyes and tried to think of something calm and soothing. The tension finally began to ease as Carlson returned and beckoned her to follow him.

Through the door into an adjoining room, she could smell chemicals, antiseptic. A masked and gowned man pushed into place a wheeled table on which lay a shrouded figure. Detective Carlson stepped close beside her, his sleeve just touching hers. "Are you ready, Eva?"

She shrugged and nodded. *Ready as I'll ever be,* she thought. She was afraid to speak, afraid the words would come out with an uneven squeak, or even worse, not at all. Gripping her purse as if it was the only rock in a surging sea, she watched as the attendant lifted the sheet and folded it down.

She felt the comforting hand of Detective Carlson as she stared down at the waxen face. It took her a minute for her brain to adjust to what she was seeing. As if from a vast distance, she heard the detective's voice.

"Do you know this man, Eva?"

She swallowed and nodded, not ready to trust her voice. Flashing through her mind were pictures of the times she'd seen him: at a distance in the rain, smiling over a teacup, opening the car door. Despite the bruises to his face, she recognized the man she hoped never to see again.

Gently, with a hand on her arm, he said, "tell me."

She couldn't identify the emotions swirling around her brain—didn't know how to react. She wasn't a stranger to the dead but she had never felt like simultaneously giggling hysterically and breaking into tears at the sight. She drew a deep breath, licked her lips.

"I—that's Phil. That's the man I told you about."

A rush of relief made her light-headed. If not for the detective, she felt certain her legs would be too weak to hold her up.

"Are you sure?"

"Quite sure. Yes. That's him."

They all stood silently; a tableau of three living and one dead. Then the sheet was drawn up to cover the body. As it was being wheeled out, Carlson guided her into the hallway, returning to the same small room they had entered when they first arrived.

"Have a seat," he said. "I'll be right back."

True to his word, he returned quickly and took the chair opposite her. He placed a file on the table in front of him and folded his hands on top. His eyes glittered in the dim light, the gentle voice and demeanor replaced by a stern gaze.

"You're probably wondering why I brought you here to view the body," he began. "It was just a hunch, but I had to follow up. We found him in an alley not far from where you're staying now. He'd been beaten. You saw the bruises. Looks like he may have died from one of the blows he took in the head." He sat back, his eyes never leaving her face. "'Course that's my best guess, until I hear different from the coroner." He opened the file, rifled through until he extracted one of the pages. "From what you told me in our first meeting, it seems likely that this was the same fellow who had threatened you and your sister's family. We couldn't find anything on him here—he doesn't seem to have a record, at least in this province. We've sent his description to the Alberta RCMP to see if they have anything. If they do, we'll see if we can find out how Bradford found him and then hired him."

He looked over the sheet he'd selected, then sat back. "Is there anything more you can think of to tell me? Has he bothered you at all? Did you see him again since our talk?"

Eva shrugged. "I... Wait. He approached me one morning not too long ago on my way to work. He said he wanted to talk to me..." She shuddered, feeling again the fear that made her heart leap to her throat. "I'm afraid I reacted and ran."

"What did you do?"

"I swung my handbag at him. Caught him in the chest— I think. Screamed at him to leave us alone."

"Us? Was someone else with you?"

"No. I meant my sister's family, too. He'd threatened my nephews."

Carlson nodded as he referred again to his notes. "Of course. What happened next?"

"Then I ran for the streetcar. It was about to pull away. I don't know what would have happened if it hadn't been there just at that moment."

Detective Carlson looked at her, as if trying to see into her soul. Raising her chin, she looked back steadily. She wasn't going to be intimidated. She couldn't tell him what she didn't know. It was his job to figure this out, not hers.

"Anything else?"

Eva shook her head.

"You should have called me right away."

At the time, the thought never entered her head. She was unaccustomed to having anyone who would come to her aid when she called. It felt strange, stranger still to know someone who would actually help. "Yes. I suppose I should have."

Carlson leaned toward her. "And then what happened?"

Eva clasped her hands together, rubbing a thumb on one knuckle as she called up the scene in her mind. There was no sound in the room; no traffic noise, no voices seeping through the walls. It was so still, she almost forgot to breathe. She closed her eyes and concentrated. "Once I found my seat, I looked out at the sidewalk by the stop. There was no one there. I almost made myself believe it was my imagination." She took a breath, blew it out. "But of course, it wasn't. And I was frightened and angry. I wanted so much to do something, but I didn't know what."

"What you do is call me. This may not be over. If anything like that happens again, let me know right away. Do you understand?"

Neither of them moved. Finally, Eva nodded. Not over, she thought. Of course not—why would it be that simple. Bradford will never give up, never leave her alone. He was like a man obsessed, and she just wanted to do anything, go anywhere, run fast enough to be rid of him.

"Eva. Do you know anyone who might beat a man so badly he ends up dead?"

Eva looked directly at the detective, anger stirring along her nerve ends. "We just want to be left alone." Her voice rose another octave. "Why would anyone think they can blackmail us into doing something whenever they feel like it? It isn't fair and it isn't right. But to kill someone? The people I know wouldn't ever do such a thing. I can't vouch for what they might be thinking, though. But no. I don't know anyone. And I'm pretty sure that if the killer is found, I would want to walk up and thank him."

Carlson pursed his lips and studied her with a thoughtful expression. Then he took the folder and stood up. "I'll take you home now. I hope this wasn't too difficult for you."

"Is that all?"

"For now. I'll do some more digging. I'll come up with something, you can bet on that. But it may take a bit of time."

He guided her back through the office, through the exit where they stepped out into the night. A light rain had fallen and the reflection of the streetlights glimmered on the slickened sidewalks. The air had been scrubbed clean, freshened by the breeze from the ocean; a welcome relief after the stuffy, stale confines of the building.

"I'd like to know who did that to him," Eva said, buttoning her coat against the chill.

"If I find anything you need to know, you'll be notified." He held the car door open.

"I'd like to be dropped at Henry's place, if you don't mind," she said as she settled in the seat. "He and Agatha should be told what happened."

"That'll save me some time and maybe it's better they hear it from you." He started the car and put it into gear. "But don't get too confident. Make sure they understand that whoever sent him may send someone else. If he doesn't report back, steps will likely be taken to find out why."

"It won't make headlines, surely."

"If the papers even get wind of it—but if so, I'll see if I can get it buried on the back pages. That may buy us some time. It'll be a while before we get any information on this guy, and who knows, maybe nothing will be said at all."

"I hope you're right."

Carlson waited at the curb in front of her sister's house while Eva walked up the steps to the door. Agatha greeted her in a faded dressing gown, her hair in curlers. With a look of surprise, she stepped back, her words of greeting unspoken as she spotted the detective's car pulling away from the curb. Agatha put her arm on Eva's shoulder and they stood in the doorway together until the car disappeared around the corner. Then without a word, Agatha strode into the kitchen.

Eva hung her coat and hat on a peg in the front hall and followed. Agatha filled the kettle and put it on the stove. Eva took a seat at the table.

When she opened her mouth to explain, Agatha held up a hand. "Hold on. Henry's already in bed. Work tomorrow. But I think I'd better get him up for this."

"Probably," Eva said. "He won't want to miss anything."

"Get out the cups. I'll be right back."

Eva busied herself setting out three cups and spoons. As she reached in the icebox for the milk, she heard footsteps behind her.

"Hey. What are you doing here this time of night?"

"Billy." Eva turned, her heart skipping a beat. Shirtless and barefoot, he stood grinning with his hands in his pockets, eyebrows raised. The ceiling light threw bright highlights on his tousled fair hair and the silver rims of his eyeglasses. One of Eva's hands automatically reached up to tuck a strand of hair behind her ear as she noticed the soft down of the hair on his chest. She felt her cheeks warming and she moved quickly to take the sugar bowl to the table. Frowning, she decided that she was simply surprised to see him, forgetting for a moment that he was staying here. "I'll get another cup," Eva said. "I'm glad you're here. You need to hear this, too."

Henry shuffled into the room, rumpled and sleep-befuddled in pajamas and dressing gown, and slumped down at the table. Agatha filled the teapot and opened a tin of gingersnaps, releasing the fresh-baked aroma of cinnamon and spices into the room.

"This better be worth getting out of bed for," Henry grumbled.

"I think you'll find it is." When everyone was seated, Eva took a deep breath and told them of her visit to the police station. "…and we won't have to worry about harm coming to the boys," she finished.

"For now," Henry said. "But what if that bugger decides to send someone else?"

"He might. Detective Carlson said as much." Eva picked up her cup, grimaced when she tasted the tea that had cooled while she talked. "But the idea was to force me into doing what he wanted. So, if he sends anyone, he'll make darn sure I know about it. The trouble is, we won't know who he is or what he looks like."

"I can't say I'm sorry about the guy on the slab," Henry said. "He had it coming, one way or another. But I'll tell you one thing, I'll sleep better tonight." He rose from the table. "Speaking of which, my day starts early. We'll discuss this more tomorrow, if needs be." Looking at Billy, he said, "you riding with me tomorrow? Better hit the sack yourself."

"Don't worry," Billy assured him. "I'll be bright-eyed and bushy-tailed. But in the meantime, I'd better see Eva home."

Henry looked at Eva, then Billy, from under lowered brows, and Eva would have given much to know what he was thinking. With a wave, he lumbered out of the room.

Billy looked at Eva. "Unless you're staying over?"

Eva was slow to answer. "I didn't even think. I just knew I needed to come and tell you all what had happened." She popped the last bit of cookie into her mouth and smiled. "Worth it for the treats. I missed dinner."

"Why didn't you say so?" Agatha frowned at her. "There's always leftovers around here."

"Not to worry. I'll survive. But I should get going—work tomorrow and I have to get some things together. I can take the streetcar." She glanced at the kitchen clock. "Oh drat—it's later than I thought. I may have to get a cab."

"Don't be silly." Agatha collected cups and saucers. "Billy, you go ahead and take her along home. The car keys are over by the washing machine."

Eva and Billy stared at her.

"What? Don't look at me. Henry is forever putting them someplace else than they should be. I just didn't get around to putting them back in their regular place." She waved a hand in dismissal. "So the good thing is they'll be right where they should be when you get back. Right?"

Billy grinned and shook his head. "Right." He turned to Eva, pushed his glasses up. "I'll just grab a shirt and we can be on our way whenever you're ready."

19

Yawning, Dani shuffled to the door in her slippers. She didn't need to guess; she recognized Vi's distinctive, rapid knock, and geared herself for another session of her neighbour's ongoing trials or tribulations.

The night before, they had all waited as long as they could for Eva to return from the police station. Reminiscing about growing up on the farm, they lingered, sipping rum until the late hour beckoned them to bed. When the men finally retired, Dani washed up the glasses and tidied until she was sure Uri was asleep. Slowly and carefully, she climbed into bed and lay wide awake, listening for the sound of the downstairs door that would let her know that her sister had arrived home safely. Not for the first time, she wished Uri would have a telephone installed. At least then, there would have been a way Eva could have let them know what she was doing and where she was.

She would rather have the morning to herself. Uri had left at dawn for work and John shortly afterwards for an early appointment, leaving her to nurse a vague headache, a fuzzy tongue and the remains of breakfast to clear up. She tossed the empty rum bottle in the trash with contempt, vowing to stick to her own little cache in the pantry in the future. Drying her hands on the dish towel, she went into the bathroom medicine cabinet and took a couple of aspirins. Her reflection in the mirror showed a dishevelled woman, dark eyes shadowed with fatigue and stress. Her cheekbones shone through her taut skin and she wondered how much more weight she could lose without having to alter more of her clothes.

Hearing the knock, she looked longingly at her toothbrush, tidied her robe and ran a hand through her hair. At the front door, she shifted her coffee cup to her other hand, opened the door and stepped back.

"There you are." Vi's cheerful voice sounded shrill to Dani's sensitive ears. Two curlers bobbled over her forehead and she was without her usual garish makeup. "I hope the coffee pot is still on." Her voice trailed along in her wake as she made her way down the hall. "I have the most exciting news. Oh, you wouldn't believe it." Turning, she surveyed her hostess. "My word, woman, you look as if you didn't get a wink of sleep last night." She leaned forward with a sassy leer, fluttering her eyelashes. "What—Uri not letting you get your beauty sleep these days?"

With a grimace, Dani followed her guest into the kitchen. This of all mornings she should be alone, listening to the silence, not speaking, not thinking. The whispers would come, she knew, and eventually she would be able to understand the words, she was sure of it. Sighing, she picked a clean cup from the drying rack on the sink. Concentrating on keeping her hand steady, she poured the last of the coffee and handed it to Vi. "Sugar and cream is still on the table."

Dani picked up her own cup and watched as Vi measured and stirred, a smile playing at the corners of her mouth. After the first sip, she sat back and looked at Dani.

On cue, Dani continued their ritual. "So. What's the exciting news?"

"It's just amazing, isn't it?" Vi settled in to dramatize the tale to its fullest. "How things just happen. One minute, a person is just strolling along, minding one's own business, then—POW—the whole thing changes."

Wishing she had remembered to comb her hair properly, Dani got as comfortable as she could and prepared to wait it out.

"It was such a beautiful day yesterday, wasn't it?" Vi lit a cigarette and blew smoke at the ceiling. "It was you that gave us the idea, when you said you were going to meet your family for a picnic. Well, we decided—that is, Claude and I— that it would be just the ticket. We packed up a picnic lunch and headed to Stanley Park. We thought we'd have lunch, then maybe go for a walk and spend the rest of the day at the beach."

Vi grinned. Dani re-arranged her face into what she hoped was a look of attentiveness and with an inward groan said, "Sounds like a perfectly ordinary thing to do."

Leaning forward, Vi lowered her voice as if the walls had ears. "It turned out not to be ordinary at all. We had our lunch within view of the ocean, watching sailing boats bobbing on the water, fed some crumbs to the seagulls, then walked along one of the trails. Just ordinary stuff, so far. There weren't too many people around." She flicked the ash from her cigarette into the ashtray and took another drag, inhaling deeply. Dani was beginning to feel prickles of irritation creep up the back of her neck.

"You know how men are," Vi said, one eyebrow raised as she nodded. "He had to step into the bushes for a moment. As I said, there was no one around, and it was quiet. Like a cathedral. Just the chirps of a bird or two, wind rustling branches, flies buzzing around—that kind of thing. You could hear the waves crashing on the beach in the distance."

Dani was reaching the end of her patience. She clamped her jaw and tried to look fascinated.

"Then all of a sudden Claude came running out." Vi sat up straight and threw her hands in the air. A curler loosened and hung at an angle. "He was all bug-eyed and shaking. He grabs me by the shoulders, 'We have to call the police!' he yells at me." She took another drag, made a half-hearted attempt at tightening the curler. "Well, I can tell you, I was some taken aback. He like to have shaved a couple of years off my life.

"'What's wrong?' I says to him. 'There's a dead body in there', he says to me.'" Vi ground her cigarette butt into the ashtray with a flourish. "'How do you know he's dead? Let me see', I says to him. 'No,' he says, all pale and frantic and looking to faint on the spot. 'It's not a fit sight for a lady.' And then he grabs my arm and we high-tail it out to find a telephone. We had to go almost all the way back into the city. They can use a few more phone booths in the park, if you ask me. Anything can happen among all those trees, for Pete's sake."

Dani was now listening intently. "Oh my," she said. She thought it best to keep her comments to a minimum until she heard the whole story.

"Anyway, the police arrived and Claude took them back along the path and showed them where to look. First thing you know, we were down at the police station, answering questions. 'Course, I didn't have anything to say, and anyway nobody seemed to want to ask me even if I did, so I had to hang around and wait while they had Claude in a room with a couple of detectives. I didn't even get to see what Claude was going on about. But they talked to him for quite a while. By the time we got out of there, it was late in the afternoon. No sense in going down to the beach now, of course. It's starting to get dark early. Days are getting shorter and soon we'll be sloshing around in the winter rains. I was so hoping to get in another day or two with the sun and sand—you know, to tide me over during the dark days of winter."

"So did you find out who the dead body belonged to?"

"Best I could figure is that it was male. Don't know what happened or how he got tossed in the bush. They weren't very forthcoming, the police. Want you to do all the talking. And that constable who seemed to be in charge, he was very good at it."

Dani remembered Detective Carlson's visit of the night before, and thought he would be just the kind of man who could speak much and say nothing.

Vi patted Dani's hand. "Thought you could keep an ear open. Uri gets around here and there on his route—maybe he would hear something. And don't forget the newspaper. There should be something in there, don't you think? I listened to the radio but there was nothing on the news." Her gaze turned solemn. "If you spot anything, you could let me know."

"I'll be sure to," Dani said. "Want me to put on another pot of coffee?"

Vi rose from the table. "No thanks, dear. I've got to be getting back. Claude should be awake soon, and I want to make him a nice breakfast." She looked at Dani, then smiled, suddenly shy. "Now don't go jumping to any conclusions, it's not what you think. He had such a hard time all day, the police questions and all, when we got back he was just petered out, poor duck. All pale and swooney. I tucked him up on the sofa. He'll be a bit stiff this morning I fancy, but he needed the rest, he was that tuckered."

Dani smiled. "I'm sure. That's a huge shock for anyone." As she walked her neighbour to the door she reflected that Vi had found the answer to help her through her recent widowhood. Apparently, her neighbour wasn't the type to grieve for long.

"True. And as you know, Claude is a bit delicate." At the door, Vi turned and took Dani's hand, leaning close. "Quite exciting, though, don't you think?" She giggled and stepped out onto the porch, hugging her sweater over her bright, flowery housedress. "Don't forget to let me know if you hear or see anything. We might get our names in the paper as discoverers or witnesses or something, and it can't hurt to check, right?"

"Don't worry, Vi. I'll keep my eyes and ears open."

Vi hurried down the walk and through the gate. Dani watched her neighbour climb her own front porch steps, already thinking what she'd say to Eva when she came home after work. With a last wave she shut the door, leaned her forehead against it, puffing out a short breath. *What'll she think of next, silly woman*, she thought, smiling, remembering her neighbor's penchant for drama. *But for all that, she's never boring.*

* * *

Eva repeated the order back to the customer to make sure she got it right. She had been distracted, had made mistakes a couple of times already, and was determined to keep her mind on her work, if only to avoid the wrath of Chang. He had finally relaxed enough to give her some breathing room, finally let her work without watching her every move. But today she saw him frowning as he watched her drop cutlery and forget to wipe the counter.

Later, she told herself. Plenty of time to think about it after work when she could concentrate. But a kaleidoscope of memories danced in her head: the body lying on the table, the sound of Detective Carlson's voice, all the unanswered questions. And to top it off there was the ride home with Billy, the way he had said goodnight and saw her to the door, his hand holding hers a little too long. She'd barely slept, the images and sounds like a radio she couldn't turn off. She'd hardly tasted her breakfast coffee, didn't even remember getting on the streetcar or arriving at the café. It surprised her to find herself in an apron with a pad in her hand and a pencil behind her ear, unaware of how it happened.

She put the latest order in to be processed and caught Sheila's eye. "Cover me?" she asked, inclining her head towards the lady's room.

"Sure," Sheila said, snapping her gum. She straightened from giving her customer an enticing display of cleavage and put the coffee pot back on the warmer. Eva smiled her thanks and hurried down the hallway beside the kitchen. Once inside, she closed her eyes, took a few deep breaths, and let the silence help to calm her errant thoughts. She splashed cold water on her face then pressed the towel against her closed eyes, willing her thoughts to put aside their clamoring until she had time for them. A few minutes later, as refreshed as she was going to get, she returned to the dining room. Two tables in her section were occupied with new customers. Picking up her pad and pencil, a friendly smile firmly in place, she walked over to take their order.

The next time she looked up at the clock, it was ten minutes past the end of her shift. The crowd was finally thinning out. Sheila was leaning on the counter, talking to a customer while she unwrapped a new stick of gum. Two habits, Eva considered, which made her charming and irritating at the same time.

Eva reached for her coat and waved to the cook, who was sitting on an overturned pail peeling potatoes, an unlit cigarette dangling from his mouth. He gestured with his head, which was all she would get from the taciturn man. With a quick wave to Sheila, Eva headed for the door.

It had started to sprinkle again. Streetlight reflections cast crooked, zig-zag patterns on the dark, wet sidewalks like the work of an abstract artist. She turned up the collar of her coat and wished she'd remembered to bring her umbrella, but the walk to the streetcar stop was short and there was a storefront doorway she could stand in while she waited. Head down, she was almost upon a solitary figure before she realized. He leaned against a car parked at the curb, his overcoat and hat concealing his features, but as she drew near, he straightened, tilted his hat back and smiled.

"Eva," John said, coming toward her. "I hoped I hadn't missed you. Care for a ride home?"

"What are you doing here? Isn't that Henry's car?"

"It is," he said, taking her arm. "He let me borrow it for a meeting on the condition that I stop by and pick you up. I was afraid I'd missed you."

"I worked a little later than usual," Eva told him. "We were busy."

"Lucky for me." John opened the passenger door. "I can't think what would happen if I couldn't carry out my part of the bargain."

Eva said nothing as he closed the door and came around to the driver's side and got in. She was tired and edgy. He wanted something other than his brother's portion of the land. Why else would he arrange to have time with her alone? Whatever it was, she'd deal with it; she'd have to. But she had a notion she wasn't going to like it. For a moment, she felt like getting out and walking home. She wanted to feel the rain on her face and pretend it would wash away the uncertainties and the ever-increasing demands of everyone around her.

John put the key into the ignition. "Actually, I'd hoped to have a moment of your time. There's something I wanted to talk to you about."

Inwardly, Eva groaned. Was this never going to end? Where could she go to find some peace? Maybe a convent? Maybe she should look into the war effort. Maybe they'd send her overseas and she'd at least see a bit of the world. She looked over at her brother-in-law. His big hands looked out of place resting on the wheel; they were more suited to holding the reins of a team of plow-horses.

As he threaded his way through the traffic, Eva slouched down and rested her head on the seat back. If she had to listen, she would at least make herself comfortable.

20

"We didn't get a chance to talk much, you and I," John began. When Eva didn't reply, he continued. "I wanted to ask you about Aleksy. You and he got into that arranged marriage, a deal between your father and mine. I knew from the get-go that it wasn't going to work. Aleksy is…well, anyway, Aleksy. And I know you weren't happy—he didn't exactly treat you like he should have."

"How do you know how he treated me?"

"I understand my brother. I know what he's like. Who he is." He made a left turn and slowed behind a truckload of lumber. "Thing is, he's still your husband. You should be there with him."

"What good would that do? He doesn't know anyone, least of all me, as I understand it."

"Maybe if you were there, it would help. Help him heal. I know he was upset when you left. I also know that he came after you when you left to work for Bradford. You turned him away. "

Eva felt anger stirring. She sat up a little straighter to keep her temper under control. Slowly, as if speaking to a child, she said, "The only reason he came that day was because his father, and yours, by the way, told him to. He just did whatever the old man wanted. You know what the old man was like—I heard what you said about him. Anyway, Aleksy had no feelings for me one way or another, and in fact, I got the feeling he was glad to see the back of me."

"Nevertheless, I…"

"Aleksy had his own circle of friends, which never included me. He seldom talked to me even when he was home, which was rarely. Usually, whenever he decided to honour me with his presence, he had one of his friends along. Maybe I could have dealt with it better if he had a lady friend on the side, but he never did, as far as I know. Likely there are those who know lots of things about him I don't. But he just hung around with his pals. Personally, I think he was too immature for marriage."

"Well, yeah, I know. He was certainly too young. And he was kind of a man's man, so to speak."

Eva snorted. "You could say that."

John glanced over at her. In the shadow of his hat his eyes gleamed, but she couldn't make out his expression. They drove on in silence, the only sound the purr of the motor and the slap-slap of the windshield wipers.

"I've been doing a lot of thinking," John finally said. "There's lots of time to think on the long drive out here from Alberta. Except going through the Rockies, o'course. Then a person has to pay attention. But it seemed to me you shouldn't have had to come all the way out here to escape the kind of life you had there."

"My family's here," Eva said. "I would have come anyway. Nothing to do with anything."

"Not even to get away from Horace Bradford?"

"Braford? What about him?"

"Uri filled me in on what happened: him coming out here and trying to get you to come back. I've met him, of course. Socially. In passing. Heard he's a bit of a loner. Anything else I heard I didn't pay much attention to. That is, before you went to work for him. If he's the only one you're concerned with, I can protect you—make sure he doesn't come around you, making demands."

"And how do you intend to do that? Did Uri also explain that he sent a man to harm my nephews if I didn't do what he asked? How far do you think he would go to get what he wants?"

"So maybe he was upset that you left the way you did. Maybe he only wanted you to come back. Maybe he really liked your cooking. Or say, maybe he was sweet on you."

Eva relaxed into the seat and blew out an exasperated breath. "Really, John. I don't know what you're thinking to accomplish here, but be assured, those things are furthest from his mind. Well, okay, he did like that I put good meals on the table, but that wasn't and never would be a reason. He's not right in the head if he thinks someone will stay on that remote homestead and cook and clean and never see anyone, talk to anyone, go anywhere without his permission. That's not the way I want to live my life."

John drew the car up to the curb and stopped the engine. He made no move to get out, staring straight ahead as if counting raindrops on the windshield. Eva was about to open the door and leave, but she paused. Curious, she waited. The cooling motor ticked into the silence, and a damp, faintly musky odor exuded from their wet clothing.

Finally, John drew a breath. Eva knew the signs; it was as if he was preparing for a lecture, and wanted to sound as patient and reasonable as possible. "You understand, Eva, that with the old man gone, I'm the oldest now. I have a responsibility. You are my brother's wife. For whatever that has meant to you or him, vows have been made and you are part of the family. Aleksy's in no condition to be any kind of husband, or to look out for you with the responsibilities of a husband. Therefore, I am charged with your welfare, for making sure you are cared for and protected. For that to happen, you must come back with me, stay on the homestead and let me look after you. You will be well provided for, and you would not have to fear anything or anyone. I give you my word."

For a moment, Eva felt as if she was in a vacuum. There was no sound, no movement. At last she began to feel the blood pulsing in her veins, hear the sound of her breath. She looked at John, who sat motionless, staring straight ahead. He'd prepared his speech and delivered it, and she had no doubt he sincerely meant every word. The dim light from the street lamp cast his face into a study in lines and angles, disturbingly skull-like. She opened her mouth to speak, surprised it still worked. Closed it again. The burn of anger stirred her gut, began to sizzle beneath her skin. She exhaled a long breath, expelling the annoyance with it.

She knew he was trying to do the honourable thing, as he'd been taught. She remembered his aunt Enna, and supposed she lived in their house, tending to their needs, in payment for a roof over her head and protection from who knows what. "I don't know what to say."

"No need to say anything. We do what we must do."

Eva suddenly felt drained of energy and emotion. In a tired voice, she said, "I've repeated this so many times, you must have heard it at least once: I'm not going anywhere. I will not go back to the prairies for any reason, least of all for some strange European family tradition that should have stayed in the old country. Maybe it works there, but not here. So consider yourself off the hook, no debt owed, no obligations. I can manage very well here, with my own family around. And while I appreciate that you've made the effort, and thank you for it, there's nothing that will make me return to that godforsaken place. Ever again."

John turned to her, his face expressionless. "Think about it. You're being here has put your family in jeopardy. I can't help you if you stay here. At least, back home, I can make sure you're safe and cared for. And your family here will be safe, too."

"John, yesterday I was called in to the police station. You were there when Detective Carlson came to the house to get me, you know about that. I identified the body of a man who was beaten to death. He was the one who had been following me, who was employed by Bradford to intimidate me into going back. He's dead. So however that happened, he's no longer a threat."

John opened his mouth to speak, but Eva hurried on. "So you see, I have lots of protection, the police know about this. If Bradford tries it again, he will be stopped again. That's how it is."

"If anything happens to you…."

"What? Aleksy doesn't care, never has. Even if he was able to remember me and my problems, I doubt he'd be able to do anything about it. And you are not, I repeat, not, responsible for your brother's wife."

"Eva, listen to reason…"

"Your reason, not mine. No. No thank you. And that's the end of it." She opened the door and got out of the car. She could hear John's footsteps behind her as they walked up the front stairs to the porch. The house was dark. John caught up to her and put a hand on her arm. "I'd like to leave tomorrow, and expected to take you with me. It's the right thing to do. Think about it. We can talk again in the morning."

Eva frowned at him.

"Just think about it. Please." His voice was soft, persuasive.

Eva turned the lock and stepped inside.

They parted at the foot of the stairs. John climbed to his room and she proceeded down the hall to the door that led to her rooms in the basement. As she passed the living room, lightning flashed, then darkness, leaving a ghostly image behind her eyes. "Dani?"

As her eyes adjusted to the dark, she made out the shape of her sister sitting in the armchair. She reached for the light switch and heard Dani say,

"Don't. Please. Don't turn on the light."

"You all right?"

"I'm fine." Dani blew her nose. "Just sitting here, thinking."

"About what?" She moved closer. "Have you been crying?"

"Don't mind me." Dani sniffed, and in the dim light, Eva saw her put her hanky in the pocket of her apron. "I'm just having a moment."

"More than a moment, if you ask me. What happened? Are you hurt?"

"Nothing like that. Don't worry."

"Then, what?"

Dani sighed. "Uri and I had a bit of a…disagreement. And I'm tired. It's been a long day."

"Where is he?"

"Out. Oh, and dinner's in the oven. Have you eaten?"

"No. Have you?"

"I usually wait for Uri. Now that John is back and you're here, we should go ahead."

Eva took Dani's hands and pulled her to her feet. "C'mon. Let's get going, then." Dani swayed, caught her balance, a smile tugging at the corners of her mouth. With arms linked, the sisters walked into the hallway. "We were so busy today I barely had time for a cup of coffee. I didn't even think of grabbing something before I left. Suddenly I'm starved. I could eat a horse."

In the kitchen, Eva observed her sister as Dani turned the light on and removed her apron, hooking it on the back of a door. Other than the evidence of tears, she looked her usual self as she took a casserole out of the oven and placed a basket of freshly-baked bread and a dish of butter on the table.

"I'd better let John know that everything's ready," said Dani, turning toward the stairway.

"Wait." Eva put a hand on Dani's arm. Lightning flashed again; thunder pounded and rumbled away to silence. "First tell me what happened. Your nose is red and your eyes are puffy. It must have been some 'disagreement.'"

Dani shrugged. "It's not important. Uri sometimes gets…I don't know. The littlest things set him off. He goes out and cools off. He'll be back. I'll keep his supper warm and everything will be fine." She sniffed. "He works hard, and sometimes he just—has to blow off some steam."

Eva looked into her sister's eyes, saw the sadness and pain. Her stomach clenched with anger. Kind, gentle Dani—she should be cared for and cherished, not used as a channel for someone else's problems and frustrations. She was going to have a conversation with her friend real soon, although she was beginning to wonder how much of a friend he really was.

She drew Dani into her arms in a hug. "I'm sorry, hon," she said. "I wish it wasn't so hard for you. If there's anything I can do…"

Dani turned her face away and shook her head, stepping away from her sister's embrace.

They both looked up as John appeared in the doorway. "Where's Uri?"

"He had to go out," Dani said. "Dinner's on the table."

"Will he be back soon? I was hoping we could have more time together before I go. It may be a while before we see each other again."

"I'm sure he won't be much longer," Dani said. "He'd be upset if he missed you."

Eva turned to help put the food out. The yeasty scent of the bread and warm cheese-covered pasta from the casserole made her mouth water. She could feel John's intense gaze boring holes into her back and she hid a smile. *He likely thinks he can get Uri to help him persuade me. He can darn well think whatever he wants. It's a free country.*

As they sat to the table, she looked at him, letting her smile blossom into a dazzling display of sweetness and white teeth. "You're going to love this casserole," she told him. "One of Dani's specialities."

Eva had never praised anything Dani had cooked in her life, but she pretended she didn't notice her sister's surprised expression as Dani turned to her, serving spoon poised over a bowl full of dilled pickles, eyebrows raised. Eva gazed back, projecting innocence. With a frown, Dani passed the bowl to John.

Eva hoped her sister would understand. If it meant keeping the conversation light, fending off any more mention of what she should do, where she should go and who she should be, she would do or say whatever it took. *Besides,* she thought after a forkful of casserole, *this isn't half bad. Maybe Dani's cooking is improving—or else I'm hungrier than I thought.*

She stole a glance at John. His eyes were on his plate, unaware of the thoughts chasing through her mind. His proposal grated along her nerve ends. He had no right to tell her how or where to live her life. She felt it was wrong that the social order dictated a woman belonged under the protection of a man, and she wouldn't accept it. She would make her own decisions. If she had to clean other people's houses, cook other people's meals, she would do it because it was her choice, and receive payment for it. She was her own person, she would make her own way, and if she decided to make a life with someone else some day, it would be her decision too. The rest of the world could think what it wanted.

No one spoke. The silence stretched until the sound of rain hissing against the windows filled the room. Finally, Dani put down her fork. "I just remembered. My neighbour, Vi, was over this morning. She always has something newsy to tell me. Seems her and her man friend were out picnicking and discovered a body in the bushes." Dani smiled as she remembered her friend's dramatic tale. "They spent time down at the police station and everything."

"Did they say if the body was identified?" asked Eva.

"All she could get was that it was a man, and his name was Phil. She couldn't remember the last name, but she thought it was long and hard to pronounce. You know how she is—she's not one for facts, and before you know it they're just fancies. I'm not even sure she got that much right."

Eva stared at her sister. "That sounds like the same man I was called down to identify. Isn't that something?"

That brought a wry smile to Dani's face. "And here I wondered she was making it all up. With her, you never know—she likes a bit of drama." She rose from the table and began gathering plates. "Pie anyone?" Lightening flashed, sending a blast of light through the window. The lamps flickered. Thunder threw boulders of sound against the house, which shuddered in response. As if on cue, the door opened and Uri stood grinning, wet hair plastered to his head, coat dripping, a backdrop of heavy rain behind him like a silver curtain.

He flourished a rum bottle in one hand, holding on to the door jamb with the other. "Lookit here," he said, wobbling slightly. "I bring you spirits to warm your insides and—and—. Aw, heck, let's all have a drink."

21

John was the first to react. "Get in out of the rain, you stupid bugger," he said. Getting up from the table, he strode to the door, pulled his brother inside, pushing the door closed with his foot. Uri staggered a couple of steps and slumped into a chair, clutching the empty bottle to his chest. Glassy-eyed and grinning, he looked from Eva to Dani, then turned his gaze on his brother. "Johnny?" A puzzled frown replaced the grin.

Eva turned to Dani. Her sister, eyes wide and dark in a face turned ashen, stood staring at her husband, the collected plates and silverware forgotten in her hands.

"You need a cup of good, strong coffee," John said.

Eva moved to Dani's side and put an arm around her sister's stony shoulders. Guiding her to a chair, she pushed her gently but firmly into it. "I'll get it," she told her. "You just sit for a moment, then you can serve the pie. Okay?" She put two heaping teaspoons of sugar into a cup and drained the last of the coffee, strong and bitter, from the pot. Stirring, she walked back to the table just in time to see Uri slump forward, the rum bottle rolling out of his hand, echoing the thump his head made as they hit hard surfaces at the same time. The bottle bumped to a stop under the table, and Uri answered with a loud snore.

"Good lord," said John, shaking his head. He turned to Dani. His voice soft with understanding, he smiled, obviously amused at the foibles of his brother. "Does he do this often?" Her pale gaze was all the answer he needed. He shook his head again, rubbed a spot at the back of his neck. "Here—I'll help you get him up to bed." Putting his brother's arm around his neck, he hoisted him up, dragging him toward the door. Uri stumbled a few steps as he roused from his stupor. "I'm holding you to that piece of pie you promised," John called as he headed for the stairs. Dani got up as if in a trance and followed. Eva watched them make their way up the staircase, then busied herself wiping the spilled rum from the floor, clearing the table and putting the leftover food into the icebox. Concentrating on her task, she managed to quell her anger and discard thoughts of knocking Uri over the head with the empty rum bottle to beat some sense into him. Even if she was capable of doing such a thing, it likely wouldn't do any good and it wouldn't solve the problem. No, there had to be another way, she reasoned, remembering the frightened face of her sister. First chance she got, she decided, she'd sit him down and have a serious talk, even if she had to tie him to a chair to make him listen.

* * *

The pale light from the small, high window cast the room in a faint gloom. Eva yawned, stretched and rolled over. Her alarm hadn't gone off, indicating that she'd have enough time to catch Uri before he went off to work. The mornings were dark now, with the coming of winter. Then she remembered—he may well have slept in, given the amount of rum he'd consumed last night. Sitting up, she reached for the alarm to turn it off, and discovered she had forgotten to set it at all, probably too upset about the evening's outcome to remember.

Leaping out of bed, she washed, dressed and sprang up the stairs to the kitchen in record time. Dani stood by the stove, pouring tea into a cup. She looked pale, her eyes smudged with exhaustion. "Morning," she said.

"It certainly is," Eva grumped, sarcasm intended as she found a cup. "Any coffee left? I wanted to be up earlier. Where is everyone?" She meant Uri, of course, but included John as well.

"Uri's just about to leave for work," said Dani, taking a seat at the table and reaching for the sugar. "John went upstairs for his suitcase. He should be right down."

Eva studied her sister's face. "You look tired. Did you not get any sleep?"

"I slept just fine. Uri snored up a storm, but I'm used to that. He always does when he's had a few."

"A few," Eva muttered, thinking out loud. "That's putting it mildly."

"Anyway, one of the reasons he did a bit of celebrating—seems he sold this place, and we'll be moving again. Got a good deal on it, apparently. He told me to start packing right away."

"Do you have another place ready to move into?"

"He didn't say, exactly. I think we may have to move into a motel or something. He didn't have time to tell me the whole story. I didn't even know he had anyone interested in this one, but then he doesn't often keep me up to date on the latest. He says it's because he doesn't want to get my hopes up when things don't turn out."

"I'll bet," Eva said, under her breath. Aloud, she said, "I imagine you'll have to store your furniture somewhere."

"Don't worry, sis," said Uri, pulling on his jacket as he came into the room. "I've got everything all arranged."

Eva looked closely at her brother-in-law. His eyes were red and he looked a bit pale, but otherwise, none the worse for wear. "I guess I'll have to find a place to stay for a while," she said.

"You have a place," said John, coming into the room with his suitcase. He placed it on the floor and folded his arms across his chest. "I don't have to leave right away. I can wait for you to get your things together."

Exasperated, Eva blew out a breath. "I'm not going anywhere. I can't just walk away from my job, even if I wanted to, which I don't. We've gone over and over this, for heaven's sake."

John looked at Uri. "Talk some sense into her, will you?" he said. "How can I protect her if she refuses to come with me?"

Uri looked from his brother to Eva, his expression unreadable. "I can look after her here just fine."

"You're about to put her out onto the street," John's face was becoming red and mottled. "How is that looking after her?"

"She'll stay with Agatha and Henry until we can relocate, then she'll be back here with us and safe again." His eyes suddenly went cold, his expression stony. He slammed his hat on in a gesture that plainly indicated an end to the discussion.

"Will you two just stop!" Eva was starting to feel like a commodity being put up for bidding. "I'm not going anywhere I don't want to go. Besides, I have a place to stay if I want."

Both men turned to look at her. "Where?" they said in unison.

She looked from one to the other. She saw sober, concerned eyes looking back and suddenly felt a bubble of mischief form. "In fact," she said, turning away to reach for a teacup in the cupboard. "I've been offered a place with Chang any time I want." She hid a smile while she poured. "I think he's sweet on me. We've been having a few…conversations."

"Really?" Uri's face became dark, and a muscle jumped in his jaw as he took a step toward her. "How long has this being going on?"

Eva patted his arm as she passed him, getting a trace of sour alcohol and stale tobacco odours that made her stomach lurch. She sat down at the table and looked up at him. "None of your business," she said, and grinned.

Uri glared at her. "I've got to get to work. Come on, John, let's go or you'll miss your train." He strode to the door and yanked it open and pointed a stern finger at Eva. "We'll talk about this later."

Eva reached for a piece of cold toast. "Yes, we will," she said, not caring whether he heard her or not, but meaning every word.

John picked up his suitcase. "I hope you won't regret this," he said. He took Dani's hand. "Thank you for everything. I hope we'll see you again real soon." He gazed at her for a moment, frowned at Eva and followed his brother out the door.

Eva looked at her sister over her teacup, the only sound the tick of the wall clock. Dani buttered her toast, examined it, then put it down. When she looked up again, her eyes were dark with concern. "Are you really going to live with Chang?"

"No, of course not, silly. I just said that to get Uri's hackles up. The two of them think they know everything, and that their decisions are right and final. I know they mean well, but I have news for them: I won't be taking orders from either of them, now or at any time."

"So, it isn't true?"

"Of course not."

Dani's shoulder's relaxed and she almost smiled. "I'm glad you aren't going with John, at least."

"Did you ever think I would?"

"I don't know. No, I guess not. It's just that I don't really like him. He doesn't feel right, if you know what I mean."

"If you'd met his father, you'd know why he strikes you like that. He's a lot like the old coot. Give him a few more years and he'll be just as domineering and stern. There's no way I want to live with that. I pity the poor woman who ends up with him. Probably end up in an early grave like his mother." Eva rose from the table and took her cup and plate to the sink. "There's more to the world out there than just being a wife and drudge, you know. And I intend to see about that. If I had to wait for someone to take care of me, I'd never know where I'd find myself, or what I'd be able to see—probably nothing, if the past is any indication. The plain fact is, I don't want to live with anyone. I'm just fine with my own company, thank you." She bent and gave her sister a hug. "I'd better get along to work, or I won't be able to afford to live anywhere."

Dani called after her as Eva reached the basement door. "I just remembered: there's a letter came for you yesterday. I put it on the hall table."

"Does it look important?" Eva asked.

Dani shrugged. "It has an Alberta postmark. That's all I know."

Eva's stomach tightened and she could barely swallow. She could think of only one person who would write, and she wondered what he thought to accomplish through a letter. It must have something legal in it, something that, in writing, would somehow achieve his goal. What that could be, she couldn't imagine. She suddenly felt very tired. It seemed that she just finished dealing with one problem and another popped up. Would it never end?

Well, maybe that's what life was all about, but she wasn't going to let it matter. She waved her hand as if it didn't. "I'll pick it up on my way out."

★ ★ ★

The envelope rustled with a sibilant whisper, calling from her coat pocket as she shifted in her seat. The rhythmic swaying of the streetcar helped direct her focus away as she thought about what she should do; a more pressing duty, in her opinion, than finding out what the letter may tell her. No matter what message lurked within the pages, opening it at a time of her choosing made her feel that she could still control some part of her life.

She knew full well that she was postponing the inevitable. She wanted to be able to have a plan, a place to live, and right now, the thought of going back to stay with Agatha and Henry seemed like the best idea. Perhaps her only option. When push came to shove, she really didn't have any choice, but moving back would endanger the boys again. Then it occurred to her, and the more she thought about it, the more she liked the idea, that she could simply rent a room somewhere, telling no one where she was staying. That way none of her family would be threatened. Why hadn't she thought of this before? There was a big world out there, she had told herself many times. Perhaps she should start believing her own words.

The paper envelope crackled a reminder again as she stepped down from the streetcar. It lurked like a glowing ember ready to burst into flame in her pocket, making her aware that no matter where she went, she wouldn't be free until the matter she feared was resolved. Eva firmed her chin with determination. If she had to deal with it, she'd do it when she was darn good and ready, and not a minute before.

Pausing at the door to the restaurant, she reached into her pocket and took out the letter. She examined it again. The postmark indicated it came from Alberta, as Dani had said. In the upper left-hand corner the paper was smudged as if a damp finger had deliberately tried to erase all traces identifying its exact origin. So it could be from anyone. Except that she only knew of one person who would even think to write to her and that person was the last human being on earth she wanted anything to do with.

Abruptly stuffing the envelope back into her pocket, she opened the door, determined not to let anything distract her, deciding that it could wait until she'd made some arrangements and was relocated. One step at a time.

* * *

By the end of her shift, Eva could no longer avoid what she came to think of as the monster in her closet. Her curiosity nibbled and niggled at her all day, and despite all her efforts to ignore it, the letter called to her from the coat cupboard beside the kitchen. During her early break she had called Agatha. They had already heard the news of the sale and impending move and Agatha assured her that she could stay with them as long as she needed to. Yes, Billy was still there. No, she wouldn't be a bother. And Agatha promised to come around and help pack Dani and Uri's household for storage. The weekend was coming up and everyone would be available to help. They'd all be relocated and settled in no time.

With her immediate future settled, Eva took a bowl of soup and the last piece of lemon meringue pie from the display shelf and settled in an empty booth, away from the kitchen and general traffic area. While she stirred the soup to help it cool, she gazed at the envelope, willing it to be an illusion, to disappear. But it sat stubbornly propped against a salt shaker in front of her, and finally she gave in, put down her spoon and ran a finger under the flap to open it.

There was a crest of some sort in the letterhead; it was typewritten, but the only thing that caught Eva's eye was the salutation:

Dear Mrs. Smeniuk, it began.

22

Eva stared at the paper trembling in her hand. Mrs. Smeniuk. No one had called her that for so long, she was hardly able to reconcile the fact that it was her legal name.

She barely managed to make sense of the words through her whirling thoughts...*to inform you that...severity of his brain injury... no longer recognized anyone.* Slowly, she began to understand what she was reading. ...*slipping in and out of consciousness... just a matter of time before he succumbs ...*

She looked at the letterhead again. The hospital in Ponoka.

Eva dropped the letter on the table and sat back, her mind a whirl of thoughts and memories, trying to make some sense out of it. *Succumbs to the inevitable.* Bradford had told her of the accident, but it hadn't seemed real at the time, her mind insisting that it happened to someone else. Certainly not someone she had known, much less lived with for a time. John had most likely given her address to the hospital the last time he was there. She had assumed he would have presented himself as the person to contact. He was, after all, Aleksy's closest relative, in both senses of the word. And she was here, far away and of no use to him that she could think of. But having heard how John felt about tradition and responsibilities, particularly when it had anything to do with their land holdings, he wasn't likely to let her forget that she was still married to his brother. She supposed that she should be feeling some concern, some remorse for not being by his side. She looked for those feelings and began to feel a bit guilty that she couldn't find anything of that nature in her heart. Wives were supposed to be at the sides of their husbands, to care for them in sickness and in health as the vows maintained.

To do that, she reasoned, one should have had a proper husband in the first place. And while she bore no particular animosity toward Aleksy, she felt no love or loyalty toward him either. That opportunity had come and gone a long time ago. As far as she was concerned, he was someone she barely knew. Someone she had shared a bed with for a time, in a manner of speaking. She smiled at that thought. She had shared a bed with Bradford, come to that, and hadn't had anyone's permission to do so. The former had shown very little interest, the latter had become proprietary. Next time, she promised herself, she would know exactly where she stood. If there was a next time. And even then, she vowed, it had better be a very, very good arrangement.

A burst of laughter coming from the next table drew her attention. Three young ladies were gathering books from a table strewn with emptied soda glasses and school cases. The tallest of them made a comment Eva couldn't hear and poked her red-haired friend. A blonde, cheeks aflame with blushes, finally gave in to giggles and they all laughed again.

Eva studied them. They looked so young, but she knew that she wasn't much older than they were. Probably from the high school down the street, she thought. As they exited the café, she tried to picture herself, walking the three miles with her sisters to the small one-room school. They had laughed together too. Until childbirth took her mother away. Agatha had already married and started a family, so Eva had to step into her Mother's place and skip that part of her growing-up years entirely. Helping Tina and Dani with their lessons, and reading books whenever she had the chance was all the education she could get. She watched the girls through the large windows until they were out of sight. Was she once that young? Ever?

It hadn't felt like it for a minute. Before she knew it, she had been married to a man she had met only once and sent off to start life as a wife and in time, if things progressed in the usual fashion, she would have become a mother, a role she was already familiar with. Now she wondered what it would have been like to have gone to a proper school, have carefree afternoons, a girlfriend to share secrets with. Perhaps even had a warm coat in the winter …

She rubbed impatient hands over her face to wipe away the cobwebs of the past, sipped her coffee, and pondered the piece of lemon pie. Thoughtfully, she cut off a forkful, considered it, and placed the sweet-sour portion on her tongue. As she savoured the bite, it occurred to her that she was about to become a widow before her twenty-first birthday.

She cut off another helping of pie. In her mind's eye, she searched her memory for her wedding day. She recalled borrowing Agatha's wedding dress, and her sister altering the length to fit her taller frame, but she couldn't picture the actual look of the garment. She'd have to see if she could find the photo taken that day. She remembered the delicate ribbon roses Dani had made and attached to the hat. The small bouquet she saved was still tucked in her bureau drawer with her stockings and one good chemise. Of the hat there was no clue, likely because wearing what looked like an overturned bucket, despite the fashion, did nothing to add to her bridal ideal. The ceremony itself was a blur. The reception, full of music, food and half-drunk relatives and friends and neighbours, some of whom she'd never met, was not unlike dozens of other community gatherings she had attended.

Other than that, being married simply had never seemed real. The husband she imagined would share the everyday toil of a small farm and raise a family with was absent most of the time and distant when he was around. The loneliness she had hoped to escape had heated the air of dry prairie summers, tinged the sunrises of silent snow-clad mornings and nestled cold, bare shadows in her empty bed.

Yes, she decided, marriage for her was just a word, so 'widow' was just another word. To have either one apply, it would involve a spouse, someone in her opinion she'd never really had. Talk is cheap, her mother used to say. Without action, words become meaningless. Therefore, she wasn't going to let it concern her, she had more pressing issues to consider. She folded the letter carefully, replaced it in the envelope and slipped it into her handbag. Gathering up the empty plate and cup, she turned her thoughts to keeping a roof over her head.

* * *

The next two weeks were so filled with packing and making plans that Eva had little time to think of anything else but work at the restaurant and the forthcoming move. Henry brought over the big car on Saturday morning, then helped carry her few possessions into their house and the small room they had used for storage. Billy had her old room, but Eva had no time for either regrets or plans in the bustle of getting settled and helping Dani with packing.

Uri had found a place for rent further around the lake and Billy had commandeered his friend Jacob and his truck to help with the move. On the designated day, Henry, Jacob and Billy filled the old jalopy to overflowing with boxes and furniture and the truck wheezed its way, radiator steaming, to the front of the small, run-down structure badly in need of paint.

The air had turned crisp, and small snowflakes drifted down to melt away on the sodden sidewalks, soon to turn icy. Eva climbed out of Henry's car, glad to be free of the crush of boxes she had been squeezed among in the back seat. She breathed deeply of the moisture-laden, frigid air. Right behind them, Uri pulled up in his newly acquired, second-hand car. The day he brought it home, he'd thrown open the front door and with a big grin almost splitting his face, had announced, "1938 Ford." Henry had grabbed his coat and both men went out the door. Eva followed her sister to watch them from the window.

"Women have their babies, men have their cars," Agatha said after a time. "Same thing, just different." Eva must have looked puzzled because Agatha patted her hand, took her arm and led her to the kitchen. "Never mind," she said. "They'll likely be a while. Let's put on some tea." Agatha had been right. For the next hour, he and Henry had examined it from top to bottom. When they came in, they were rosy with cold and grinning from ear to ear.

Eva looked at it again as Billy opened the trunk. The front bumper was missing, rust had chewed holes in the rear fenders and there was a large dent in the passenger door. Despite the rich shine to the dark blue paint and the slightly decrepit look, it was serviceable and paid for.

Everyone selected a box and carried them in a fine procession up the weed-infested sidewalk. Uri unlocked the door and threw it open. A faint, musty smell reminded Eva of the sparse little house she had entered as a bride. She shivered, shaking off the ghosts of the past and stepped aside as Henry entered the room, carrying a huge box which he put in the middle of the floor with a grunt.

Sleeves rolled up to his elbows, arms akimbo, he looked around. Frowning, his glance went from the peeling wallpaper in the tiny kitchen to the threadbare carpet in the living area to the ceiling with the water stain in one corner. Eva couldn't read his expression and would have liked to know what he was thinking, but if he was true to form, he'd let everyone know soon enough. Finally, he shook his head and shrugged.

"Nothing here that'll scare the horses," he said. "Or that a little fresh air and soap won't cure. Guess it'll have to do." With a grunt, he picked up his box and made for the back room.

Dani came in behind Eva in time to hear their brother-in-law's pronouncement. She rolled her eyes at the remark and the two sisters shared a smile, knowing who would be wielding the mop and broom. They took their boxes to the back room and Dani placed hers on the pile with a reluctant gesture. "Guess I won't be needing the Christmas decorations this year," she said, her voice wistful. Eva turned to her, eyebrows raised.

"Well, just look around," Dani said, spreading her arms to include the tiny rooms. "Where would I even put up a tree to begin with? There's little enough space for the kitchen table, and the sofa will have to do if we need anywhere else to sit." She looked longingly at the box and sighed. "Heaven help us, I hope we find something else soon."

Eva knew how much Dani loved Christmas. She usually went all out, decorating hallways and doors, windows and mantels and even had hung a wreath in the outhouse in their prairie home. Now that she had a complete indoor bathroom, her embellishments knew no bounds. But she also knew that Uri wouldn't budge from this place until Dani had scrubbed, cleaned and redecorated all she could. Even though he had told them it was rented, Eva had an idea that he would somehow turn it to his advantage.

"Never mind, love," Eva said, placing an arm around her sister as they walked out to get another box. "Agatha will have a big tree, and I'm sure she'd love some help decorating her house this year. And I tell you what—let's have a shopping day. We'll go out early, have lunch, spend the whole day. We'll make it a special event for just the three of us, if Agatha wants to come. Then maybe we'll do it every year."

"We already have a day when we cook Christmas dinner together. I love that we sit and chat while we make the cabbage rolls and pyrogies. Sometimes we even get together for the shortbreads and cakes."

"That's as may be, but it doesn't ever take the place of shopping."

"True."

By the time they walked arm and arm back to the truck, it was mostly unloaded. Jacob was standing on the curb, cigarette hanging from his mouth, thumbs hooked in his suspenders as he watched the others come and go through eyes slotted against the smoke. As the two woman approached, Jacob stamped out the butt and straightened, smiling.

"All finished up in there?" he asked Eva.

"Just about. Thanks again for lending us your truck. It saved us a lot, and we're grateful."

"Aw, it don't make no never mind." He reached for his tobacco pouch. "I wasn't doing anything else useful today anyways."

"Well, we're glad you could come," said Dani.

"We certainly are." Uri came up from behind and pushed in between the two sisters, an arm around each. "Thanks again."

Billy walked past the little group and hauled the last box from the back of the truck.

"Be with you in a minute," he told Jacob. He looked at Uri and the two girls, his face stony. "There's still a couple of small boxes in the car. Then I think we're done."

"I'll get them," Eva said, wriggling out of Uri's grasp.

"I'll help." Dani was right behind her. Uri laughed. "See," he said to Billy. "That's what a woman will do if you train her right." He put his hands in his pockets and sauntered up the sidewalk and through the front door.

Billy and Jacob exchanged a look, Jacob's face broadened into a wide smile. "Aw, he's okay," he told Billy. "His problem is just that a few of his pages are stuck together." He gave Billy a wink. "He'll get over himself. Give him time."

Billy just shook his head, hefted the box to his shoulder and with his face a study in black looks that bored into Uri's back, he followed him into the house.

23

Trying to get ready for work is an exercise in frustration, thought Eva. With the extra boxes piled in a corner, the small cot and dresser, there was little room to turn around. And she had to even be careful lest she bump her head on the slanted ceiling. A room tucked under the eaves was less than perfect, to say the least, but at least it was rent-free while she looked for something more suitable.

Flipping the blanket on the bed to straighten it, she grabbed her handbag and promptly bumped her head again. *That's it,* she said to herself as she stomped out. Today is the day I'll find something, or else.

"Good morning." Billy's cheerful voice was loud in her ear. His ability to appear at her elbow from anywhere in the house was disconcerting, and starting to become downright annoying. "Slept well?" His sunny smile never ceased to irritate her at this time of the morning. It wasn't even light out yet. The windows wept raindrops, indicating the sun wasn't likely to make an appearance anyway, but that wasn't the point.

She tried a smile in his direction, failed, and continued down the stairs. Billy followed behind, whistling cheerfully. Another reason, Eva decided as the happy trills grated along her nerve ends, to have her own place as soon as possible.

As Eva approached the kitchen, the aroma of freshly-brewed coffee filled her nostrils and made her stomach growl. The best of compensations, she observed as she filled a cup, was for someone to have it ready and waiting.

"Got time for breakfast this morning?" Agatha stood stirring porridge, apron tied over her dressing gown. Her two sons slumped into the kitchen,

153

book bags dragging and shirttails untucked. She busied herself getting the boys in order while Eva sipped her coffee and nibbled on a piece of cold toast.

"This is fine," she said around a mouthful. "You have enough to do." She watched her sister adeptly do two things at once and wondered if she'd ever have the opportunity to experience such loving chaos. "Oh by the way," she said as she started toward the hallway. "I'll be a bit late. I'm going to stop in and see about a new job I saw advertised."

The sudden silence from behind her made her turn back. Agatha stared at her and Billy stopped his reach halfway to the sugar bowl. At least the boys ignored her, concentrating on their cereal and continuing their shoving match under the table .

"Hold on there, lady," Agatha strode over to stand in front of her. "What position? What are you planning now?"

"I'll tell you all about it later," Eva tried to squeeze past her sister. "I don't want to be late."

Agatha grabbed her arm. "You have lots of time. You can take a minute."

Eva made another attempt to step past and met Agatha's glare. "My house, my rules." Agatha folded her arms and blocked the doorway, eyes dancing with mischief and curiosity. Eva turned to see Billy and the two boys staring at her. With a sigh, she gave in. "I saw an ad in the paper for a housekeeper and cook at a small hotel downtown. It'd be nice to be able to do what I enjoy, get a better paycheck. Maybe I'll even be able to find a place of my own soon."

Agatha studied her for a moment, trying to look stern, then she smiled. "Well, then. Good luck." She returned to the stove. "I'd like to be there when you tell Chang, though. That ought to be interesting."

"He'll get over it," Eva said. "Serve him right for not giving me the grill like I wanted." She grinned at her sister. "I haven't got the job yet, so let's not get ahead of ourselves, shall we?"

Billy stood up. "So—are we still on for tonight?"

Eva looked at him, embarrassed at the surprise that must be showing all over her face. Then she remembered. "Oh yes, the pictures. There'll still be time later, I'm sure." She shrugged. "Or I might have to cancel. Depends." His bereft expression changed her embarrassment to guilt. "I'm sorry."

"Never mind," Billy said, brightening. "We can always go tomorrow night. Or another time." He looked disappointed, Eva thought. They had talked about it last night after dinner, and he had been so excited about the new film that had just come out. She couldn't recall the name or the actor he'd gone on about, but at the time, she thought it would be good to get out of the house. If she had to spend many more nights in the tiny cubbyhole where she slept, she'd lose her mind.

"What did you say was showing, again?"

"The Westerner. Gary Cooper is the star. You'll love it, I'm sure."

"I'm sorry, Billy. Really I am." He had really looked forward to it, and from the look on his face she felt as if she'd betrayed him. "I'd really like to go. We'll figure something out, I promise."

He brightened at that, his good humour returning with his smile. "I'll hold you to that," he said. "See you later then."

"Right. See you later."

* * *

As Eva waited at the streetcar stop, a dark sedan pulled up at the curb. The door opened and a young man, dressed in the brown uniform of a soldier, got out and offered his hand to an elderly woman from the back seat. She wore a long fur coat, her silver hair styled in stern waves beneath an elegant hat complete with veil and feathers. The old woman pecked the soldier on both cheeks. He reached for the door handle and suddenly turned back, enclosed the woman in a hug, then hurriedly got in the car. She stood motionless as the car drove out of sight, then the woman straightened, hefted her cane and walked away, head up, a lone figure casting a dark statement in the early morning light.

Eva was moved. *That's how we all end up sooner or later,* she thought. *Walking alone, with no one but ourselves to see us through to the end.* As the early morning mist swallowed the woman from sight, Eva suddenly became aware of the subtle heartbeat of the city pulsing under her feet, the rhythmic swish of the car tires against damp pavement as they slowed and stopped, started again. In the distance, she heard the seagulls screaming and the rotting-salt smell of the sea reached her through the moisture swirling in the air. The city harboured its inhabitants in a box of tall bulwarks of buildings, floored with miles of cement and pavement. Bunched clouds stretched from apex to dome like spun cotton. People wove their lives from door to corner, spinning invisible threads, connecting, disconnecting; part of the city, in tune with the electric hum of progress and industry as she had now become. Eva tried to remember feeling as one with the vast emptiness of the prairie, the silent song of the distant stars, the sighing of the wind, but the images had become unclear and vague. She knew for certain that she could never go back. No matter where she settled, the city was part of her now, and she a thread within its tapestry.

The arriving streetcar brought her thoughts back to reality. Finding her seat, Eva realized how much she had been looking forward to the movie with Billy. The ad for a new job where she might have a better chance of getting ahead had completely blocked it from her mind. Now the initial excitement was interrupted by an unfamiliar feeling, one she had time to take out and examine while the streetcar made its way across town. She had enjoyed Billy's recent attentions, his good humour and gentle teasing. Even, if she was being honest with herself, his cheery disposition in the mornings. Suddenly she knew she didn't want to give that up and she promised herself she'd find some way to make it all work.

* * *

Eva thought her shift would never end. Without preamble, she donned her coat, tied her kerchief around her head and grabbed her purse. Outside, the air was fresh, a tinge of frost skipping through the moisture-laden air. As she started toward the streetcar stop, a parked car turned on its lights and started its engine. A horn blared. Looking over, Eva recognized the dents and rust marks that defined Billy's car.

"Hey, want a ride?" Billy yelled through the open window.

Feeling her face flush for no reason she could think of, she walked over to the car and got in. "I hope you remember I'm going for a job interview," she said.

"Where to, ma'am?" Billy was grinning at her. "I'm here to serve."

She shouldn't be testy, she told herself. He was just trying to help. "Sorry. I'm just surprised to see you, is all."

"I came straight from work. Thought if I gave you a ride, we might have time to get a bite and catch the movie after all."

Eva could smell burnt metal and sweat, the familiar odor of foundry workers that Billy and Henry came home with each night. In the half-light she could see that he'd washed his hands and face and made himself as presentable as he could. For all she knew, her clothing reeked of fried bacon and old coffee grounds, the thought making her stomach growl. She swallowed a giggle. *I hope it doesn't do that at the interview*, she thought. *On the other hand, maybe they'll think I'm starving to death and give me the job.*

She thanked Billy and gave him the name of the hotel. He put the car in gear and pulled away from the curb while she mentally reviewed her list of all the things she thought she might need to say.

As they approached the intersection, Eva glanced at the passenger-side mirror hanging at an odd angle. It showed a figure in a hat and overcoat, standing on the sidewalk beside the space they had just vacated, appearing to watch them drive away. As they turned the corner, Eva shook her head at her assumption. *Probably just someone waiting to cross the street*, she chided herself. *You're getting paranoid, girl.*

She glanced over at Billy. If he had seen anyone, he made no comment. She dismissed it from her mind and returned to her mental preparations.

* * *

By car the hotel was only a few minutes from the café, but Eva was grateful for the direct route, rather than the round-about system of the streetcar or the time spent walking. A fine drizzle coated the landscape with a layer of moisture, trading the cool tease of winter for the ordinary coastal humidity. She shivered, glad she would arrive warm and dry.

"I'll likely be a while," Eva said.

"I'll wait. Take your time. I'll just sit here and work up an appetite, then we can either celebrate or drown our sorrows in a nice, thick steak from our favorite greasy-spoon."

"Deal."

The hotel sat in the middle of the block, its painted wooden sign the only indication that it wasn't one of the other retail stores on either side. The cozy lobby had plain wood panelling, a thick carpet, and a feeling of welcoming calm. It smelled of oiled wood and fresh pine wreaths. Garlands wound with red velvet ribbons and hung with silver globes were suspended in loops along the front desk. Through a door to her right, she glimpsed tables set with white linen, and tall chairs with upholstered seats.

Mrs. Baumgarten, the owner, greeted her with a smile so big it almost hid her eyes in the folds of her cheeks. "Call me Mrs. B," she said, and indicated that Eva follow her into the office behind the front desk. Mrs. B heaved her considerable bulk into a chair behind a desk strewn with boxes and papers and indicated that Eva should take a seat across from her. Her penetrating gaze made Eva feel as if she could probe the inside her head to expose her every thought.

"So tell me about yourself." The large woman folded her hands over her girth, tucked her chin into the multiple creases of her neck and looked as if she was prepared to listen to a Sunday sermon. When Eva finished speaking, Mrs. Baumgarten didn't move. Eva couldn't tell if her potential employer was impressed or uninterested. The vague thought crossed her mind that the woman had fallen asleep with her eyes open. Finally, Mrs. B shifted in her seat and blew out a breath in a snort.

"Ya'll be expected to live on the premises," the woman said in a voice softened with a southern drawl. "Be in charge of seeing that the rooms are in order, the laundry is up to par, and the chambermaid, when I can hold on to one for more than a couple of days, are properly doin' the job. In between times, you will take charge of the kitchen." She narrowed her eyes, as if trying to read the reaction to the duties she had listed. "Now, I got a cook that comes on in the afternoons, does the prep work and then puts up the dinner menu, so you don't have to worry yourself about that. Yours is just the breakfast and lunch, which is pretty light. But the ordering and stock for that'll be up to you." She lifted a chubby finger adorned by an onyx ring and pointed it at Eva. "It ain't as scary as it sounds. This here's a small hotel, and we don't get a big rush of travellers. We bin here for enough years so's we have our regular clients, travelling salesmen and the like, a few new out-of-towners, and they don't make much fuss. So things should go along pretty smooth if you get a handle on it. Do a good job, an' along with room an' board, I figure the job is worth in the neighborhood of eight dollars a week to start you off."

She sat back and folded her hands. Faint sounds of traffic filtered in from outside the window.

"Well." Eva said, not knowing exactly what she was supposed to say, but guessing from the long silence that it was her turn. She hadn't expected the job to include quite so much, but she was determined to take it on and do her best. She'd hoped she would be making a bit more salary, but knew once she got started, she'd make herself worth a lot more to them. "I think I'd be able to handle it."

Mrs. B nodded. "Good. You look a little young for the job, but you didn't blink when I told you what you were up against, so you might do just fine. So here's what I'd like to happen. Come on down here and cook us up a breakfast. It'd have to be on your day off, I reckon, but I'll pay you for it. The cook I had up and quit, so's I've been doing it my own self. If that comes along good, the job is yours." Her face creased up in a grin. "Ya'll get around without burnin' anything, we may have ourselfs a deal."

"I'll have to give my notice. When did you want me to start?"

"You do what you have to do. I wouldn't worry about Chang too much. That old fool's been stealing my dinner customers for years. Time I had a turn, taking somethin' of his. Anyways, plenty of his gals has up and quit on him. He doesn't seem to worry none about it." The older woman struggled to her feet and gently guided Eva to the door. "The sooner the better around here, of course. Five'll get you ten he'll fire you on the spot when he finds out, anyways. Just let me know right away. I'm pretty done with making breakfasts 'n' I got better things to do than try'n run the whole shebang around here."

"I'll come in this Monday, if that's all right," Eva said.

"That'll do fine."

Stepping outside into the dark, rainy street, Eva was glad to see Billy's car at the curb.

"So," he said as she got in. "How'd it go?"

Eva closed the door and slumped against the seat. "Oh my. I don't know what I've put myself into this time. I think I may have bit off more than I can chew."

"So that means you got the job?"

"I think so. I'll know for sure in a couple of days. There'll be a few loose ends to tie up."

Billy put the car in gear and turned into the traffic. The windshield wipers kept up a quiet rhythm as they drove.

As they waited at a traffic light, Billy turned to her and took her hand. "I'm sure going to miss you in the mornings."

Eva laughed. "I'll bet. You'll probably appreciate the peace and quiet. I'm not exactly your 'Little Miss Sunbeam" at 6 a.m."

Billy grinned. "I'm cheerful enough for both of us. I'd like to think I passed a little bit of that along."

Eva lightly squeezed his hand. "Thanks for doing this, Billy. For taking me to the hotel, that is."

"Gotta get in all the time with you I can before you're gone."

She felt his reluctance to let her go in the way he slid his hand from hers as he parked in front of a restaurant two blocks from the theatre.

24

Eva hurried up the front steps of her sister's house; she hadn't had time to visit in the last couple of weeks. She and Billy had been doing a lot of things together since the night of the movie. It was hard not to smile when she recalled how they couldn't seem to stop talking all through the meal at the restaurant, and all the way home. She couldn't remember when she'd had a more relaxing evening. No reason not to, she told herself—they were, after all, good friends. She was almost humming as she entered the front hall.

"You made it." Billy hung his scarf on a hook on the mirrored storage bench beside the door. "I hoped you would before the fog gets any thicker out there."

Eva took her gloves off and put them in her pocket. "It's pretty bad. Won't be able to see your hand in front of your face, soon."

"True. The colder it gets, the more everyone stokes up their stoves and furnaces. Keeps the wood and coal suppliers in business, though." He took her coat and hung it on a hook beside his own. "I just made it back from an errand for Agatha. Good thing I didn't have too go far."

It had a homey feel to see their coats hanging side by side after a long day, and finding Billy at the door when she came in added to her good humour. For just a moment, standing beside him felt like something she would like to do a lot. She gave herself a mental shake. She couldn't let herself trust too much. That's a place she didn't want to find herself in again, leaving herself open to disappointment and heartbreak. But still, it was rather pleasant.

She had thought a bit, now and then, about settling down with someone. Some day. But with Billy? She studied his profile as he hung her scarf on the last vacant hook.

Billy reached into his pocket for a hanky and began to polish his glasses, looked up to see her studying him and winked. Eva pretended not to notice and concentrated instead on a sudden fluttering in her solar plexus. She felt as if she had been caught with her hand in the cookie jar. She took a deep breath and tried to relax, amazed at herself that she wasn't sure what to do next.

"Mmmmm…. Smells good in here." With relief, Eva seized upon the subject of dinner waiting in the next room. She inhaled the hearty aroma of roast beef with overtones of apples and cinnamon. "I'm looking forward to some good old home cooking." They should move on into the dining room where she could hear her family making preparations, but for some reason, she didn't want to end the moment. Billy's gaze held hers, and for a moment the world went away.

"I thought I heard voices." Eva peered out from behind Billy to see Uri standing in the doorway.

"About time," her brother-in-law said. He nodded briefly at Billy, then turned to Eva with a smile. "I'm starving. Agatha said if the two of you weren't here in the next ten minutes, we were going to go ahead without you." He exchanged his smile for a long-suffering expression. "I'm sure I wouldn't have lasted another minute."

Eva noted the almost-empty glass he held and his glassy-eyed gaze as he approached them. "Well, at least you've been making good use of the time while you waited." She linked her arms between the two men. "Let's not keep the gang waiting."

Henry was standing at the head of the table, carving knife and fork poised as Agatha brought in the roast.

"Sorry I'm late," Eva said as they took their seats. "I'd guess the boys have already eaten. You all shouldn't have waited for me."

"Oh lordy." Agatha affected a mock frown. "She's beginning to talk like her Yankee employer already."

"I can't wait to hear about your new job," said Dani as she placed a large gravy boat on the table, full to overflowing.

Eva groaned inwardly, hoping the gravy wasn't as lumpy as usual. "It's been interesting, that's for sure. I got to meet Mrs. B's husband the third day."

"That would be Mr. B, I guess" said Agatha.

"Not to Mrs. B," Eva said. "She refers to him as 'the husband'. I don't know his first name, even. He's a wraith of a man, and I mean that kindly. He comes up to his wife's shoulder in height, skinny as a barn cat with a beaky nose and sad, droopy eyes. He appears and disappears so that you're given to wonder if he's real at all. One minute he'll be at the foot of the stairs, the next you'll find him at your elbow."

"Sounds pretty creepy, if you ask me," said Dani.

"Oh, he's nice enough. Just that he's very quiet. But if you need something done he'll see to it right away. I think that old building is attuned to him and runs on his own personal energy. Now that's creepy."

"So how do you like working there, generally?" asked Henry.

Eva speared a carrot with her fork and gave it a thoughtful inspection. "I like that I have charge of the kitchen, for sure. It feels good to plan meals even if it's only breakfast and lunch. The other cook comes in early and does his own prep. He was a bit snooty at first, but he's come around. I don't leave him a mess to clean up and he does the same for me. We get along."

Over the clatter of knives and forks, Eva told them about life in a small hotel. She had a few anecdotes about the chambermaids and laundress, but they were mostly curious about the indomitable Mrs. B who ruled the staff and her spouse with a fair but iron hand.

"…and she doesn't mind pitching in where needed," Eva continued. "If one of the chambermaids doesn't show up, she fills in. When the mangle iron in the laundry got jammed, she was right there to get it fixed. Heaven forbid the sheets aren't done properly."

"As long as she isn't hard to work for," said Dani.

"Not at all." Eva said. "She seems to be tireless. One of the waitresses has a small room behind the kitchen, where she stays with her little girl. It's no more than a closet, really. When the child was feverish, Mrs. B made her take care of her and served the customers herself. Her husband helped as well, of course. It's certainly been interesting so far."

"That's a lot going on in just the two weeks you were there," said Henry. "Sounds to me like you don't have a minute to be bored."

"It's been an experience that's for sure."

"What about Chang?" said Agatha. "I never did hear about what happened when you told him you were leaving."

"I'm not sure exactly how he took it. Hard to tell, with him. I told him when I picked up my pay. He didn't say much. He just shrugged and told me not to come back. I have an idea he was waiting for me to leave—I don't think he trusted me after I didn't show up that first day."

The conversation turned to the latest news about the war, and when the last of the gravy, for once entirely lump-free, was soaked up with home-made dinner rolls, Agatha went to the kitchen to get dessert. Eva came behind her with a load of dirty plates and Agatha beckoned her to one side. "Glad you could make it today," Agatha said. "I want to talk to you." When Eva raised her eyebrows, Agatha continued, "It's about Dani and Uri. I think something's going on. Neither of them is saying much, but I can just feel it. Something's not right."

"Are you sure you're not imagining things?" Eva balanced four of the pie plates on her hands and arms. "There was a time when I thought something was wrong, remember? You were sure there wasn't. Then you came to me with that tale Dani told you about the abuse. But honestly, I didn't see anything like that the whole time I stayed with them. It's hard to believe anything else but that they're a normal couple with normal problems."

"I know my sister. And I'm getting to know her husband a little better, too. I can't say I'm much impressed with what I'm looking at, there."

"I wondered what was going on with you. You kept giving him strange looks all during dinner."

"I'm just keeping an eye on him." Agatha swept up the last of the pie-laden plates and a platter of cheese slices and started towards the door. "Mark my words. I know strange when I see it. And I smell trouble."

"He has been drinking a bit too much lately, come to that," said Eva. "More than he usually does. That alone is bound to make a person do some strange things. Nothing I noticed that was harmful to Dani, though. Maybe he just bit off more than he can chew with the deal on the house and now he's having trouble with it."

"Well, that's too bad if that's the case, because it's affecting Dani. She won't say a thing about it though, but anything that I can do to make it easier on her—I swear he works her to death, and he's probably taking his frustrations out on her, too. I'm going to get to the bottom of it. And I need your help." Arms full, Agatha backed her way out of the room. Eva puffed out a breath, exasperated. While she was delighted that Agatha was finally starting to take her role as big sister seriously, Eva hoped she wouldn't make matters worse by interfering where she shouldn't.

At the table, Uri was pouring the last of the wine, and Eva noticed his glass was the fullest. As she passed out the plates of pie, she gave Dani's shoulder a comforting squeeze. She'd always wanted the best for her little sister, and hoped she would have the kind of life she deserved. Dani tensed beneath her hand, and flinched away. She didn't look up.

Eva moved back to her seat, thoughtful. If something was wrong, they'd get to the bottom of it soon. As the talk turned to general matters and coffee cups refilled, Eva started to form a plan.

Head full of ideas, Eva didn't notice Billy standing beside the kitchen door as she went back to finish clearing the table.

"Sorry," she said, before looking to see who she had bumped into. She put up her hand and backed away. Billy took her hand and held it. "You can bump into me any time," he said.

Flustered, Eva didn't know what to say. Billy's calloused hand was warm and he smiled down at her, not moving. He smelled of spicy after-shave and whiskey. She wondered again how strange it felt to look up into his eyes. Not many men she knew were taller than she was. It felt right, somehow, to stand close to him and the warning bells faded away.

"When's your next day off?" Billy asked, breaking the spell. "There's a new 'western' showing at our theatre. Interested?"

Eva nodded. Why standing close to Billy made her feel like smiling, she didn't know, but she enjoyed the way it made her insides seem to glow. "I'm trying to get Sundays off. But with the holidays coming, there's a lot to do. I can let you know as soon as I can."

Billy returned her smile, eyes twinkling behind his glasses. "Just say when."

* * *

Eva finally got Dani alone on her first day off after the family dinner. With Christmas looming, dinners needing to be planned and shopping had to be done. Agatha had one of the boys home sick with a fever, so the two sisters went ahead with their anticipated all-girls day without her.

Dani balanced the tray on the table and Eva removed the soup bowls and coffee cups, and gave them each a utensil set she had brought from the counter. The clank and clatter of trays and dishes wove through the conversations of the crowded cafeteria. Through the window they could see the department store where they had spent the morning.

"This is one of my favourite places," said Dani. "Every time I shop at Woodwards I try to stop in here."

"Good choice," Eva said, blowing on a spoonful of hot creamy liquid. "After spending all our hard-earned money, we're lucky to have enough left for a bowl of soup." The colourful illustration of clam chowder on the wall boasted of lots of vegetables and fresh clams, but the reality failed miserably, in her opinion, to live up to expectations. She reached for the salt.

"Do you know why it's called White Lunch Cafeteria?" asked Dani.

Eva nodded. "All I ever heard about this place was that there was a labour dispute a couple of years ago. The employees shut it down for about six months. Something about working conditions and wages."

"Well, I heard that they only hired white folk, and they wanted to cater to white people only. That was what the strike was about, I think."

"Really?" Eva looked around to make sure no one was listening. "Are you sure?"

Dani shrugged. "That's what I heard. I'm not positive. Makes a good story though, don't you think?"

"I'm beginning to think nothing could surprise me." Eva gave up on the soup and reached for her coffee cup. "You in any hurry to go home? There's a movie just out that I'd love to see. The theatre up the street has a matinee. It would be a lovely way to spend the afternoon. What do you say?"

"I don't know." Dani said, putting her empty bowl aside. "I should get home. And besides, you said you didn't have any money left."

"Well...." Eva tried to look contrite. "I always tried to save enough for a movie."

Dani gave her sister a knowing grin. "You've become quite a fan of the silver screen, haven't you?"

"That's all Billy's fault. He started it. I absolutely love the stories. I can sit in a theatre for hours. He likes Westerns, though—I'm not sure he'd appreciate a soppy drama." Eva leaned forward. "C'mon, sis. Let's take a break from all this Christmas shopping. You'll get home in time to make dinner—we won't even have to tell anyone."

Dani was almost persuaded, Eva could tell. The more time she spent with her sister, the more chance she had to find out what, if anything, was going on.

"We'd have to drag all these packages along with us."

"Oh, come on." Eva waved the objection away with the toss of her hand. "Be a sport. We don't often get the day to ourselves. Let's make the most of it."

· It hadn't taken much more persuasion, and when the movie was over, Dani was full of the romantic fantasy. The dashing leading man put stars in her eyes, and the plight of the tragic heroine moved her to tears. She was still reliving the experience as they walked up the steps to her house. There hadn't been an opportunity for Eva to ask her sister about Agatha's concerns without spoiling the easy mood they were enjoying together. Agatha had asked Eva to be tactful. Confronting Dani hadn't worked before and she'd just made more excuses, then refused to talk any more about it. Eva had tried to find opportunities to ask questions, but Dani seemed so relaxed and happy, perhaps it was best not to spoil the day. So when Dani had asked Eva to accompany her home and help with the gift wrapping, she had agreed. Perhaps she would be more forthcoming in the privacy of her own home.

Dani was about to put the key in the lock, then paused. "I'm sure I didn't put the light on before I left."

"It may have been a good idea if you did," Eva said. "It gets dark so early now."

Dani continued to hesitate. "What if there's a burglar inside?"

"A burglar?" Eva gave her a nudge. "Look at this place. Do you think this is where a burglar would think to come and get a big haul?"

Dani blew out a held breath. "I guess not. I probably did leave the light on. Thinking ahead, and all that." She grinned. "Imagine me."

In the hallway, they put their bags in a jumble on the floor and hung up their coats, giggling about Dani's fears.

A sudden snarling voice froze them to the spot. "Where the bloody hell have you been?

25

Agatha sipped her hot tea, feeling the liquid soothe her sore throat. She was grateful for the dimness of the dining room, making her red nose and watery eyes less obvious to the casual observer. Through the window she could see flakes of snow among the raindrops , confirming her decision to wear her heavy woolen coat and hat. Heavy woolen stockings and fur-lined boots kept her feet warm, and she glanced fondly at the gloves she had knitted herself lying beside her purse.

Reaching for her hankie, she sneezed as discretely as she could, not for the first time wishing her boys would stop sharing their germs with her. Henry seemed to be immune. *Probably,* she thought a bit resentfully, *because of the iron dust he breathes at the foundry all day.*

She looked at her wristwatch again, frowning, then looked up with relief to see Eva finally slip through the side door and hurry to the table.

"Sorry," Eva said. "One of the chambermaids needed a bit of help. She's not too bright, but a good worker for all that, and I'm sure once she sees the way of it, she'll be fine."

"Ever the mother hen," Agatha said, trying to speak plainly through plugged sinuses. "So tell me—what was so urgent you had to see me right away?"

"It's about Dani and Uri." Eva chose a seat on the far side of the table, hefted the teapot, then beckoned to the waitress, indicating she should bring another cup. "The other night when we came home from our shopping day, Uri was already home. He was unbelievably angry, raving mad because Dani wasn't there, waiting for him when he got home." She shook her head, remembering the fury in the eyes of a man she once considered a friend, and how she had tried to understand why he was so upset and offended. "Honestly, you'd have thought she'd gone away for a week. At first I thought he was concerned. You know, maybe thought that something had happened to her, but it soon became obvious that wasn't the case. I could hardly believe my ears. Imagine being furious because she took some time to go shopping and take in a movie."

"I remember our father doing something the same," said Agatha. "Almost as if he was looking for an excuse to berate and intimidate mother."

Eva thanked the waitress and reached for the teapot. "And if I remember correctly, Uri's father had a similar attitude. Always wanting to be in control—no one could make a move without his consent."

"Well, at least Uri comes by it honestly."

"Agatha! This is serious."

"You want serious," Agatha blew her nose into her hanky and wiped her eyes. "I'll give you serious. In fact I was going to try and meet with you before I came down with this stupid cold." She leaned forward and lowered her voice, although the nearest occupied table was on the other side of the room. "Dani is afraid to leave the house. It seems Uri comes home at all hours and checks up on her. And to add to that she has a bunch of new bruises."

"I didn't see any bruises when we were out shopping the other day."

"Well if you think back to what she was wearing, she likely dressed so nothing showed. And did you happen to notice that she wears more makeup lately? I saw plenty when I dropped in unannounced the other day and found her with a paintbrush in hand. Her short-sleeved dress gave me all the evidence I needed. Her upper arms were black and blue. She tried to give me some lame excuse, but I know better."

"I don't see how Uri can come and go like that," Eva said. "Doesn't he have to be at work?"

"When he's out making deliveries, I guess he can slip away any time he wants." Agatha rummaged in her handbag for a fresh hanky. "I tell you, it's just not right. I'd like to see if we can talk her into packing up and leaving him. If he's abusing her, we have to find a way to protect her. She's terrified of him."

"We can't do anything if she doesn't want to leave."

"Well, we'll just have to make her see that she shouldn't have to put up with such nonsense. If he's going to treat her like a slave…well, she just doesn't deserve that. She needs to understand that's no way to live."

"No argument there. But what should we do?"

Eva rubbed her forehead, as if to make her brain produce a solution. "For one thing, Uri could use a good talking-to. Maybe if he knows we're on to him, he'll smarten himself up."

Agatha grimaced, sneezed into her hanky and wiped her eyes. "If I thought for a moment that would do any good, I'd be right over there before you could say 'skedaddle'. But I'm afraid it's going to take more than a scolding to make him behave like a human being. If he was a proper husband, this wouldn't be happening in the first place. Not to mention that this has been going on for a long time."

With a thoughtful frown, Eva stared into her teacup. "We have to do something to help her. We've talked about it long enough. We'll make her realize that she should go away from him for a while. Maybe—maybe then he'll see that we're not going to let him get away with the way he's treating her." She chewed on her lip. Her sister's predicament hung from her heart like a weight. She had always felt responsible for her younger sisters. She wasn't there when Tina needed her, and now her youngest sister was gone, but she'd do everything she could to protect Dani, and even Agatha if she had to. She'd have to find a way.

"My next day off I'll go and talk to her," Eva said. "Christmas will soon be here. I don't want to start anything that will spoil the holidays, but maybe I can give her something to think about. How about I go over there, first thing in the morning after he leaves, and see what I can do. I'll try and persuade Dani to come away. If he's there, I'll talk to the two of them—actually, it'll be hard not to take a strip off his hide."

"What if he turns on you?" Agatha asked. "You used to be friends at one time, but it seems to me that the situation has changed radically. If he gets violent with you..."

"I can't see that he would." Eva heard a slight flicker of doubt echoing in her own words. "Anything's possible, I guess. But if he does, I'll see to it that he'll regret it, that's for sure."

"Well let's hope it won't come to that. And I think she'd be more likely to listen to you than me, but I could come with you."

Eva smiled at her sister with sympathy. "If you're feeling better, why not. But if you're not, you may be more of a hindrance. Let's just see what happens."

"Let me know what I can do," Agatha sniffed.

Eva patted her sister's hand and poured her more tea. "You just get yourself better. You have to be well enough to host Christmas dinner; we can't have you mashing your germs into the potatoes."

* * *

Billy splashed on some Old Spice after-shave lotion, humming the catchy advertising tune he'd heard on the radio. The balm had been on the market a couple of years, but he'd only just heard of it. A lot of the fellows at the foundry were using it, and if it worked as well as they said, it just might let him get a little closer to Eva. Grabbing his jacket, he hurried downstairs. It was her day off, and he'd made plans. One more day until Christmas Eve and family activities will be in full swing, no time to get her alone so he could talk to her. For a few hours today he'd have her all to himself.

In the hallway, he shrugged into his overcoat and reached for his hat, going over in his mind all the things he wanted to say. This time for sure, he was going to tell her how he felt. No holding back, he firmly told himself. Squaring his shoulders, he reached for the doorknob just as he heard a knock and opened the front door to find Detective Carlson, shoulders hunched against the icy drizzle.

"Afternoon," he said. "Is Agatha at home?"

Billy stepped back, inviting him in. "In the kitchen. I'll call her."

"Don't trouble yourself," the detective said. "I'll just go on in. I assume Henry's at work?"

"He's on the early shift. Should be home any time now."

Carlson looked Billy over, face expressionless. Billy felt an uncomfortable twinge, as if the man was reaching into his mind. He didn't understand how the detective did it, but he could make people feel as if they'd been up to something. And if they hadn't, he would know if they were going to be. He had a moment's pity for those on the wrong side of the law. "It's my day off. I was just about to go out."

Shrugging out of his raincoat, Detective Carlson spared Billy a cursory glance, hung up his coat and hat. Billy noted the bags under his eyes, the tired slump to his shoulders and the wrinkled suit. It appeared to him that being a detective was an occupation he wouldn't want in a million years. He'd rather be hauling logs or bending iron, at least he could walk away without carrying his job on his shoulders.

Carlson made his way toward the kitchen. Staring at his back, Billy wondered what the visit was all about. Then he remembered that Henry and Carlson were old friends, and this was probably just a social call. Then why did he feel it was something more?

He put those thoughts aside as he left the house, jangling his car keys. He had other, more enticing things to occupy his mind.

The lobby of the hotel was gloomy and empty, no one attending the desk or occupying the bulky, sagging chairs. A damp odour permeated the room, mixed with the scent of furniture polish.

Billy walked into the dining room. The melodic murmured conversations of a few guests sounded counterpoint to the staccato handfuls of freezing rain the wind scattered across the front windows. He decided he might as well wait at a table; perhaps have a cup of coffee. Eva had promised to be on time, but he knew how last minute duties or circumstances might prevent that from happening. He sat down, and when it looked like it might be a while before someone showed up to take his order, he began to fidget.

Finally, he gave up. He was too tense with anticipation to sit with nothing to do. He got up and retraced his steps to the lobby. Maybe he could find someone who knew what was keeping Eva.

The proprietor, Mrs. B, now stood behind the reception counter, her bulk taking up considerable space. Billy took a seat, preparing to wait in comfort. Unable to settle, he looked around for a magazine, crossed and uncrossed his legs, cleared his throat. Finally, Mrs. B appeared to notice there was someone else in the room and looked over at him.

"Can I help you?" she asked.

He stood up and walked over to the counter. "I'm waiting for Eva. I'm Billy. She said to meet her here."

Mrs. B's face dissolved into a series of rolls and wrinkles as she smiled. "Well, now young man, I've got a message here from Eva. She says to tell y'all she had to go over to her sister's place. Something that couldn't wait, apparently, so she left a little early." Mrs. B squinted at the note, holding it up to the scant desk light on the counter. "Sez here to meet her at her sister's place if y'all want, or just sit tight and she'll be along as soon as she can."

She put the note down and leaned on the counter and Billy imagined he could hear the wood creak in protest. "Now, I reckon she took herself off to the streetcar to get there, so if I was y'all, and I had a car an' all that, I'd take myself down to where she went and pick her up from there when she's done."

Billy grinned, pleased to be in action at last. "Well then, that's just what I'll do." He started toward the door but turned back. "By the way, did she tell you which sister she went to see?"

"Well now, she didn't mention that, come to think of it." She turned her head at a small man who had just slipped in from a side door. "Say, you hear tell the name of the sister Eva went to see?"

The man shook his head, glanced at Billy from under bushy eyebrows. Taking a ledger from a drawer behind the counter, he scurried back through the door, closing it softly behind him.

"I expect she figured you'd know which one." A chuckle rippled through her, and Billy was almost sure he could feel a slight tremor.

"I've got a pretty good idea. Thanks a lot."

On the way to the car he made his decision. Detective Carlson didn't make social calls, now that he thought about it. If what he had to say had anything to do with Eva's previous employer, or her husband, she would probably want to be there. As he made his way through the traffic, he wondered why she hadn't called to tell him of the change in plans. *She likely didn't think of it or maybe she did and thought I'd probably already left*, he mused. *I really don't know how we managed without telephones back on the homesteads. Things would have been so much easier.*

He was halfway back before he realized he could have called to see if she'd already arrived.

26

Eva hurried up the sidewalk and pushed open the sagging gate to Dani's house. Her mind was made up.

She'd spent a sleepless night, tossing and turning as her concerns for Dani grew larger and more urgent. It seemed every time Eva and Agatha got together, all her sister could think about was the times Dani had looked pale and withdrawn, had worn clothing inappropriate to the weather and circumstances, and how their little sister was being treated. It made their visits full of worry and stress rather than the carefree times they used to have. Maybe Dani needed her help. Maybe she didn't. Maybe Eva just needed to take herself to Dani's house, talk to her and find out what was going on once and for all. As the moon rose though a break in the clouds, she made up her mind. She was going to get this cleared up before Christmas, so they could have a proper family gathering without the black pall that had hung over them these last few months.

Finally, just before the dawn birds stirred to sing their morning paeans, she had dozed into a fitful sleep. When her alarm rang, she dragged herself from her bed, determination seeing her through her duties at the hotel. When she asked if she could leave a bit early, Mrs. B. must have seen from the set of her chin that she wasn't to be argued with. Her employer simply nodded, took the note to Billy that Eva handed her, and slipped it somewhere into the voluminous folds of her smock.

Eva was halfway down the block to the streetcar stop before she remembered that she could have telephoned Billy, telling him where to meet her. They had made plans for the afternoon and evening, but until she had seen this through, she could think of nothing else but her sister. Now, as she knocked on the door, she squared her shoulders and firmly decided that she wasn't going to leave without clearing the air. Then she could phone Billy and they could have a nice, quiet evening. A nice, normal evening.

Waiting for her knock to be answered, she went over in her mind what she would say. Dani seemed fragile at times; she would withdraw and no amount of questioning or cajoling produced a response. It was as if she slipped into another place where what was being said didn't apply to her. Eva would have to phrase her words carefully so Dani wouldn't get defensive and shut her out. Once Eva was satisfied there actually was a problem, they could all deal with it.

When the door opened, she stopped short in surprise, and her heart jumped as she thought she might have knocked on the wrong door in her distraction. A small, blonde woman stood smiling, severely plucked, painted eyebrows raised in question.

"Um…" Eva looked around. *Yes, this was the right house.* "Is Dani at home?"

"Of course she is." The woman smiled, crinkles appearing around her eyes that added a few more years to her appearance. "You just come on right in. I was just getting my coat when you knocked." As if to demonstrate, she reached for a bright blue coat crowned with an enormous fur collar. "Dani and I used to be neighbours, you know. We visited quite a lot, and I sure do miss having her right across the street. Now when I have some news to share with her, by the time I get here, I'm about ready to burst."

Eva remembered Dani telling her about some of the times she had with her neighbour. She caught a whiff of alcohol on the woman's breath as she spoke, and noticed her eyes were a little bit red and puffy. She wondered if the news had been sad. It didn't matter anyway; it was nice to know that Dani had a friend.

"I hope I'm not interrupting anything," Eva said.

"Not at all. I'm glad to finally meet one of Dani's sisters. Which one are you?"

Wondering how she knew she was Dani's sister rather than a nosy neighbour, Eva said, "I'm the oldest. Eva. And you are?"

"I'm Vi. Dani may have mentioned me."

"I think she may have. Nice to meet you."

Before Vi could respond, Dani came into the hallway, wiping her hands on a tea towel. "Eva. What a nice surprise. I thought you and Billy were going somewhere today."

"We are." Eva hung up her coat and made room for Vi to finish putting on her hat and gloves. "Later. I thought I'd drop in and see you first."

"I was just about to start dinner. I know it's early yet, but I like to be prepared." Dani looked past her sister to her friend. "Vi, you don't have to go yet, do you? We could all have another cup of tea."

"Tea. Of course." Vi paused, looking from one to another. She opened her mouth, closed it, considering, while Eva and Dani waited for her to make up her mind. "I think I'd better go along," Vi said at last. "By the time I wait for the streetcar…." She reached into her pocket for a hanky with which to cover her nose and mouth, flapping her other hand in dismissal. "Thanks, but perhaps another time." Sniffling loudly, she opened the door. "You take care of your own self, now." And she was gone.

The two sisters stared at the closed door for a moment, then Dani shrugged. Eva turned to her sister. "Is that the woman you told us about who discovered a body and had to go down to the police station?"

Dani nodded. "She's been going through a lot lately. First that, then she had a bit of a to-do with the man she's been seeing. Seems he's determined to be a part of the war effort, and is going to try to enlist in communications or something." She turned to the kitchen, waving Eva to follow. "He packed up and left yesterday, and she's been in quite a state. I think she was rather fond of him."

"Didn't you mention she was a recent widow?" Eva asked. At Dani's nod, she continued. "Maybe she's just lonely."

Dani waved a dismissive hand. "I don't know. Maybe. Personally, I'm not interested in her doings." A smile turned up the corners of her mouth. "She is rather entertaining, I'll give her that."

Eva grinned. "I'll bet. I well remember some of the things you've told us about her. It would be nice to have a friend like that, though, who would come all the way over to visit. Even if it's just to tell you her troubles." She sat down at the table, peering closely at her sister to see her reaction. They'd been having a bit of a nip, she'd wager. Dani's eyes were sparkling, but she was otherwise just herself. Perhaps they'd had a couple, no more. "Better than being alone all the time," Eva continued.

"Oh, I'm not alone so much," Dani examined her hands, rubbing the knuckle of her thumb as if it had become a priority.

"Really?"

"Well. You know. Uri's job. He's in and out. It's always such a nice surprise to see him in the middle of the day. He doesn't do it very often, really."

"I guess so, if that's what you like." Eva shuddered at the thought that someone would always be popping in to see what she was doing. "As long as he doesn't get underfoot and start telling you what you should be doing, I suppose it's a good thing. But I meant—you know, a woman to talk to. Someone to confide in, share a secret or two."

"Oh, I don't worry about that," Dani said, still refusing to meet Eva's eyes. "I have as much company as I need."

"What do you mean?"

Dani shrugged and bit her lip as if she had said something she hadn't meant to, but she didn't raise her head. Eva noticed her cheeks had become flushed.

"C'mon. You can tell me. We used to talk about everything, remember? Back when we only had each other?"

The tea-kettle began to whistle. Eva couldn't remember Dani putting it on, but she must have done so at the time Vi answered the door. Now Dani poured water into the pot and taking her cup, she disappeared into the pantry. She came out with an opened tin in one hand and her teacup in the other. She put both on the counter and began to pile muffins from the tin onto a plate. Eva held her breath, trying to be patient. Mindful of what she had planned, she relaxed against the back of the chair and waited.

Dani put the plate on the table and as she poured the tea, Eva reached for a muffin and broke it in half. Eva looked closely at her sister and made a decision. "You don't have a lover, do you?" Not if Uri was arriving unannounced, Eva reasoned. But the statement had the desired effect. Dani's head snapped up, eyes wide.

"What….whatever made you think that, for heaven's sake?"

Eva popped a piece of muffin in her mouth. *Not bad—she hadn't had time for lunch.* "Well, you're holding something back, I can tell. What else could possibly make you not care if you spend long days alone, painting and papering; redecorating…or so you say."

"Now, you're just being ridiculous."

"So you say."

They glared at each other across the table. "Well?" Eva prompted, all thoughts of tact and diplomacy forgotten.

Dani emptied her cup in one long draught and reached for the teapot. Eva narrowed her eyes with suspicion. Her own tea was too hot to drink. Her sister had obviously not had that problem, and she had an idea she knew why. It would explain her frequent visits to the pantry, but that could wait until later. For now, she stared at Dani. She had a strong feeling she was about to get the answers she wanted. "Well?" Eva said again, determined to do whatever it took to force Dani to confide in her.

Dani stared into her cup. "You probably wouldn't believe me," she said.

"Try me." Eva leaned over and put her hand over her sister's. "Come on. You know me. We grew up together, remember? We used to tell each other all kinds of things." She leaned back again, eyeing Dani carefully. "Unless it's something really weird or too horrible. And if it's either of those, you should tell me so I can help."

"I've been seeing…" Dani shook her head. "She's everywhere."

"Who?"

"Tina."

Eva kept her voice level and quiet. Dani had mentioned ghosts before, but hadn't been specific. "Our sister? Our Tina?"

Dani did another inspection of the hands in her lap. She nodded.

"And?" Eva prompted, her voice gentle, persuasive.

Dani raised her head and stared at her sister. Eva looked back, keeping her face expressionless as she sipped her tea. "She have anything to say?"

A flash of surprise crossed Dani's face. "You believe me?"

"Sure. I saw her a couple of times, shortly after her funeral. Remember the time I came back to your place after the service? You were making tea in the kitchen. I saw her then. I always thought she had come to say goodbye." Eva reached across the table and took Dani's hands. "I used to see a lot of things when we were at home. Since I came here, to the coast, I haven't, for some reason. Just occasional dreams, and half the time I don't even know what they mean."

Dani raised one hand to cover her mouth as she stared at Eva.

"Tell me about it," Eva said. "What does she do? Does she say anything? I used to think that sometimes when I saw things I heard voices, too. Whispers." She saw her sister's eyes widen. "Oh, I know. It sounds like I'm a candidate for the funny farm. But mother used to tell me that she saw things sometimes too. Probably runs in the family. So you see, you're just normal." She smiled. "Sort of."

Dani continued to stare. "Well?" Eva prompted.

When her sister didn't reply, Eva told herself to hold on to her temper or she wouldn't get anywhere. She tried another tactic. "You realize that's it's just her ghost you're seeing, don't you?"

Dani nodded. Finally after taking a deep breath she lowered her head, not meeting Eva's eyes. "She follows me around the room. Whispering. She says it's my fault she's dead. If I had taken better care of her, got the help she needed sooner. She says that I deserve to be punished, and that's why Uri is…the way he is, sometimes."

"And how is our dear Uri?"

Dani raised one shoulder as if to defend herself from a blow. "He can…" her voice was a whisper, the only sound beside the soft ticking of the clock. "He can be a bit…thoughtless."

"Does he push you around?"

Dani nodded, then ducked her head even lower, staring into her teacup. "Tina says I deserve it. She wouldn't be here if I had paid more attention to her, looked after her better…"

"She actually said that?"

" Not exactly. But I know that's what she means."

"But you can't say for sure, can you?" Eva fought to keep her voice low and calm. "Have you ever thought she's trying to tell you to get out of here before you end up wandering around whispering to people too?"

Dani raised her head. Her expression told Eva she hadn't even considered it.

"Look. You need to start thinking about yourself. If Uri is being abusive, he has to stop. You don't deserve to be treated like that. Husbands care for their wives, they don't control them, mistreat them." Eva knew all about that. There were different ways to go about it, but it was all the same in the end. She covered her sister's hand with her own. "You need to go away for a while. Just so he can see what it would be like without you. Maybe then he'll realize that it's time he started doing better by you." It was all Eva could do to suppress the fury that boiled up when she thought that the man she used to think of as a friend turned out to have such a dark side. She still found it hard to believe he had changed so much. To her he had always been kind and helpful.

When Dani didn't reply, just looked at her, eyes wide, Eva squeezed her hand. "Come with me, Dani. Just for a little while. I'll help you pack a bag.

We can go now, before Uri comes home. I'll leave him a note telling him where you are, and that we have to have a talk before you'll come back."

She could see Dani beginning to soften. "You have to do something," Eva pressed on. "Things can't continue this way without something happening, and that something could be serious if we don't put a stop to this. Please. Let's go pack a bag. Let's do something. Now."

A tear rolled down Dani's cheek. She rose from the table, nodded, the movement so slight, had Eva not been watching, she would have missed it.

Eva rose and went to her sister, putting her arms around her. "It'll be alright, I promise." She smoothed her hair the way she used to when they were children and Dani woke from a bad dream. "Let's go get packed," she said.

27

"I didn't know you still had my old suitcase," said Eva as she watched her sister close the lid. "Good thing you kept it."

Dani tried a smile, but Eva saw her chin tremble. "It's just about to fall apart. Lucky I don't have much to pack. Still, it's an awkward old thing."

"If you knew how much I paid for it—second hand, yet—you'd be more appreciative." Eva took the suitcase from the bed and walked out into the main room. "Better dress warmly, I think. Looks like it's going to get cold tonight, maybe even snow. Wouldn't it be something if we had snow for Christmas. I didn't realize how much I miss it this time of year."

"Ha. This isn't the prairies, you know. Snow over Christmas is almost impossible, and if we do get it, it turns to slush in no time. I'd rather have rain than have to slide around in that stuff. That's why we wear galoshes instead of snow boots."

"Well, Agatha will be happy to see us when we show up on her doorstep, that's for sure," Eva said, trying to distract Dani and encourage her to look ahead. "She can always use extra help making her big dinner on Christmas Eve. She already started a week ago. You wouldn't believe some of the dishes she's already prepared; I swear she gets more elaborate every year."

Eva handed Dani her coat and took hers from the peg beside the front door as a gust of wind blew cold air into the room. Uri stood in the opened back door. His puzzled look changed to a smile as he spotted Eva halfway into her coat.

"Hey, what a nice surprise," he said. "Haven't seen you for a while. You just get in?" His smile widened as he spotted the suitcase on the floor. "You moving in?" Closing the door with a foot, he threw his coat over a kitchen chair.

"We don't have a whole lot of room—but don't worry—we'll figure something out." He looked at Dani, then back at Eva with a puzzled expression. "You lose your job or something?"

For a second, Eva stood frozen, her sister motionless beside her. Then she put her coat on the rest of the way with a sigh. This was going to be a lot harder than she'd counted on. Once Uri starts in on Dani, he'd talk her in to staying. Maybe even force her to change her mind. "We were just leaving," she said.

"Leaving?" He walked over to the icebox, opened it and took out a bottle of beer. He watched them as he reached for an opener. "It's a little late in the day, isn't it?" Directing his gaze at Dani, he unerringly flung the bottle cap into the sink. "I come home from work, I expect my dinner on the table like usual. Or at least some indication that it's on the way." He took a drink. "So when was that going to happen?"

"Why not, just for tonight," Eva said, "you make your own dinner."

With a laugh, Uri flung himself on the couch. "That's what my wife is for."

"So you're telling me," Eva took a couple of steps toward him, her tone careful, reasonable, "that you married my sister so you could have someone to make your meals? That's not what it looked like to me at the wedding."

Uri's grin turned into a grimace. His eyes glittered with a cold light. "Some days that's pretty much all she's good for. Funny how quickly things can change, don't you think?"

Eva could feel fury spark along her nerve ends, but she kept her voice low, even. "You're joking, aren't you?"

Uris eyes flashed, daring her to challenge him, then he relaxed, dangled the bottle from his fingers, and returned her gaze. Eva's fury settled into a dark rage. "And what are you good for, may I ask? Pushing around someone half your size? Does that make you feel like a big, grown-up man?" That wasn't what she meant to say, at all. Damn, she wasn't prepared for this.

When Uri didn't reply, she pulled her kerchief from her coat pocket and refolded it. She'd put it on when they got outside. "Come on, Dani. We're leaving." She turned to Uri. "And we'll stay away until you start putting some common sense into that empty head."

Uri straightened, suddenly serious, glaring. "My wife isn't going anywhere."

Eva spun around. "Your wife—my sister—is coming with me where you can't get at her. We know what's been going on here. We know how you've been treating her. And it stops now."

"You don't know anything," Uri stood and put the beer bottle on the table. "You're so busy in your own little world you can't see anyone but yourself." He turned to Dani. "Get back here. Put your coat away and do what you're supposed to do. You're my wife and you'll do as I tell you. And right now you're going to stay right here and make my supper."

Having stood still all this time with her coat half on, Dani began to take it off. Eva put a hand on her arm. "Do you want to stay here, Dani? You know what will happen after I leave." She had to get Dani away while she still could. Frantically, she groped for something to say that would help her decide. They couldn't stay here much longer.

Dani looked from her sister to her husband, her dark eyes swimming in tears. Eva drew her arm all the way into her coat and pulled Dani back, glaring at her brother-in-law. She'd have to change her plans, talk to him. Just for a minute. This would be as good a time as any to have that conversation. She took a breath and tamped down her anger.

"What's happened, Uri?" she asked, voice low and even. "We're friends… used to be. You were never like this. Remember when you came to the farm, helped me when I was alone?"

"I helped you alright," Uri said. His eyes bored into hers, his knuckles white as he clutched the bottle. "I've always been there for you." His lips pulled back into a snarl. "You never noticed how I felt. You were married to my stupid brother, for all that he never appreciated you. He never cared for you, but I did. It should have been me. I should have been the one."

"You're not making any sense. What are you talking about?"

"I asked papa to give you to me, but he seemed to think he knew what was best for everybody. He thought that marriage would make a man of out of Aleksy, but he was never a man. The little prick doesn't even like women." He looked at Eva and smiled. His voice grew soft and sly. "You didn't even notice, did you?"

Stunned, Eva stared at Uri as he walked to the icebox, finishing his beer as he went. She could feel Dani holding onto her arm, heard her whimper. Absently, she patted her sister's hand, groping for something to say, but her mind was a maelstrom of confusion and disbelief. Uri brought out another beer and opened it. He walked over to the cupboard, leaned on it, crossing his ankles.

"We didn't talk about things like that, did we?" he continued. "Nobody did. But everybody knew." He shook his head. "You're pathetic, you know that? You couldn't even see what he was."

Still shaken, Eva tried to regain some footing. "What has that got to do with this? I don't understand how that gives you the right to treat people like dirt. If you didn't want Dani, why in the world did you marry her?"

"Doesn't matter. It's done and there's no changing things. But she's not going with you. You're not taking her away from me, too."

"And if she stays here, what are you going to do?"

"That's between her and me."

"Not any more, it's not," Eva said. She had to get away before it was too late, and Uri talked Dani out of leaving. She pulled her sister toward the door.

* * *

Billy parked behind Detective Carlson's car and hurried up the walk just in time to meet the detective coming out the door. Carlson nodded, pulled his coat collar up against the sudden, icy blasts of sleet-laden wind and got into his car. He drove away as Billy opened the door.

In the living room, Agatha put cups and the remnants of a plate of cookies onto a tray. She looked up, eyebrows raised, as Billy walked in.

"Eva here?" he said.

Agatha straightened, concern wrinkling her brow. "Why, no— I thought you were going to pick her up at work. What happened?"

Henry walked in from the kitchen, smelling of hot iron and fresh soap, the former so embedded into his pores that the latter had no defence against it. He greeted Billy with a heavy hand on his shoulder. "You lost, old son?"

"I got to the hotel," Billy explained, "only to find that Eva had left a note saying she was coming to see her sister and that it was urgent. So I thought, what with that detective come to call just as I was leaving, that it was something important so I came back here, straightaway." He looked from one to another. "So I take it she isn't—wasn't here?"

Henry took a swig from a bottle of beer. "Nope. Haven't seen her." He looked to his wife. "You?"

Agatha shook her head. "She likely went to Dani's. We've been talking about—um—we think there's a problem there, and we were trying to figure out how to help with it."

"Well, that's where she's gone then. I just picked the wrong sister."

Agatha made sure he saw her quirk an eyebrow. "No offense," he said. She smiled, satisfied that she had caused his cheeks to redden.

"She shoulda been here though," Henry said. "Carlson was asking more questions about that fellow they found. You know—the one they had down in the morgue. Guess they still haven't figured out who he really was so he went over everything again, hoping we'd remember something." He walked into the living room, sprawled on the couch. "He really questioned me about it—gave me the third degree. Did I see him, where was I the night of...Stupid questions like that. As of he hasn't known me for years." He inspected the bottle of beer, drew it up to his mouth then changed his mind. "Guess that goes out the window when there's a murder."

"What'd you tell him?" Billy asked.

"Told him I didn't have anything to do with it, o' course. Told him I'd of done a whole lot better job of it." He glowered at the beer bottle, than at Billy. "He corner you as well?"

"He already asked me a bunch of questions down at the station. You know, the time Eva and I went down and she identified the body. Guess he figured out I was pretty harmless."

"Yeah, right," Henry snorted, his good humour returning.

"He wanted to know did he have any weapons, like a gun or a knife," Agatha offered. "He should have been asking Eva that, not us. She was the one who saw him close up, but I guess Carlson figured she might have said something to us that she forgot to tell him when he questioned her before." She looked at her husband. "I don't think we even ever saw the man; it was Eva who had the most to do with him. And anyway," she gave the coffee table one more swipe with her cloth. "I don't know why he's asking those questions all over again. Maybe he's got a new lead, or something."

"He's probably on his way over to Dani's right now," said Henry.

"No," corrected Agatha. "I think he said that he had to stop off at the station house first. Then he would pay them a call right after."

Henry frowned at his wife, but nodded in agreement. "Well, something like that, anyway." He turned back to Billy. "I guess it may be time my old buddy should pack it in, if he can't even make up his mind what he's looking for...A gun, for Pete's sake. Where'd he come up with that idea? I thought he said the dead guy was beaten up. Next thing you know, he'll be chasing his own shadow. Or maybe he should transfer back to the prairies where there's only a few harmless stubble-jumpers with an illegal still or two for him to worry about." He chuckled. "Anyway...seems he dropped in at the old place first. The people that bought it weren't very cooperative. Or else they don't know exactly where Dani and Uri moved to, so he came here. I guess he didn't even know she took a job at the hotel, 'cause he was over asking at Chang's, first off. See, that's what I mean."

"I'll get going then," Billy said. Henry often spoke about the ongoing one-upmanship of the two old friends, but he wondered if he'd ever get to know when Henry was serious and when he wasn't, and if there was more between them than just friendly rivalry. "I'll meet up with Eva over at Dani's house. She's probably waiting for me now."

Henry motioned with his beer. "Got time for one before you go?"

"Thanks anyway." Billy shook his head, regret and resignation in his smile.

"When you get there, maybe you ought to wait until Carlson comes by. Tell her he's wanting to talk to her. You've got lots of time—Carlson isn't going to get there before you do, that's for sure."

* * *

Dani seemed turned to stone; Eva tugged at her arm but she didn't move. Dani's cheeks ran with tears, and she started to tremble. It broke Eva's heart to watch her sister suffer. Ever since she could remember, her little sister seemed to be unable to hold on to happiness. She had seemed to feel every hurt, both physical and mental their father had visited on their mother. He had been hardest on Dani, maybe because he knew she felt more pain. He had seemed to feed off it, revel in it. Eva was sure that once her sister had someone to love and care for her, she would at last bloom into the woman she was meant to be. She deserved better; she'd done nothing to merit this.

The sadness that took hold of Eva was almost too much to bear, but it served to fuel the anger she had held at bay. Furious, she firmed her grip on her sister's arm and reached for the door with her other hand.

"Stop." Uri's voice, soft and menacing.

Turning, she opened her mouth to tell him what he could do with the rest of the day, and her suggestions wouldn't be pretty. She was so angry she wasn't sure if the words would come, but they backed up in her throat along with her breath as she saw the gun in his hand.

28

Stunned, Eva could only stare at her brother-in-law. Finally, she found her voice, but could only manage a whisper. "What are you doing?"

He took so long to answer, she wasn't sure he'd heard. "The same as I always do. Looking out for what's mine. Taking care of things." Uri didn't take his eyes off them as he drank. Carefully, he set the empty bottle on the counter. "And you're not, after all I've done for you, gonna just walk in here and expect me to stand by while you take what belongs to me."

Eva didn't move. A frisson of fear jolted up her arms and lodged in her chest, making it hard to breathe, but she clung to her anger as if to a lifeboat. She heard Dani whimper and felt her hand begin to slip. Eva tightened her grip and held on. *He's just trying to frighten us.*

"You've got a gun. Where did you get a gun, of all things?" She was pleased that her voice was quiet, almost calm, despite the panic making her stomach clench.

Uri hefted it, then pointed it directly at them, his hand trembling slightly. "From your sleazy little friend. He drew a knife on me, but all the while he had this in his pocket. An unexpected gift. For taking care of things, I suppose." He grinned. "See, I was looking after you again. Making sure you were okay. Keeping that dumb jerk from getting to you—and the boys." He tapped the muzzle of the gun against his chest. "Me. I did. Nobody else was going to take him on—do anything about it. So I took care of things. I got him out of the way."

It was like a stranger spoke with Uri's mouth. His eyes were glazed; beads of sweat covered his forehead. Eva couldn't believe he would even think of such things. "What are you saying? Are you talking about the man who threatened us?" Suddenly she couldn't get enough air into her lungs. She coughed then breathed deeply, dragging the air through her nose with effort. "You took care of him? What did you do— are you telling us you killed him? Did you kill him?"

"I didn't mean to. I just wanted to rough him up, show him who he was fooling around with. Make sure he understood that we take care of each other, and there's no way he was going to fool with us." He wiped the sweat from his face with his sleeve, shifting from foot to foot.

"What happened?"

"Oh, I don't know. It was all so sudden. One minute I had him so's I could tell him what would happen if he kept bothering you. Next thing is, he pulled his knife on me. Slipped it out slick and fast and snapped it open. Almost skewered me, the sneaky bastard. Made me mad. So I hit him." Uri shrugged, waving the gun. "A little too hard I guess. He went down. I made sure he didn't get up." He ran his hand through his hair. "I didn't mean to, dammit. He just made me so mad."

He stood looking from one to another. "You know me, right? You know I'm a good guy. I don't go around killing people." Started to pace. "It's just that…sometimes—sometimes things don't go as planned." He held out his hand to Dani. She cringed and crept closer to Eva, her trembling body almost throwing Eva off balance.

"Put the gun down, Uri. Please." Eva heard her voice, still calm and quiet. She wondered at that, since her insides felt like they'd tremble apart any minute. "You're scaring us. You have to turn yourself in, Uri. You can't carry this around with you."

He stared at her with a puzzled expression.

"The gun and the guilt. Nobody can carry stuff like that around with them. It's too hard. In time, it'll make you crazy."

"And how am I going to do that? Do you know what could happen to me?" He nodded his head, as if agreeing with something only he could hear. "They'll put me away. Throw away the key. I can't tell anybody." He pointed the gun at her head. "And neither can you. It was an accident. Self defence. And there's no proof I was even there, either. And if I go to jail until they prove different, who's going to keep a roof over Dani's head? I'll lose everything—the house— everything I've worked for." He pointed a finger at Eva, frowning. "If you say anything, I'll tell everyone you're just saying that to get Dani away from me. No one will believe you. You don't know anything, either of you. They'll believe me, not you. And in the meantime, you'll just cause trouble."

"You're right. I won't tell anyone, Uri. I promise. But if it was self-defence, it wasn't really your fault, and once everyone understands that, it'll be okay. We appreciate what you did for us, really. But we can't stay here now. Dani and I will bunk in with Agatha until this gets straightened out. Then everything will be back to normal, okay?"

"You can't go anywhere now," Uri said. "I shouldn't have told you. See, now that you've made me spell it out, we're all in it together." He held out his hand. "Just come on—take off your coats. Dani, you can start making supper."

"And then what?"

"What? It'll be just like always. We'll figure it out." He looked back and forth between them. "We'll just…"

Be careful. Careful, Eva told herself as she began to move slowly for the door. Trying to be unobtrusive, she inched her hand toward the doorknob.

"Well, come on. What are you waiting for? Take off your coats and let's get going."

"Uri, be reasonable. I'm supposed to spend the afternoon with Billy. He'll be looking for me. What will you do if he shows up here—will you hold him, too?"

"Damn it." Uri aimed a kick at the corner of an easy chair, missed and hit a side table, knocking an ashtray to the floor. His face twisted in a dark scowl. "Stop making things difficult. Just do as I tell you. Come on. Move."

"Uri, please…" If she could just stall him, maybe she could talk him out of this. That hope quickly drained away as his face twisted in a snarl and he took a step towards them, then another. Fear leapt into her throat. Eva's hand found the doorknob and twisted. She pulled, but the door wouldn't open. Frantically, her heart pounding loud enough to drown out all sound, she twisted the doorknob back and forth, pulling again and again. She needed both hands but she dare not let go of Dani. Panic gripped her chest with icy fingers and she couldn't catch her breath. Finally, she felt the lock click free and she yanked the door open. Relief drenched her with sweat. She leapt for the opening, pulling her sister after her. But she couldn't seem to move fast enough. Time seemed to slow. She saw Uri coming towards them and a bright flash made her eyes sting. Sound exploded all around her, and she felt a sharp jab at her shoulder. Why would her sister fight her, push her away? Couldn't she see they were in danger—that she was trying to take her to safety?

MOON UNDER WATER

The world went grey; her arm began to go numb. Her grip loosened and she felt Dani's hand jerked from hers like a cork from a bottle. A rush of cold air hit her cheek, then she was falling, tumbling. Pain ripped through her knee and shoulder, bright sparks erupted behind her eyes.

Time stopped; there was no sound or movement. Confused, she could feel one side of her face, cold against a hard surface. In her line of vision, lazy snowflakes drifted down, white against a wall of slate, settling in front of her as in a dream; she could feel their quiet coolness on her face. Through the curtain of white beginning to form a blanket before her, a muffled sound, like the faraway rumble of thunder, sounded once and again, echoing against the inside of her head. Then all went still. Somewhere in the vast distance almost beyond hearing, drops of water pinged a drip-splash rhythm. She began to feel cold but she didn't want to move. She'd rest here just for a moment, then get up and…what was she doing? She couldn't remember. Everything seemed so blurry, so distant. Did it really matter, after all? A fluffy snowflake settled on her eyelash, blurring her vision. She blinked the world into darkness.

* * *

Billy turned on the windshield wipers and defrosters. The car skidded slightly as he negotiated the corner, gearing down to compensate for the slush that was beginning to accumulate on the road. As he peered through the fat flakes of snow, he went over the list of afternoon plans to allow for the changing weather. Maybe they'd just take in a movie, leave the walk in Stanley Park for another day. On the other hand, if the snow covered the paths and trees in the park and didn't turn to rain, it might be a lovely walk. In the twilight, the harbour lights shining on the black ripples of the ocean always gave him a feeling of peace and contentment. He hoped Eva had galoshes with her; otherwise, they'd have to drive back to Agatha's to get them. It would turn cold later, too, probably, so warm coats were in order, in place of rainwear.

Then again, there was something to be said for sitting in a comfortable, warm theatre, sharing a bag of popcorn and maybe holding hands as they watched Spencer Tracy or Hedy Lamarr on the screen.

Stopped at a red light, he listened to the slap-slap of the wipers as they removed the fat splats of snow. He made a list of the places they might like to go for a bit of supper. He'd heard that the same fellow who ran the hot-dog lunch counter at Prospect Point in the park had opened a restaurant on Granville Street. It was called the White Spot something-or-other. Oh yeah, White Spot Barbeque, that was it, and one could drive up and order and eat without getting out of the car. He'd always enjoyed the hotdogs at the food stand, so the food would probably be good at the new place as well. That would work in weather like this, he decided. On the other hand, he might have to keep the car running and the heater on and the hot food would fog up the windshield. It was probably better to go inside. Then again, he could always let Eva decide. She was more interested in how cafés and restaurants ran than he was. As far as he was concerned, as long as he was in her company, he didn't really care where they went or what they did. As long as he could finally find the courage to tell her how he felt.

Whistling as he pulled up to the curb, he thought how nice it would be to bring her some flowers. He discarded the thought, deciding it was probably too late in the season to find anything decent, and maybe that should wait until he found out how she felt before he got into serious courtship. He was dreaming anyway, he chided himself. There weren't any fresh flowers available this time of year. He started up the sidewalk, puzzled at the strange shape in his path which lay obscured in the deepening twilight and covered with snow. As he approached, he recognized Eva's coat. Kneeling, he looked into her still face and his heart seemed to stop, his breath clumped in a hard knot in his chest. A ribbon of blood had crept across her forehead and his heart turned over with dread.

"Oh, god—Eva? Are you alright? What happened?" He shook her gently. When she didn't respond, he lifted her in his arms and carried her into the house, pushing the half-opened door open the rest of the way with his foot. The house was silent and dark save for the dim light of a lamp. Billy placed his burden on the sofa and took her hand, feeling it cold and still. Frantic to think what to do, he began rubbing her hand and wrists. She stirred slightly, and he felt the blood rush to his head with relief.

"Where's Dani?" he said. "What happened here? Eva. Answer me." The slight rise and fall of her chest told him she was still breathing and he could feel the throb of her pulse. He let go of her hand and found a dishtowel in the kitchen. He dampened it and placed it on her forehead.

"Just stay here and rest," he said. "I'll go for help." He didn't know if she heard him, and he cursed under his breath at people who didn't have enough sense to install a telephone.

Reluctant to leave her, but knowing she needed care, he debated with himself for a moment if he should just pick her up and take her with him to go get help. As he reached for her hand again, he saw a dark stain on the front of her coat. He stared in horror, realizing that he'd best do something fast. He had to get her to the hospital. He looked around for something to wrap her in, finding an afghan tossed across one of the easy chairs. Reaching for it, he noticed the overturned coffee table, and beyond, the dark shape of what looked like a body. Carefully, he approached. Dani lay on her side as if she was napping. Uri sprawled on his back a bit further away, half his body off the living room rug. They looked so peaceful, Billy thought, realizing as soon as the thought crossed his mind that it was far beyond the ridiculous, since part of Uri's face was missing.

29

White. Eva opened her eyes to soft, white mist, featureless, dreamlike. She seemed to float in a timeless void. She relaxed and let herself sink deeper.

When she again awakened, she saw only white curtains enclosing her space, heard only the hushing echo of hallways unused. White sheets and a coverlet encased her as she lay on a narrow bed. Comfortable, warm, there was no reason to move or think or act. Time was nothing and everything, meaningless and profound in turn. Asking her for nothing, letting her drift in a void of silence. Beside her, a window displayed soft winter twilight and she watched, fascinated, the spiralling patterns of falling snowflakes. Moving to get a better look at her surroundings, she felt a sharp pain in her arm, and she gasped in surprise.

"You're awake."

With great effort, she turned toward the sound. Hair dishevelled, blonde stubble on his cheeks, Billy peered at her through slightly-askew glasses.

"Billy." At least that's what she meant to say, but the word was no more than a croak.

"Here," he said. "You must be parched." He lifted her head and helped her take a sip of water.

"You're in a hospital," he said. "Do you remember what happened?"

"What happened?" This time, the words were a whisper.

"That's all right, take your time." Billy's hands were warm as he carefully enfolded one of hers, his thumb gently stroking her wrist. "Whenever you're ready."

She closed her eyes, willing the images to tell her how she came to be here. Her mind was as blank as the curtains that hung in front of her bed. Opening her eyes, she looked at Billy, questions starting to crowd in. What was she doing here? How did she get here? What was she doing before she…

Try as she might, the answers just wouldn't come. "I'm sorry," she said. "I just don't…" A movement behind Billy caught her attention, and Eva looked up to see Detective Carlson shifting his weight as he leaned against the wall beside the door, arms folded, watching with narrowed eyes.

"What's going on?" Panic began to take hold. "How did I get here? I have to know." She tried to sit up. "Ow," she yelped, pain flashing in her shoulder and down her arm.

"Try to relax." Billy's voice was soothing as he pushed her gently back on the pillow.

"You were at your sister's house," said Carlson, coming to stand behind Billy's chair. "Try to remember what happened while you were there. If you just relax, take a breath, it'll all come back. Just be patient. I got all day."

Feeling as if she had somehow walked into a bad dream, Eva could only stare at him.

"Take your time," he said.

Eva had a feeling that he would rather she didn't take any time at all. In fact, she was just as anxious as he was to know how she came to be in a hospital bed, with two men pretending patience, waiting for answers.

Her sister. Dani. Suddenly, memory came rushing back, hitting her in the stomach and taking her breath away. Fragments of scenes came and went. Uri, the gun, trying to pull Dani with her; trying to get away. They had to leave but the door wouldn't open, then the world exploding. The pain, the falling into darkness as if at the end of a nightmare. Waking here. "Dani," she said. "Where is she? Is she alright?"

"She's being looked after. The doctors say she'll pull through well enough."

"What happened?" Eva clutched Billy's hand. "Tell me. Please."

"The doctors are taking care of her. You mustn't worry."

"And Uri?"

Billy shook his head. "I'm sorry."

"You're sorry? Why? What happened to him?" When he didn't answer, she looked at Carlson. "I don't understand. What happened?"

"Uri shot Dani and then shot himself. For some reason, he didn't do a very good job of it, because Dani survived. Barely. But he didn't." The detective came to stand next to Billy. "Look. I'm sorry, Eva. But I have to know what happened, what led up to it. If you can remember anything, anything at all, I would appreciate it if you tell me."

"Eva's been shot too," Billy said to the detective, making as if to rise from his chair. "She needs to rest."

"I'm sorry," Carlson said. He put a friendly but firm hand on Billy's shoulder. "But this is my job. The sooner I can clear this up, the sooner I'll get out of your hair."

"Shot? I've been shot?" Eva settled back against the pillow, only now realizing the extent of the pain that crawled down her arm from her shoulder.

"The bullet only grazed your arm, Eva," Billy said. "Just under the shoulder. Luckily, it didn't hit a bone or a vein, or even luckier, another place more fatal."

Eva turned to the window; she wanted to start over again. The snow had turned to rain. She brought her gaze back to Billy, feeling her frown smooth out and relax as she realized he was trying to be comforting. Closing her eyes, she tried to focus her thoughts, but could feel again Dani's hand slipping away from her…falling…

She put a hand to her forehead, as if to physically pull the memories out, but instead encountered a bump, covered by a bandage. She must have fallen—that would account for the vague headache that had plagued her since she awoke. Then one by one, other images came. Not many, just enough. After a minute, in a voice soft with tears, she told them all she could. In the hours to come, little by little, she remembered bits and snatches, and she wrote them down on the pad Detective Carlson left on the small stand next to her bed. By the time she was ready to go home, she had told them most of the story. Whether the whole picture would come back, in time, remained to be seen.

* * *

As the weeks went by and Eva returned to work, she was constantly distracted with worry over Dani's progress. Out of hospital a couple of weeks later, Dani moved in with Agatha, spending hours enclosed in the little upstairs room and saying little at mealtimes or the few occasions when she had visitors. When she did try to be social, she would often fade away from the conversation, her attention drawn to some scene that only she could see.

One afternoon shortly after the New Year, Agatha arrived in the dining room of the hotel. Eva hurried over and the two sisters found a secluded table where they could talk. As they seated themselves, the waitress brought over a gin and tonic and placed it in front of Agatha.

"What's this?" Eva knew that Agatha didn't drink this early in the day unless she was at her wits' end.

"I'm at my wits' end," Agatha confirmed after taking a sip. "Not to mention, I'm so angry I could chew nails." Eva prepared herself for the worst. What that would be, she couldn't imagine.

"I got a visit from two men just before lunch today," Agatha began. "Sleazy-looking brutes they were, too. They were looking for Dani. Well, actually they were looking for Uri, but they traced down what had happened and now they're after his wife."

"Whatever for?"

"That nincompoop got himself up to his eyebrows in debt," Agatha fumed. She took another gulp of her drink, and Eva was grateful, from the look the waitress gave her when she had put it on the table, that it wasn't too strong.

"Dani's going to lose the house, and likely have to sell off most of the furniture to pay his debts. And I don't even know if that'll be enough."

"I thought they were renting," Eva said.

"Apparently not. Just another of Uri's less-than-brilliant schemes, as it turns out."

Agatha picked up the glass but put it down with a thump. "Honestly, I don't know where this is going to end. What else is going to happen? What else did that lame-brained, god-forsaken idiot get himself into. Trying to be a big shot—all he did was make a huge mess that everyone else has to clean up."

Eva reached across the table and put her hand on Agatha's arm. "Relax, kiddo," she said. "We'll deal with it. We'll get it all straightened out. He wasn't smart enough to do too much more damage, I'm sure." With all her heart she hoped she was right. And with a feeling of profound sadness, Eva realized that the man she once thought of as a friend, who she thought she knew could be counted on to help, had created a disaster that would affect them for the rest of their lives.

As she walked Agatha to the door, Eva put her arm across her sister's shoulders, feeling them relax, anger tempered now that she had shared it. She hugged her sister, reassuring her that she would be there for her, as would Henry, and even Billy. They'd put their lives back together as well as they could, and go on.

* * *

After a family dinner on a Sunday in late May, Billy and Eva walked down to the lake. The mild, softly-scented air was redolent with the fresh odor of new grass after an overnight shower. The park was quiet—she and Billy were alone save for the soft chirps and rustles of the hidden night creatures.

Billy started to spread a blanket on the ground, then picked it up as he became aware of the dampness of the grass. He invited her to sit on the bench and draped the blanket around her.

"You'll catch your death," he said. Then he looked aghast. "I'm sorry. Bad choice of words. It just slipped out…what we always say…" He shrugged. "I'm sorry."

"Never mind, Billy," Eva said. "It doesn't matter." *Does anything matter?* "There are worse things than the wrong choice of words."

"I'm glad you're here," Billy said. "Glad you're safe. I'd like to try and keep you safe, if you'll let me."

"You've got a plan?"

"Not really. Well, sort of. I just think that two heads are better than one. That is, I mean to say…" He enclosed her hand in his. "I'm not very good at this. But I think that, say, the two of us, we could be good together. Look out for each other, like. I thought we could go up north—you know, to where I've been working at the camps. You could get a job as a cook, and me, well, I'll do whatever job's available. In fact," he continued after clearing his throat. "I got a lead on a job with a guy who owns his own small logging company. Name's Woody. We've had a few beers together up at the hotel on a Saturday night, but I didn't know who he was at the time. His actual name is Woodruff McPherson. He's just like one of the guys, really. He's got an opening at the camp, needs a cook and a faller. You could have the cookhouse all to yourself. Not too many men to cook for—maybe ten or twelve. His son, Eggy, now there's a nickname for you—don't know what it stands for—seems like that family has weird names just so they can have weird nicknames. Anyway, he's going to come along to help out, peel potatoes, run errands and so on."

He paused for breath, looking closely at Eva. She looked back, interested to hear more.

"The good thing is, anyone looking for you, and you know who I mean, won't be able to find you. We wouldn't be hiding, exactly. Just, you know, we'd be…"

"Safe?"

"Yeah, safe. At least so hard to get at he'd give up and go away, not bother you again. We could do just fine, you and me, and we could get a grubstake, pool our money and get a nice house somewhere..." He fumbled to a stop as she turned her face away. "The war won't last forever. But by the time it's done, we could be in a good position to...to..."

His blue eyes looked into hers through the misty lenses of his glasses with something she hadn't seen before. "Your glasses are fogging up," she said. She'd often wondered what it would be like to have someone who cared for her unconditionally. Now it seemed that she might find out. If she wanted to.

He let go of her hand and reached into his pocket for his hanky. He took his glasses off and polished them carefully, concentrating on each mark and speck. She studied his profile as if it would tell her everything about him. His tousled blond hair needed a trim, he smelled of soap and another pleasant scent she couldn't identify. He'd been there for her, just when she needed someone. Now he was offering to...what?

"What are you trying to say, Billy?"

He looked into her eyes. "I just, well, I thought...I'm very partial to you, Eva. I've thought about this for a long time, and I think we should be together."

"Like partners?"

"If that's all you'll give me, I'll take it."

"How about friends?" she smiled. "Lovers, perhaps?"

"That's what I was hoping for. And if you want, we could even get married."

There was something about this man that always made her feel secure, comfortable. Now she realized that there was a spot within herself that felt warm and right when they were together. Yes, she could do worse. Heaven knows, she had. But, she discovered as he took her hand again, this could be better than she'd ever thought possible. Much better.

"Can it wait until Dani's on her feet again? I feel like I should be here to help take care of her for a while. In the meantime, we can make some plans. Would that suit you?"

"That'll suit me just fine. But Dani's on the mend; what she needs now is time. Woody will want an answer soon, or he'll find someone else for the job."

"We'd better get back and start getting organized, then," she said.

"In a minute." He put his arm around her and she relaxed against him, her head on his shoulder.

They sat listening to the night, the croak of frogs, the vague hum of traffic in the distance. The park was full of shadows and moonlight. The wind stilled, and the lake turned into a looking-glass where a silver disc appeared, duplicating the one that sailed the black sky above it. Something rippled across the water, breaking the image into bars and shards of quicksilver. From a hidden branch, an owl hooted, eerie in the near silence.

Eva shivered and wrapped her arms around her middle. "People think they're like the moon, Billy," she said. "Whole and bright and full of light. But we're more like the reflection; we can be torn apart without reason. And then we have to try and put ourselves back together again. That's what each of us is: a moon under water, a poor imitation of the real thing. Broken and patched, broken and patched—until we finally can't be put back together again."

Eva thought of Dani, how far her sister had come in such a short time. She still had moments of distraction, when her attention wavered and she saw or heard things, or seemed to, that no one else did. She spoke little and smiled less, but most of the time, she was happy to do what she was bid, like a child learning new skills. It would take time, the doctors said, and they promised there was hope.

Her thoughts turned to Uri. They had been friends. What had happened to him that the only place he could find refuge waited at the end of a gun?

Billy put his hand over hers. "Not you. You're strong and full of the kind of light that makes everyone around you feel strong, too. You can't be broken like that; I've seen how you hold yourself and everything and everyone else together." He edged a little closer to her. "We are like the moon, Eva. No matter what shadow we're standing in, in the end, we're the ones who decide what happens next, if we want to come out bright and shiny or not."

His words surprised her a little. It appeared that there were depths to him that would be worth looking into. They sat, silent, watching the twin moons floating across lake and sky.

The tension that had wrapped around her like a shroud loosened a little. As the moon rode higher in the sky, the night sounds became muted and calm. Her body warm against his, she allowed herself to dream.

Made in the USA
San Bernardino, CA
28 May 2014